LARKSBURY RINGS

Sheila Spencer-Smith

CHIVERS

British Library Cataloguing in Publication Data available

This Large Print edition published by AudioGO Ltd, Bath, 2013.
Published by arrangement with the Author

U.K. Hardcover   ISBN   978 1 4713 1678 4
U.K. Softcover   ISBN   978 1 4713 1679 1

Printed and bound in Great Britain by
MPG Books Group Limited

CHAPTER ONE

Although the forgiving May sunlight couldn't disguise the flaking paint of the white fence or the weeds choking the brick path, Elisabeth Turner gazed at Marigold Cottage, entranced.

Two hundred years-old the advertisement said. The roof must have been re-thatched several times since 1757 because it looked in good shape. There was something about the property that appeared cosy and aloof at the same time. She thought of chilly autumn afternoons with the scent of wood smoke filling low-beamed rooms while the rest of the world was shut out.

She loved it already.

At a sound behind her she turned. Crossing the lane towards her was a tall fair-haired man in a sports jacket that looked lived-in with its scuffed leather patches on the elbows.

'Miss Turner?' His voice was warm and the faint lines round his eyes deepened. 'I'm the owner, John Ellis. I was expecting someone older.'

'Does that make a difference?' Her friend Bella had warned her that she looked positively elfin in her green dress and far younger than her twenty-nine years but he didn't look much more than thirty.

He smiled. 'Not a bit of it.' His hand felt

warm in hers.

'My bus was early so I had time to look round the village. Mellstone looks a charming place.'

'On a day like this certainly.'

'I was thinking of windy afternoons with the leaves swirling from the tree I passed on the green.'

'The Tidings Tree.'

'It looks old.'

'It's certainly that.'

She glanced down the lane towards it and saw that from behind the thatched cottages haze was rising from the downs. She took a breath of delight. 'Very paintable,' she murmured, flexing her fingers and wishing she had brought a pad and charcoal with her so she could sketch it straight away.

Someone else was hurrying along the lane now, dressed in black and with her arms full of leafy branches.

John Ellis smiled. 'That's Alice Pengold who lives opposite. She does peculiar things with roots and berries.'

Elisabeth's laugh had an element of panic in it. 'What a subject for a portrait!'

'You're an artist?'

'I love to paint.'

'Alice would never stay still long enough to be painted. She'll be off to clean the church soon, I expect. She cleans the school too. It's the building next door.'

Elisabeth nodded and did her best to concentrate on the practical details of viewing a property. 'That's handy. And so is the wooden chalet you have in the back garden. Could you show me that first please, Mr Ellis?'

'Certainly, if you wish.'

They followed the brick path to the back of the cottage and he stood back for her to climb the steps onto the lawn ahead of him. In the far corner, backed by some tall trees on the other side of the wall, stood a large cedarwood building. Sunshine reflected from the large windows and seemed to turn the walls to gold.

He produced keys and stood aside for her to enter. The wooden floor was spotless and she stared around with pleasure. 'There's plenty of room here for all my painting equipment,' she said. 'This is where I shall work. So much light. It's so right it's unbelievable. Exactly what I'm looking for.'

His lips twitched and she could almost see the amusement bubbling up inside him. 'You sound very sure for someone who hasn't seen inside the cottage yet.'

She waved his words aside as of no consequence, smiling at him. 'I know it's just the place for me.'

He smiled too and she looked away. Too much enthusiasm was not a wise thing in the circumstances. Her friend, Bella, would have told her that but she simply couldn't help it.

3

'It's important for me to have somewhere suitable to work because I want to become a full-time painter.' It was a reasonable aspiration, she thought, even if it did sound odd to other ears than her own.

'Surely you must see inside the place before reaching a decision?'

Sensible man. Cautious too by the sound of it. He didn't look the sort to throw security aside for the sake of a dream as he seemed to think she was doing. She wondered what he did for a living.

She allowed him to show her the downstairs rooms of the cottage. In the kitchen she glanced briefly at the gas stove that was part of the fittings and then, remembering what was expected of her, pretended an interest in the larder and the wall cupboard. She didn't register anything about either because her eyes were drawn to the window as she pictured the chalet up on the lawn with masses of space for her painting paraphernalia that was threatening to take over their tiny flat where they had lived for the last four years. Here she and Jenny would start a new life, grateful that the money she inherited from her great aunt had made this possible.

'Upstairs?' he said at last.

She followed him up the narrow staircase into bedrooms with sloping wooden floors and faded wallpaper where the scent of lavender lingered. She moved to the window set deep

4

in the wall to look across the lane to the row of terraced cottages opposite. From one of them the black-coated Alice Pengold emerged carrying a garden fork she proceeded to use with energy in her small front garden.

'You realise that the rates are high in Mellstone?' John Ellis said. 'The fire insurance too because of the thatch. It's none of my business, of course, but you do know what you're doing?'

She gazed at him in surprise that he should point out the drawbacks when he was trying to sell the property. 'I feel it's right for me,' she said.

'You don't look ruthless and determined enough if you don't mind my saying so. I should consider this very carefully if I were you.'

'Are you trying to put me off, Mr Ellis?'

'Well no. Your future plans are none of my business. I apologise.'

'Marigold Cottage is the place I most want to be,' she said. 'And so will my little girl when she sees it.

He frowned. 'Your . . . little girl?'

'Jenny will be eight in a week or two. She's been with me since she was three. Her mother was my cousin.'

'I see.'

There was a slight awkwardness in the atmosphere now. Maybe she should have made this clear from the beginning instead of detailing why she needed space to paint. Jenny was the main reason for moving to a larger place when the opportunity came. She mustn't forget that.

He smiled as he made a movement to go. 'My solicitor will be in touch with yours in due course.'

'There's just one thing, Mr Ellis. It's a pity but we won't be able to move in just yet.'

'You mean you've been house-hunting too soon?'

'Not too soon,' she said hastily. 'I'm so pleased it's a price I can afford. I knew I had to view right away in case someone else got in first.'

'And?'

'I've a very dear friend who's in trouble. It's complicated. I promised to help out until she can make suitable arrangements to take her sons abroad. And she's been ill so we won't be able to move in for some months, possibly a year. I'll let the place meanwhile. I could do that, couldn't I?'

He looked doubtful. 'It's not a good time to let property at the moment unless you can be quite sure whoever moves in will honour the lease.'

'I'll take the risk.' Elisabeth was aware of sounding too optimistic but sometimes it was necessary. She had no doubt on this occasion that this was the right thing for her to do and it would work out as she planned.

He said nothing but she could see that he didn't approve.

* * *

The morning in early July when Elisabeth and Jenny eventually moved in to Marigold Cottage was as hazy and beautiful as the day she had first seen Mellstone. Her tenants had left the cottage in good order, sad to be going when their tenancy expired.

Jenny was helpful in spurts but a lot of the time she was racing in and out, delighted to have a garden and wanting to know if she could grow flowers like the white roses on the trellis at the back.

As soon as the furniture van left, Elisabeth sank down on the window seat in the living-room and gazed around her with pleasure. Their things were old and worn but already they looked happy in their new home. She would need a rug in front of the fireplace but that could wait until she sold a painting. When they were straight she would fill a vase with some of those white roses to place on the runner on the table.

'Someone's come to see us,' Jenny cried, bursting into the room and sending a pile of papers flying. Her red hair was dishevelled and her cheeks flushed. 'She's carrying things and she wants to see you. She's called Mrs Cameron. She says she lives opposite us and

7

saw us moving in.'

The front door was open and on the step stood such a friendly-looking person that Elisabeth felt immediately at ease. Soft grey hair framed her smiling face and she wore a baggy blue cardigan the same shade as her eyes.

'I had to come across as soon as the van went, dear,' she said. 'No, no . . . I won't come in. You're busy. John said to call to see you were settling in.'

'John?'

'My sister's boy. Sadly passed away now. My sister, I mean, not John. He's a good boy to his uncle and aunt. Always has been. I meant to wait until later but I saw your little girl and I brought some sweeties across for her. And these are for you.'

Elisabeth took the two jars from her and swallowed the lump in her throat. 'You're kind, Mrs Cameron, so kind and . . .'

'Bramble jelly,' Mrs Cameron said with pride. 'And green tomato chutney. No, don't thank me, dear. We'll like having some young life in Marigold Cottage, Donald and me. He doesn't say much but he sends his regards and said not to hold you up so I won't, not now. Jenny will be going to the school I expect. It's a shame Miss Bryer won't be there this afternoon or you could have called in to see her. She's the headmistress.

Elisabeth smiled. 'Tomorrow, I think.'

'They're interviewing someone at the vicarage this afternoon, a new teacher for the little ones. I hope they'll find someone nice. It's a lovely school. I'll go now, dear. If there's anything you need just come across.'

Still bemused at Mrs Cameron's kindness Elisabeth thanked her and walked with her to the gate. Then she turned and gazed at the front of the cottage. It looked warmly welcoming with the sun slanting across the thatched roof. Her home, hers and Jenny's . . . she could hardly believe it even now.

When Jenny's parents were killed four years before on their way to the West Country, their car struck by an out-of-control lorry careering down a steep hill, she had been living in their North London home as part of the family. She was devoted to Jenny who clung to her at that terrible time. It had seemed right to continue looking after her and eventually apply to adopt her legally. No one else in the family was in a position to do so even though they offered financial support when she gave up her teaching job. She had never regretted it for a moment.

And now Jenny would have a country upbringing while she was free to paint. Even Bella, hoping to sign the contract of her dilapidated barn of a place in Cornwall that had stood empty and neglected since the war, couldn't argue with that.

'We won't ever leave here, will we?' Jenny

9

said breathlessly.

Elisabeth looked down at the anxious face at her side and smiled. 'I hope we never have to, my love.'

* * *

Catherine Mellor sat on the edge of her chair in her best suit and brown velour hat and wished she were anywhere but here.

The vicar and chairman of the school governors cleared his throat. 'Miss Mellor,' he said in a voice that sounded deeply reassuring. 'Would you mind waiting outside, in the garden perhaps, while we consider your application?'

Cathy got up rather too quickly and almost overbalanced. Flushing, she looked round for her handbag and found it by her feet. 'Of course,' she murmured.

The interviewing panel weren't all old, of course, but had seemed so to her first anxious glance. Mr Moore, the vicar, younger than the others, had welcomed her with kindness when she'd pulled at the bell rope outside the open door of the vicarage earlier. His height was heartening and beside him she felt, for once, slim rather than lanky. This was a good feeling and her confidence lasted until she was sitting opposite the interviewing panel.

Most of the questions had nothing to do with her prowess as a budding teacher. One man's eyelids began to droop, another with a bristly moustache asked if she had any plans for matrimony in the near future and then seemed to lose interest when she said she hadn't. Another wanted to know how long she planned to stay in Mellstone if her application were successful.

She hadn't seen much of the village yet, of course, being far too interested in the longer view as the taxi drove down the steep road from the town of Hilbury on the last stage of her journey. Stretching far into the distance on her right was the vale, Thomas Hardy's Vale of little Dairies. She thrilled to see it. And it was easy to imagine the soft turf and the sheep bleating off in panic from anyone walking on those rounded hills to her left. One of them was ringed with grassy embankments and looked intriguing.

So as they swept through open gates of the vicarage and pulled up outside an ivy-covered house she'd only glimpsed a few thatched cottages and a huge tree on a triangle of grass and knew she had arrived in Mellstone.

Miss Bryer, the headmistress, sat at the end of the table tapping a fountain pen on her pad. Her intent gaze had been disconcerting. Even though she looked at least thirty she was still attractive with dark wavy hair. But there was something about the way she held herself like a coiled spring that made Cathy wary.

'So have you anything you would like to add,

11

Miss Bryer?' Mr Moore had asked her when the questions faltered to a stop.

She considered and then frowned. 'Perhaps you could you tell us what you like doing in your free time, Miss Mellor?'

Cathy hesitated. The education lecturer at college had stressed how important it was to have outside interests. Would it be best to say she had no free time because she worked hard every single minute or come out with something that made her seem less boring like lion taming or a lover of trapeze stunts?

'I like walking,' she said. 'And reading.' *Please don't ask my favourite authors. My mind's gone blank.*

Now outside in the grass-scented air a little spurt of excitement filled her because Mellstone School needed a new teacher for the Infants class and it could be her.

The eldest of three sisters, she had looked forward to branching out on her own away from their influence when she left training college. The two years she had been away from home had given her something she hadn't known before. Not confidence exactly. She had never had much faith in her ability to do things on her own.

She began walking to and fro on the spongy grass. She had seen enough of the surrounding area now to feel pleased she was really and truly here, the only candidate. But why she was the only person being interviewed? Was this a

12

good thing or not?

The headmistress had said little but had obviously studied her application with care. Once or twice she had caught her impatient expression at some of the questions asked by the others. Her own had been brief and to the point. She had approved of the training college's modern approach to teaching methods and the policy of continual assessment of the students rather than exams at the end of the two-year course.

Cathy stopped prowling and walked across to examine the sundial on the stone plinth in the centre of the lawn. She ran her fingers along the surface, liking the feel of the rough stone. The shadow fell just before five o'clock. That late? But no. No one had informed the sundial that the clocks had gone forward in the spring. She checked her watch. Nearly four. Ten minutes had passed since she'd left the interview room, surely enough time for them to come to a decision?

*   *   *

Karen Bryer picked up the fountain pen on the table, released the cap and then screwed it up again. 'So that's that,' she said as the last of the other members of the interview panel left the room.

'Indeed.'

Although he was standing at the other

13

end of the table such was Robert Moore's personality that she felt that he loomed over her. His expression was brooding as if deep thoughts filled his mind.

She tapped her pen on the table. He had appeared satisfied when there was a unanimous decision to offer the position to Miss Mellor but she wasn't sure she was.

'What else could we have done in the circumstances?' he said. 'As you know hers was the only application we received from someone who is a communicant member of the church.'

She stared at him for a moment. He surely needn't have sounded quite so anxious?

'And leave that pen alone,' he said.

She dropped it as if it were red hot, startled at his unexpectedly sharp tone. 'You're right of course,' she said as she got to her feet and began to gather her papers together. 'I was hoping for someone more vibrant and bursting with ideas to bring Mellstone School out of the Victorian age and into the nineteen-fifties.'

'More like yourself, you mean?'

She looked at him quickly. 'A criticism?'

'No, indeed. But you exaggerate.'

'Miss Snell has been with us so long, all her teaching life. In fact all her school life as she never left Mellstone School.'

'She's a fine woman.'

'I'm not disputing that. She's devoted to the children and they love her. But things have

14

changed. We need new blood, new ideas. I have a feeling this girl might be a bit of a drip.'

'He raised his eyebrows. 'That's a harsh judgement surely? Miss Mellor has good reports from her training college. A conscientious girl it seems, pleasant-looking too. I think she will fit in well here and that's important.'

'If you say so.'

'I'm willing to suspend judgement.'

'And obviously I must give her the chance to prove her worth. At least I was invited to be present at the interview.'

He bowed slightly and she knew she had him to thank for that. Some governing bodies didn't consult the heads of school before making appointments.

'I'm aware that the numbers on roll are dropping with a larger contingent of eleven-year-olds than usual off to school in Hilbury,' he said. 'The new child coming to live in Marigold Cottage will be starting here next term, of course, now that she and her guardian are moving in at last.'

'So I heard. I wish John Ellis could have been here.'

'John Ellis isn't a school governor.'

She shrugged. 'I value his opinion, that's all.'

He said nothing. She bit her lip and wished she had kept quiet. She could tell by his expression that any mention of John, her dearest friend since childhood, was not

15

welcome. Valuing John's judgment as she did she would have liked to call at Nether End Farm on her way home so that she could discuss the outcome of the interview with him. He would give his measured views in such a way that she would feel at peace instead of disappointed. But it wouldn't do, of course, because all that had passed here this afternoon must be held in confidence.

The vicar placed a chair against the wall and began to move another.

'Let me help.'

'No need,' he said. 'Bob Lunt is coming later and he'll see to it. It's a pity Miss King and Miss Buckley are not in this afternoon but it's good they're willing to take a lodger. I've given Miss Mellor their address so that she can contact the ladies in due course. I'm sure she'll be all right with them.'

Karen nodded, anxious now to be off. Her mother would have forgotten she would be later than usual because of the interview and would be fretting if she didn't get home to Haymesgarth soon. Otherwise the bitter interrogation would last for hours until they were both exhausted.

Lucky Catherine Mellor moving in to Lynch Cottage and starting a new life in the place of her choice!

16

CHAPTER TWO

With Jenny safely in school Elisabeth should have found it easy to get out looking for suitable locations for her work but she discovered in herself a reluctance to venture far from Marigold Cottage.

Her premonition of disaster was ridiculous. Today she must make a supreme effort and get herself and her painting gear up on the downs before the weather worsened and she was forced to remain inside.

She took the lane that lead up to the track that climbed up through Hodman's Hollow. Birds sang and butterflies dipped and fluttered among the bordering grass, brown speckled ones and a yellow Brimstone that shone out like a flicker of sunlight.

She paused half way up to get a view of Mellstone through a gap in the overgrown hedge of hazel and dogwood. She could see the downs, some of whose names she had learnt from Mrs Cameron who lived in Ivy Cottage opposite her own with her husband, Donald. Uckdown Hill, Hodman Down and Larksbury Rings. She felt inspired by them, but it was the village down below with the vale stretching beyond darkly mysterious that she wanted to sketch today.

Dewdrops from the overhanging bushes

showered her hair as she went through the gap into the field beyond. Knee-deep in damp grass, she stood and stared .The silence was profound, a deep satisfying emptiness in the quiet air. Then in the distance a dog barked, drawing her eyes outward across the vale so that she knew she must get this down at once before she lost the moment.

For some time she was engrossed as she worked away with her charcoal to get the shape of the picture she wanted. In the distance the church tower was a wonderful focal point. She tried different positions, different angles, but in all the sketches the tower stood proudly beautiful.

A wave of optimism surged through her and set her smiling as she worked. All the oil paintings that resulted from these sketches would sell, she felt sure. Her certainty lent speed to her fingers.

She glanced at her watch at last and hastily began to gather her things together, aware for the first time that her hands were cold. She realised too that she was being watched.

A trickle of apprehension ran down her spine until the ragged figure of a gypsy girl turned to vanish through the gap in the hedge. Ashamed of her reaction to someone who had as much right to be there as she had herself, she almost ran down the track that seemed so much longer now than when she had trudged up a few hours ago. Her morning's work had been inspirational but now, of a sudden, the practicalities took over. There was no hope of success without hard grind and a big part of that was finding outlets for selling her work. So far she had none.

'Can I give you a lift?' a deep voice asked as she paused at the bottom of the track where it joined the lane. Looking at her from the Land Rover that had pulled up alongside was a pleasant-faced woman whose short straight hair, greying a little at the temples, looked neat. 'You've come to live in Marigold Cottage, I believe?'

Surprised, Elisabeth acknowledged this with a smile. She indicated her bag of art materials. 'There isn't far to go now, this is rather bulky so I'd better walk. Thank you all the same.'

'Fair enough. I'm Jean Varley from the farm down the road.'

Elisabeth liked her no-nonsense approach. She seemed like a breath of fresh air. 'Elisabeth Turner,' she said.

'I've been meaning to call on you. Come in and see us this evening, my dear, why don't you? And bring your little girl. Nothing formal. Sandwiches and coffee in the kitchen or something stronger if you like. Martin, my husband, will be back from market and our son Ralph is still with us. I'd like them to meet you. Ralph goes back to his agricultural college on Monday. Do come.'

It sounded more like a command than

19

an invitation and difficult to refuse. Good working time lost, though. But Elisabeth smiled and thanked her.

Jean Varley indicated the large black dog slobbering all over her shoulder. 'This one's Bruno and he's in disgrace. Subdued now, would you believe? I've had to go after him and bring him home. He does this sort of thing periodically. One of his really bad points, clearing off to Larksbury Rings. I'd say he had a lady love up there if the only animals weren't sheep. But of course that's the problem and why he had to be brought home whether he likes it or not.'

She smiled and Elisabeth laughed too. From the look of his adoring brown eyes and lolling tongue Bruno looked only too pleased to be driven home in comfort and knew when he was well off.

'We'll see you later, then. Bruno's bark's ferocious so tell your little girl he'll be locked away tonight. Serve him right, the wicked creature.'

Heartened by the encounter, Elisabeth hurried on her way with the brief feeling of doom quite gone. Mellstone was the place for them even though Bella had tried her best to persuade her of the delights of Cornwall.

*　　　*　　　*

Cathy was up early on the first day of term,

20

unable to swallow much of the scrambled egg on toast Miss King dished up with an excited flourish. Both ladies waved Cathy off at least half an hour before she needed to be at school.

The smell of damp grass in the lane and the sound of birdsong in the hedges gave Cathy a spurt of delight that helped smother her nervousness. As she got closer she was pleased to see a small black car parked outside that she suspected was Miss Bryer's. So she wasn't too early after all.

She walked across the empty playground and in through a lobby into the main classroom that smelt of polish and new wood and something else she couldn't quite place.

The headmistress rose from her desk. 'Ah, Miss Mellor.' Her smile seemed to Cathy to be forced but perhaps that was her imagination.

She smiled tremulously back. 'Good morning, Miss Bryer.'

'Come through to your room.'

The door in the partition between the two classrooms was stiff and creaked a little as she pushed it open. This room was smaller than the other but the desks were arranged in the same straight rows, each with room to seat two pupils. The teacher's desk at the front was the usual sort with drawers on either side divided in the middle with space for legs. Not that she would be seated much, Cathy thought. Sitting down for any length of time had been frowned upon at college.

21

Miss Bryer opened the top drawer and took out a bunch of keys. 'You'll find the stationery in one of the cupboards, the pencils and the plasticine. Poster paints too and all you'll need. I'll leave you to it to sort things out before the whistle blows.' She paused, frowning. 'Is something wrong?'

Cathy hesitated. Then she said with a rush: 'The desks . . . they look so formal like this. Would I be allowed to arrange them in a different way?'

'How exactly?'

'I'd like to have them in groups, two or three pushed together to make tables. Not at first, but after I've got to know the children a bit.'

'I don't see why not.' There was silence for a moment until there were sounds of someone entering the room next door.

Miss Bryer moved to the door. 'That'll be the new child and her mother. I'll have to see to them. Arrange the desks as you think best.' This time her smile looked genuine. There was a sparkle in her eyes, too.

Cathy, relieved, checked the other drawers in her desk and discovered the register and red and blue fountain pens. These she placed ready for use. Then she wandered round the room, seeing in her mind's eye how it would look when arranged exactly as she wanted it. She would have bright pictures on the walls, flowers on the window sills.

After a while she heard the whistle blow

outside in the playground and braced herself in readiness for the start of her teaching career.

*   *   *

After school Karen Bryer drove off quickly, her mind on the girl who had started her teaching career today in Mellstone. So far so good. She had tried to keep her under surveillance surreptitiously. Miss Mellor had been nervous at first but by the afternoon seemed to have got into the swing of things in the classroom next door and afterwards had said she was looking forward to the next day.

Down at the main road Karen stopped, checked both ways and then drove straight across along to the lane that lead to the top of the downs past Nether End Farm, John Ellis' home.

John would be at market today so she wouldn't call in and return the book he had lent her. All the same she slowed down as she neared the entrance to his property. Peering in through the bars of the gate was a short figure she recognised instantly.

She pulled up and wound down her window. 'Jenny Finlay?'

The child spun round, startled, her bedraggled red hair looking as if she'd been though a holly bush several times. Her gabardine raincoat was splattered with mud

23

and had a button missing.

'What are you doing here, Jenny?'

'Walking, Miss.'

'Does your mother know where you are?'

'I'm looking for good places for her to paint.'

'So far from home?'

The girl looked at her solemnly. 'I went further than I meant to, Miss.'

'I'd better drive you back.' Karen released a handle so she could push the passenger seat of her car forward. 'Get in.'

Jenny slid inside and sat on the edge of the seat.

'So what's your mother doing?'

Jenny mumbled something Karen couldn't hear and she didn't press it. Elisabeth Turner had come to Mellstone to attempt to make enough to live on with her painting as everyone knew and wondered at. She'd be in her studio now engrossed in her work. The villagers, suspicious to a man . . . or woman . . . of this strange way of life looked on her askance and muttered about her among themselves. Apart from the vicar Karen suspected that only Mrs Cameron, John Ellis' aunt who lived opposite Marigold Cottage, had anything good to say about her. But she pushed that thought to the back of her mind as she reversed the car and began to drive back the way she had come.

'And did you find any suitable places?' she asked the silent child.

24

'No, Miss.'

'A waste of time then.'

Jenny didn't answer and Karen was aware that she had slid further down in to her seat.

'Go straight home from school next time,' she said.

She waited until she had seen Jenny run indoors before setting off for home once again.

And now she really was late.

She thought of her own first teaching post within travelling distance of home. Her father, a solicitor, had died of a heart attack in his sixties and had left his widow and daughter well provided for. When the headship of Mellstone School was advertised nine years later she had applied for and obtained the position. Now at thirty two she seemed settled there for the foreseeable future because her mother's worsening arthritis and general state of health made this necessary.

She parked the car at the front of the house and stood for a moment looking up at it. Built at the beginning of the century it was far too large for herself and her mother. Too dark and gloomy, too.

She sighed and opened the heavy front door.

*   *   *

Later that day, as she walked along the lane with Jenny, Elisabeth wondered what the inside of the Varley home was like. She had

25

seen the farmhouse from outside standing square and grey in its small front garden close to the road. Mrs Cameron had told her that Martin Varley farmed three hundred acres spread round the village and had a herd of sixty dairy cows, mostly Friesians.

Jean Varley welcomed them into the farm kitchen where low beams gave a cosy feeling to the place and logs crackled in the stove. A girl was seated nearby whom Mrs Varley introduced as Cathy Mellor, the new teacher at the school. Elisabeth settled down beside her, finding her pleasant to talk to and glad to exchange notes on being newcomers to Mellstone.

'I hope you'll feel free to call in and see me sometimes,' said Elisabeth. 'I'd like that.'

'Me too,' said Cathy, looking pleased.

As the evening progressed others arrived. Ralph Varley, the son of the house, his thick fair hair falling over his face, brought a new friend with him, Arnold Bronson, a forestry student at present based locally on his uncle's farm, a fellow bellringer.

As Arnold Bronson stepped forward Elisabeth saw that he was a year or two older than Ralph and half a head taller. Perhaps it was his moustache and the way he gazed round with such confidence that gave him that air of maturity she found off-putting. Ignoring the empty chair beside Mrs Cameron with a shudder of distaste he found another beside

Cathy.

*   *   *

'Not off already are you?' Arnold Bronson said
later as Cathy moved slightly in her chair. 'I
trust we haven't put you off wanting to learn
the art of bellringing?'

'Oh no,' said Cathy breathlessly, flattered by
his interest.

Arnold downed his drink in one gulp and
wiped his hand across his moustache. 'We'll
escape to the pub. Coming Ralph? Cathy?'

'But . . .' Cathy began, wondering if Mrs
Varley would mind them leaving so early.

Ralph's fair hair shone in the lamplight as he
sprang up but Cathy got up slowly as if doing
so would render her invisible. The slight guilt
she was feeling made her stumble against the
door and grab at the handle with a clatter. She
followed the others with a strange anticipatory
excitement.

Outside Arnold caught hold of her arm and
she felt a tingle of pleasure as they crossed the
yard.

The Swan Inn down on the main road was
dimly cosy with highly polished horse brasses
and warming pans on the wall between the
lighted carriage lanterns. As they went in
Cathy's eyes began to water in the smoky
atmosphere and she could hardly see across
the room. They found seats in the corner and

27

she sat with her back hard against the wall while Ralph went to the bar with their order.

For a moment Arnold inspected the carriage lanterns and then gave a snort of disgust as he sat down beside her on the cushioned bench. 'Amazing how they flicker so realistically,' he said. 'Who'd have thought of seeing anything so sophisticated in a dump like Mellstone?'

'Don't you like it here?' said Cathy, surprised.

'Do you? If things don't soon look up I might have to think seriously of moving on.'

She felt a stab of disappointment. He made her feel interesting and alive. It was incredible that he was paying her so much attention when he seemed to regard most people as fools.

'So where will you go?'

He shrugged then smiled. 'I've a feeling now that I won't need to after all.'

She felt warmth flood her cheeks and hoped he hadn't noticed. Ralph was back now with the drinks and a man leaning on the bar came across to join them.

'Tom Barnet, Tower Captain,' Ralph said with a flourish. 'Tom meet Cathy. We're persuading her to come up the tower on practice night.'

Tom's dark hair was thick but the top of his head looked as if it had been battened down with a mallet. He pulled up a spare chair and sat down heavily.

With a tremor of delight Cathy felt the

pressure of Arnold's leg against hers and hoped her expression didn't give her away.

The Tower Captain, his ruddy complexion deepened by the warmth, leaned forward and the talk turned to bellringing.

'Bill Gedge is here somewhere,' Tom said as he placed his empty beer mug on the table.

Arnold picked it up. 'Same again?'

'Thanks, lad.' Tom raised his voice. 'Come on over here, Bill. The young lady wants to hear some of your ringing tales.'

'Oh aye?' The old man hobbled towards them on legs that seemed too frail for his weight. 'Well, Miss, it were like this.' His voice sounded shaky as he cleared his throat. 'Jimmy were a Mellstone Ringer forty year ago. He caught his thumb in the end of the rope one night and couldn't get 'un out. It were wrenched right off and he never saw his thumb no mwore!'

There was roar of laughter at the horror on Cathy's face. She took a gulp of Babycham.

'What about that young chap who thought he knew it all?' Ralph prompted as he leaned back in his seat, his eyes bright with laughter.

When it was time to go Arnold caught hold of Cathy's arm and propelled her outside into the windy night, calling goodnight to the others.

'Don't be put off by old Spindleshanks and his stories,' he murmured. 'I like my girls to show some guts..'

29

The significance of that remark made Cathy thoughtful as the cold air hit her. Arnold, stumbling a little on the rough ground, pressed her close to him to steady himself.

'I'll see you home,' he said.

The beams of his torchlight made uneven patterns on the lane as they walked past the invisible Tidings Tree, its leaves rustling from the branches swaying overhead. He clicked the torch off when they reached Lynch Cottage.

In the sudden darkness Cathy felt Arnold's nearness and wondered, her heart lurching, if he would kiss her.

'See you Practice Night then,' he said as he moved away from her. He snapped his torch on again.

She looked back as she went inside but he had gone.

*   *   *

'Jenny Turner, Jenny Turner, Jenny Turner's a slow learner!'

With hot colour enflaming her face Jenny spun round and glared at Joe Barden. In the rising wind her hair stung her eyes and she brushed it back angrily.

'Jenny Turner's a sl . . .'

'I'm not, I'm not!' she screamed, stamping her foot on the asphalt playground. 'I'm not!'

'Jenny Turner's a slow . . .'

She sprang at him but he held her off with

30

one hand and grinned down at her, his eyes vicious.

'I'm not Jenny Turner,' she shrieked as she kicked out at him.

He grabbed her round the throat and struggling to be free she lost her balance and fell. She heard a blast from the whistle and then Miss Bryer was standing over her.

'Jenny Finlay, get up at once.'

Jenny's head swam as she staggered to her feet.

'Now, what's going on?'

'She kicked me, Miss.'

'I'll see you later, Joe Barden. Get into school, both of you. And Jenny, have the sense to keep away from the big boys.'

A flash of compassion filled Karen for a moment as she looked down at the child's white face. She'd had the rough edge of Mrs Barden's tongue herself more than once and Joe took after his mother. He had certainly got it in for Jenny.

'I did kick him, Miss,' Jenny admitted. 'He called me names. Then he strangled me.'

Karen sighed. 'Off you go, Jenny, and remember what I said.'

At least the child was truthful, she thought as she rescued an empty paper bag hurtling across the windy playground. In her place she would have done the same although kicking was too good for the likes of Joe Barden. She thought of the cane on the top shelf of the cupboard always kept locked. It might well get an outing before long if she had more trouble from him.

CHAPTER THREE

Elisabeth stood at her studio window and gazed out at the windy garden. The movement out there was superb and the smoke from the cottage chimney hid the thatch in bursts of blue haze. Here was inspiration for future paintings and she reached for her pad and charcoal to make lightning sketches so she wouldn't forget.

She ripped off page after page, wanting to get it all down while she had the chance. A black cat cringed out of the bushes with its body close to the shivering grass. Wary green eyes looked in her direction before it disappeared with its fur blowing the wrong way.

The wind was blowing the branches so that before she had sketched them one way they switched momentarily to another like mad dancers. Wonderful! She smiled as she sketched the patterns they made against the sky. Their infectious excitement made her want to throw open the door and battle her way to the bending trees themselves.

But she must stay here and work because it

was the life she had chosen and she couldn't let up even for a moment. For as long as she could remember she had longed to live in a beautiful place with the freedom to paint but had never thought it could happen until her great-aunt's legacy had made it possible.

So, a thatched cottage in Dorset . . . idyllic or pure madness? Now she knew it was neither because of the hard work involved merely to exist. With luck she could manage financially until Christmas but after that it was up to her. She fought down a stab of panic as another gust shook the trees.

And there was the cat again emerging from behind the dahlias. He leapt onto the wall and jumped down the other side into the school playground but not before she had sketched him as he poised ready to leap. She smiled, pleased with her work.

The door bell rang on the studio extension. Who could be calling on such an afternoon as this? She threw down her pad, went out and ran head down across the lawn.

She paused for a moment to regain her breath before opening the front door. On the doorstep, his large frame cutting out the light, stood the vicar.

Surprised, she stared at him. She had seen him about the village once or twice and wondered at his comparative youth. He had stopped on one occasion as she sat at her easel beneath the Tidings Tree and admired her work and this had pleased her because she appreciated hearing the reaction of others to her paintings.

He cleared his throat. 'Miss Turner?'

'Mr Moore.' She smiled. 'Won't you come in?'

She looked bemusedly round the living-room where the scent of pot pouri and Michaelmas daisies mingled with the smell of wood ash. A layer of dust decorated the bookcase in the alcove and papers were strewn on the window seat. She was aware, suddenly, of her paint-smeared dirndl skirt and put up a hand to push her hair out of her eyes.

'Ah splendid, a wood fire!' His voice had a confident ring to it. 'Such a windy day. Just listen to it.'

She smiled. 'I love it, don't you, all that wild movement of air?'

He nodded his agreement. 'Indeed, I found myself enjoying battling against it as I came round the corner. I believe it's getting worse and there will be damage done somewhere. That was an especially loud roar, wasn't it?'

'A good day to be indoors,' she agreed.

'I hope I'm not interrupting your work, Miss Turner? I trust it's going well for you?' He looked at her intently, screwing up his eyes so that his bushy brows seemed almost to meet.

She nodded. 'I've been sketching the effect the wind has on the surroundings.'

'An interesting subject.'

34

Won't you sit down, Mr Moore?' She indicated the armchair by the fire and seated herself on a low stool to reach forward to the log basket.

'What a splendid painting you were doing a week or two ago of the view of Mellstone from the Tidings Tree,' he said.

She flushed with pleasure. 'Thank you.' She felt that the painting was one of her best but it hadn't yet sold. 'A beautiful September day, balmy and still.'

'It was indeed.' He leaned back in his chair and sighed. 'The tree looked so different this afternoon creaking beneath the black sky and its leaves flying. It will lose them early this year, I fear.'

She raised her face. 'But I like painting the tree in all its moods. It's magnificent. We're so lucky to be living here.'

He looked towards the window as a strident sound rose and fell in the distance above the snarl of the wind. An ambulance here in Mellstone? There were voices now too, shouting.

Elisabeth sprang up in alarm at the same time as Mr Moore. 'What's going on?' she cried as they rushed out into the strong air and looked towards the Tidings Tree.

At first she could see nothing but a blur of fallen branch and foliage and people crowding round.

'I hope no one's hurt,' he said as they ran

towards it.

Then Elisabeth saw the ambulance but people were crowding round and hiding everything apart from the huge branch that had been wrenched off the tree.

'Who is it?' Robert Moore demanded.

A way was made clear for him and through it Elisabeth was able to see someone lying on the ground in a grey skirt and green jersey. A child? *'Jenny?'* She rushed forward and threw herself down on her knees beside her. Rough hands were pulling her back and she tried to fight them off.

'Are you the mother?' someone asked.

She nodded and brushed stinging hair out of her eyes.

'Stand back for a moment. We're doing all we can.'

She felt helpless in the hands of these men who were lifting Jenny onto a stretcher.

'She's not dead?' she whispered through fear-stiffened lips.

'She's unconscious. We're getting her to hospital as quickly as possible.'

And now Jenny was in the ambulance and they were signalling to her to follow. Inside, Elisabeth gazed at Jenny's white face, thankful there didn't seem to be a mark on her even though her hair was a tangled mess of leaves and twigs. She tried to move some of them but her fingers trembled too much. She ought to pray but she could not.

Vividly the memory of their first morning in Mellstone invaded her mind . . . Jenny's blissful excitement, her own joy in the sparkling grass and the uncurling marigolds by the wall. There was no thought then that the beauty was illusory. How naive she had been, so ready to see only the surface loveliness.

They set off, slowly at first until they reached the main road and then they gathered speed. With a sickening heart she was aware of the siren while all the time she gazed at Jenny lying motionless beneath a red blanket.

Much later, in the hospital waiting room there was the murmur of voices at her side. The vicar, Mr Moore, pressed her hand and was gone.

Instead she saw the anxious face of a woman whose face she knew. Elisabeth stared at the blackberry stain on the sleeve of the mauve cardigan and listened to the soft voice that seemed to flow to her through a fog. She was Mrs Cameron who lived in one of the terraced cottages opposite and had been kind to her the day they moved in.

'I said to John . . .' Mrs Cameron murmured. 'We came running out when we heard the noise. And there was the branch down and little Jenny near it. So lucky, dear, that the vicar was with you. John drove me here at once to be with you . . .'

John? Oh yes, Mrs Cameron's nephew who was sitting on the other side of her. She had met John Ellis only once when he showed her round Marigold Cottage and she had seen Mellstone for the first time.

Elisabeth clasped and unclasped her hands. A sob broke from her and she bit her lip.

After a while the seat beside her became vacant and John took it. She heard Mrs Cameron's voice talking to her in words that were soothing in their triviality.

A nurse approached them. They would take good care of Jenny and would be in touch immediately if there was any change.

'I must stay here,' Elisabeth said. 'I can't go home and leave her here.'

John was talking to the nurse now in a low voice. He turned to Elisabeth and she saw the sympathy in his eyes.

'Aunt Ruth will look after you,' he said.

She felt stifled in kindness but all her instincts cried out that she couldn't go home when Jenny needed her. 'You don't understand,' she said.

His voice was unruffled as he said, 'Think of Jenny. What good will you be to her if you don't look after yourself? For her sake you must be sensible.'

Sensible? How was it sensible to leave Jenny among strangers? 'I'm staying here,' she said.

She thought he might take her home by force. His face was stern, his eyes steel-blue. Then he relaxed and smiled briefly. 'It seems that you are more stubborn than I am,' he said.

When the school bus had gone and the last of the children had left the playground Cathy went back inside to her silent classroom. She still felt numb from the shock of hearing the clatter in the next room earlier when Tom Barnet had come blundering in. She had opened the intervening door in time to hear his reason for being here, that a child was injured by the falling branch from the tree and was gone to hospital. The child from Marigold Cottage.

Hardly aware of what she was doing Cathy shut the door and concentrated on sounding calm and reassuring. She had got out a story book and started to read aloud and one by one the children had become involved with the story they were hearing until it was home time.

Now the air felt chill and Cathy shivered. She reached for the window pole, closed the top window and then dropped the pole with a clatter against the wall. The water from one of the jam jars on the nature table smelt rank and she went out to the cloakroom to change it.

There was no sound from the junior classroom, no scraping of a chair or cupboard doors closing. She pushed open the intervening door. Miss Bryer, who sat slumped at her desk, straightened and looked up. Her face was white.

39

'Yes?' she snapped.

Cathy hesitated. 'Is there anything I can do for you?'

'Such as?' The tone was brittle.

'Can I see to any clearing up?' Cathy looked round and saw that nothing was out of place and the blackboard was wiped clean.

'I have to wait here for Mr Moore. He's sure to come when he hears what's happened. He'll need to see me on my own before Mrs Pengold gets here. You get off home. There's nothing you can do here.'

Or anywhere else for that matter, Cathy thought. Useless as usual. She opened her mouth to offer to make a cup of tea but then shut it again, knowing it would be refused. 'If you're sure?'

'I'm sure. About that at least.'

Outside sheets of drizzle swept across the playground. Cathy pulled her jacket closer round her, dreading looking in the direction of the Tidings Tree for what it had done to Jenny. She couldn't imagine how it would be now with a branch down. So different but just the same? Eerie and worrying.

At the school gate she met the vicar. He looked drawn and worried as he stood aside for her without his usual polite greeting.

'Indeed this is a bad business,' he said.

She nodded. 'I'm so sorry . . .'

'Is Miss Bryer still here?'

'She's waiting for you.'

'I see. Thank you.'

With a slight bow he moved off. She remembered, suddenly, that she had left her bag in her classroom. But this was not the time to retrieve it and eavesdrop on the confrontation in the next room.

As she walked along the deserted lane against the swirling wind, Cathy thought of the poor child lying beneath the fallen branch. Tears filled her eyes. She was glad of the rain to disguise them even though there was no one to see.

Mellstone seemed like a ghost village, shocked by recent events.

* * *

If Jenny dies, Karen Bryer thought, *I shall be blamed*. In her head she heard again the clamour of voices and the tapping of paint brushes on jars before the deathly hush as Tom Barnet came rushing into the room to tell them about the terrible thing that had happened. His rugged face was pale. The children had sprung to their feet and were motionless. It was like a ghastly game of statues as they waited to hear him blurt out why he had come.

A swift automatic count of heads had been her first reaction. Then incredible horror. Tom was unable to tell her much but it was enough. Oh yes, it was enough to know that serious

41

repercussions would follow.

The atmosphere was electric.

'Sit sown everyone,' she had ordered.

There was a shuffling of feet and loosening of tongues. Two girls began to cry.

'Stop that!' she had snapped as she sat down too. She must establish immediately how it was that no one had seen Jenny slip out of the classroom. But no one could tell her that. Then she harangued them, making them promise to keep well away from the tree on the way home. They would have taken no notice, of course.

The classroom door opened and Karen got up and stood with one hand pressed down on her desk to give her strength. Attack was the best form of defence, she thought.

'The child had no business to run out of school like that,' she said.'

The vicar looked down at her, his brows drawn together. 'I'd like to know exactly what happened here.'

She felt sick. 'Has she . . . is she?'

He seemed to hover over her. 'We don't know anything yet,' he said, his voice gruff. 'Mrs Cameron and her nephew are staying with Miss Turner at the hospital.'

Karen's mouth felt dry. 'I don't know why Jenny ran out of school on a day like this. There was no good reason.' She glanced at the window. The shaking trees on the far side of the wall gave glimpses of angry sky.

'It was sheer perversity. We had painting this afternoon which they all like. They were going to and fro changing their painting water in the cloakroom. They weren't all in the room at the same time so no one noticed.'

'I see. So you don't know how long she was missing?'

She gripped her hands together so tightly that her knuckles showed white. 'And what good would it be if I had?' she demanded. 'Anyone I sent after her would have been injured too.'

Robert Moore looked suddenly tired and much older. 'We must wait for what she can tell us when she gains consciousness.'

'She will come round . . . won't she?'

He gave a small shrug. 'She's in God's hands. We can only pray.'

Karen moved some papers from one side of her desk to the other and then looked at them as if she didn't know how they had got there. 'It was entirely Jenny's own fault.'

'Miss Turner may not see it like that and . . .' He broke off and clutched the side of the desk.

Karen looked at him in concern. 'Are you all right, Robert?'

'Yes,' he said. 'Perfectly.'

He certainly didn't look it. His cheeks had lost their colour and his eyes were dazed.

'Why don't you sit down?' She reached for a chair. 'Have you eaten since this happened?'

He moved his hands and stood upright. 'It

43

doesn't matter. We'll keep to the matter in hand, if you please.'

'Yes, well. The Parish Council and the Highways people . . . aren't they responsible? They must have known the tree was becoming dangerous.'

'No doubt it will be looked into.' He rubbed his hand over his forehead. 'Are you quite sure there was no reason for the child doing such a thing?'

'I've already told you. There was no good reason. I suppose financial worries and the odd way they live is all rubbing off on her and causing the child to do odd things. Why can't Miss Turner paint as a hobby instead of making such a big thing of it?'

'I admire Miss Turner for what she does.' He spoke stiffly. 'Something like that takes courage.'

'Sheer self-indulgence,' Karen burst out. 'Why can't she get a job like everyone else? It's Jenny who suffers . . .'

'So you're blaming Miss Turner?'

'Why should she blame me?'

'She hasn't yet,' he reminded her.

She would want someone's blood, Karen thought *especially if the child dies. Oh God, it couldn't happen, could it?'*

She looked at him bleakly. 'Wouldn't you be better comforting Miss Turner instead of coming here accusing me of negligence?' she said.

He gave her a swift penetrating glance as he turned to leave. 'We'll discuss this again later,' he said.

*   *   *

Outside the school Robert paused to feel in his pocket for his phial of tablets. The pain in his chest was still there. Not for anything would he have taken a tablet in front of her and have to admit that he was unable to cope without them.

His pride was as great as hers, he thought. As Chairman of the Governors he had visited the school to offer his support in this difficult situation but she would have none of it.

He crossed the lane and lifted the latch on Mrs Pengold's garden gate, tapped on the door and waited for permission to enter. She was huddled in a chair by the empty grate.

At once he was down at her side. 'Are you ill?'

She glanced up at him. 'You won't get me at no church service again, Vicar, if that's what you come for. I told you that when my Bert died.'

'I've come about the accident, Mrs Pengold.'

'He shouted, Tom did. The little maid were there and down it come.'

'You were there with her? Can you tell me what happened?'

She pursed her lips and was silent.

45

Something was worrying her because she wouldn't look at him but no amount of questioning from him would bring it to light if she chose not to tell him. Her stubbornness in blaming the Almighty for not intervening in her husband's death was proof of that. Although she still cleaned the building every week he suspected that the vow she made at the funeral never to set foot in the church for a service again would stand firm until her own.

He got up and rubbed his knees. 'Everything is being done for the child. You mustn't worry but I can see you're not well. I'll ask Mrs Barnes to sit with you while I telephone the doctor from the vicarage.'

'The likes of me can't afford to be ill.'

Robert took no notice. He plugged in the electric fire and filled the kettle to put on the stove. 'It was your day for cleaning the church, wasn't it?' he said with his back to her. 'Did you see the child before it happened?'

But she said no more. He was relieved, though, that she made no further attempt to prevent him from fetching her neighbour.

*   *   *

The narrow hospital bed that was eventually made available to Elisabeth was hard. Sleep was impossible. She stared up through the darkness at nothing and in her mind saw the Tidings Tree swaying and creaking in the wind.

46

When she had first seen it she had thought it beautiful in its ancient glory of fresh leaves. Now she knew that the reality was ugly.

Jenny couldn't tell her why she had run out of school, just that the wind made her do it. She had wanted to run and shout in it and so she had slipped out when no one was looking

Fearing to upset her, Elisabeth had said no more but had assured Jenny that she was all right now and was being looked after and would soon be home.

Now Elisabeth thought of that first time when she had arrived at Marigold Cottage with an appointment to view. She had felt that she was being judged by the vendor, John Ellis, and found wanting when he tried, surprisingly, to put her off purchasing the cottage. She had watched him walk down the path to his car afterwards, a tall lean man who looked supremely sure of himself. And she had been sure of herself too as she and Jenny began their new life in Mellstone. But now . . .

The Tidings tree was at the very heart of Mellstone and gave the village its identity. Everyone loved it. Over the long years it had been growing here it had witnessed so much.

And now the Tidings Tree had injured Jenny and it was impossible not to imagine that Mellstone was rejecting them because they didn't belong here.

CHAPTER FOUR

John Ellis walked across the lawn that stretched to the bottom of the hill behind Nether End Farmhouse. His dog, Fly, moved ahead and then looked back at him with puzzled brown eyes.

'It's all right, boy,' John said. 'A change of plan today, that's all.'

He had rung the hospital. The child was to stay in for at least another night but Miss Turner should be taken home. He had arranged to pick her up at two o'clock and then to drive her back for evening visiting time.

He glanced at his watch. There was time for a brisk walk up the hill to inspect wind damage now that the gale had blown itself out. He quickened his pace.

A slight nip of autumn in the air made his face glow as he climbed. It was a time of year he loved, the first tentative feel of the changing seasons.

They were near the top of the hill now and he paused to look back. Unlike Mellstone, Nether End had been lucky with no damage to speak of. Through the trees he could see the sunshine smoothing the turf on Larksbury Rings and the shadows deepening the hollows to grey-green.

He got his pipe out of his pocket and began to fill it as he gazed across the vale, remembering the disappointment to his six-year-old self on discovering that it wasn't the dark mysterious place that distance lent it but on closer inspection a place of tree-bordered fields and pleasant villages drowsing beneath the wide Dorset sky.

He had so many memories of both here at Nether End and of Mellstone where his mother's family had lived for years in Marigold Cottage. When the last tenants left he had offered it to his aunt and uncle in exchange for Ivy Cottage as it was bigger than their own. But Ivy Cottage had been their home since their wedding fifty years before and they didn't want to change.

He looked down at the pipe in his hand, knocked it out in a tree stump without lighting it and placed it in the pocket of his jacket.

He had had no choice but to put one or other cottage on the market because of the necessity of providing for Stephanie after their divorce. The land he was looking down on was his since the death of his parents. To lose any of it was unthinkable and to know that anyone should seek to take it from him was deeply hurtful.

Never again would he get himself into that position. Nether End was his, all thousand acres of it and so it would remain. It would have been good to have been able to pass it on

49

in due course to a son but it seemed it was not to be.

Change was inevitable and now Marigold Cottage was gone. He was relieved that it wasn't bought as a weekend cottage. Or worse, as a holiday let. Aunt Ruth was happy too because she liked the new occupants.

'Come now, Fly,' he said. 'Time to go home. We've seen enough.'

* * *

The wind was a loud whine, rising and falling, rising and falling, the monotonous scream of a tree in pain. After a short silence it started again with a skirl that hurt Elisabeth's eardrums and set her teeth aching.

She jerked awake in the afternoon daylight and ran to open the window. For a second the noise was more insistent until it stopped again. She looked towards the tree and stared in horror at the giant stalagmite of the bare trunk that was left.

She thought in anguish of the golden early September morning when she had painted the flickering sunlight on the thatched roofs nearby. It had been the feeling that mattered to her, the slight movement of air that had set the leaves rustling. And now they would never rustle like that again.

So engrossed had she been then that she was unaware of passersby until the changing shadows meant that it was time to go. A small elderly woman had come stumping along, cleaning paraphernalia clutched in both hands and her grey hair scraped back in a bun.

She hardly paused at Elisabeth's greeting. 'You'll be the new lady at Marigold Cottage,' she said, daring her to deny it. 'Straight already, are you?'

Unspoken criticism had hung between them.

The woman sniffed. 'I'm Alice Pengold as lives opposite. I got to get off now to clean the church. Black as the pot as like as not and me not fit to do it with them old screws playing me up.'

Rheumatism? Full of sympathy Elisabeth had watched her go stalking off, carrying her broom and mop like fixed bayonets. And that was only a few days ago yet seemed a lifetime.

Now, suddenly the tears came and when at last Elisabeth was ready to go downstairs she felt drained.

Mrs Cameron emerged from the kitchen, a tea towel stretched round her waist for an apron. 'I've made soup,' she said.

She smiled with such sweetness that Elisabeth felt tears in her throat again. She blew her nose. Mrs Cameron's cheeks were as pink as the cardigan she wore today. The scent of lavender about her soothing.

'Miss Bryer called,' she said as she carried the bowl of soup to the table. 'The vicar too. I told him John was running you back for visiting this evening. Men have been busy on the tree with their machines. Come and get started, dear.'

Elisabeth hardly recognised the tidy living-room as her own. This was how it would be if she hadn't spent all her time painting, she thought with a stab of guilt.

She sat down at the table and let Mrs Cameron put the soup spoon in her hand. 'I'll have to go into school after this and see Miss Bryer,' she said.

Mrs Cameron looked at her anxiously. 'Are you sure that can't wait until tomorrow, dear?'

Elisabeth finished the soup and got up before her courage failed. 'I must go now,' she said.

The last thing she wanted was to enter the building from which Jenny had run out in to the cruel wind yesterday but it had to be done. As she went in she glanced at the coat-filled pegs in the lobby and at the wellington boots scattered on the stone floor. One of the pegs was empty, no doubt Jenny's.

The classroom door opened and the headmistress came out. In her grey suit and with her dark hair pulled back from her face she looked pale and hollow-eyed. 'It was the child's own fault,' she said before Elisabeth could say anything.

'But why . . .'

Karen Bryer bit her lip. 'It's nearly playtime. I'll let the children out. We'll talk in the classroom.'

As soon as the room emptied she turned to Elisabeth, her expression anxious. 'I trust she'll be all right?' She seemed to hold her breath as she waited for the confirmation.

Elisabeth nodded. 'I hope so. I believe so. Can you tell me why she ran out of school like that, Miss Bryer?'

Karen's face hardened. 'I didn't send her out if that's what you mean. The first I knew about it was when Tom Barnet came rushing in to tell us.'

'So that's why no one went after her?'

'No one has ever done such a thing in this school before, I assure you. No one. I fail to understand how a normal child would do such a thing on a day like yesterday. I was hoping you could tell me why, Miss Turner. Is everything all right at home? No problems she may have picked up on and worried about?'

Elisabeth looked at her in silence. She had come to reassure Jenny's teacher and hadn't expected to be verbally attacked like this.

'Are you quite sure you can't throw any light on something?'

Elisabeth flushed. 'I'm prepared to say to anyone you like, Miss Bryer, that what happened was Jenny's own fault,' she said. 'I don't hold you responsible.'

Karen shrugged and turned her face away for a moment. When she looked back at Elisabeth the relief in her eyes was apparent.

53

It would have been cruel not to have made her decision clear, Elisabeth thought as she turned to leave, but after the ungracious reaction she was tempted to change her mind. Miss Bryer might at least have thanked her. Instead she had made her dislike of Jenny unnecessarily obvious, a hurtful thing to do at such a time.

*　　　*　　　*

Later that day John Ellis smiled as he leaned across to open the passenger door in his car for Elisabeth. She turned to wave to the stout figure of his aunt who appeared, beaming, in the doorway of Marigold Cottage.

Elisabeth knew what to expect as they passed the tree but it was still a shock to see its shorn trunk. A knot of people standing nearby stared at the car and it seemed to her as if their malevolence was directed at her. Even the low cloud obscuring the downs looked menacing.

'They're blaming me!' she cried.

'Nonsense,' John said as they drove down the lane past the church. 'It wasn't your fault the branch came down. The tragedy was that Jenny was underneath it at the time.'

Elisabeth took a deep breath and struggled to be reasonable but she couldn't forget the grim-faced woman and the old man's threatening gestures. She shivered.

'Concentrate on Jenny getting better, why don't you? I understand you went to see Karen Bryer?'

'I didn't do much good there. She doesn't like Jenny.'

John smiled briefly, his eyes on the road ahead. 'It's a bad situation for Karen. She doesn't mean half she says, you know, and she's bound to be worried over this.'

'I realise that, of course.'

'Our mothers were close friends. I've known Karen for years. We played together as children. She didn't have too happy a time of it with that father of hers.'

He said no more and she was grateful for the silence.

*   *   *

'Wait, Jenny,' Elisabeth called as Jenny ran ahead of her along the lane, her red hair awry and her green gabardine raincoat bright against the thinning hedge. This was their first proper walk since Jenny had come home from hospital and she didn't want her to overdo things.

'You're so slow. We'll never get there,' Jenny cried.

There was no sign of fatigue about her now but Elisabeth still felt anxious, unable to truly believe that all was well. Tomorrow Jenny would be back at school and life could continue as before. She smiled as she caught up with Jenny, willing herself to think positively and be thankful.

This afternoon they had chosen to go up past Nether End to see if they could find the footpath that led up to Larksbury Rings. As always Elisabeth was on the look-out for scenes to paint, ready to fix them in her memory for future inspiration.

'Not so fast,' Elisabeth said, laughing. 'See that spider's web on the hawthorn shining in the sun. It's beautiful.'

Jenny gave it only a cursory glance before dancing ahead and nearly missing the stile half-hidden in the hedge. She skidded to a halt. 'Is this the way?'

'I think so,' said Elisabeth doubtfully. 'We'll try it anyway.'

She waited for Jenny to climb over first and then followed. The grass was soft underfoot now. The path they were on led up and across a field and then veered to the right alongside a hedge and seemed to be taking them away from Larksbury Rings. But it didn't matter. They had come out to explore this afternoon and that's what they were doing.

Jenny tugged at her arm. 'Look,' she said urgently. It's *her*. She's there picking things.' She gave a frightened gasp.

Ahead of them on the path a figure appeared in a black coat, a flowered overall showing beneath.

'That's only Mrs Pengold, Jenny,' said Elisabeth.

'But what's she doing?'

'She's just out for a walk up here like us.'

'But she's picking things.'

Mrs Pengold had an armful of grasses and twigs and a single scarlet-berried head of lords-and-ladies in the middle. Jenny stared at it wide-eyed. 'It's horrible,' she said. 'Like blood.'

The old lady held the bunch close to her as they came near. 'In the churchyard she was,' she muttered, pointing at Jenny. 'Running and dancing like a mad thing.'

Jenny cringed behind Elisabeth.

Mrs Pengold gave Elisabeth no chance to speak but stumped off down the hill muttering to herself.

'She made the branch fall off the tree,' Jenny said miserably.

'Nonsense, Jenny. It was the wind that did that.'

'Why is it called the Tidings Tree? Is it because people always met there to tell their news?'

'Something like that, I expect.'

'But they won't be able to do that now.'

'Why not? They say the tree will sprout out and grow again one day.'

'Will Mrs Pengold make it grow?'

Elisabeth looked at her anxiously. 'No human being can make it grow, Jenny. It'll grow on its own.'

She had seen Alice Pengold several times about the village but today she seemed furtive as if she had something on her mind. There was something about Jenny, too, that was worrying. Could it be that the accident had affected her in some way that made her believe Alice was responsible?

'You're tired, Jenny,' she said. 'And I'm not sure this is the best way to go. It looks as if we should have started off up Hodman's Hollow to get to Larksbury Rings. We'll go home now and try another day.'

Jenny nodded, subdued, and took hold of her hand.

Elisabeth glanced across at the Iron Age hillfort that was Larksbury Rings. The olive green grass looked shiny in the afternoon sun but had no power to inspire her now.

*   *   *

Cathy sat at her open bedroom window and looked down into the back garden of Lynch Cottage, the home of Miss Buckley and Miss King, where she was lodging with the two retired librarians.

'Just temporarily, dear,' Miss King, had whispered to her on her arrival as if by keeping her voice low she felt it was quite respectable to be paid for the board and lodging they provided.

'You may find somewhere more suitable before our little flat is ready for you,' Miss Buckley had growled, the glint in her eye daring her to do so.

Not that she would even consider it, Cathy thought as she watched Miss King pottering about down below. When her accommodation had been suggested by the vicar after her interview it was thought that the small flat being converted from part of the ladies' rambling home would be ready for the start of the Autumn Term. Now it wouldn't be ready until after Christmas. She was quite happy to lodge with them meanwhile and was beginning to get used to their extraordinary ways.

Miss King, small and twittery and clad usually in baggy trousers, threw herself into transforming the large overgrown garden while Miss Buckley who always wore thick tweed suits summer and winter, prowled about indoors petting their bad-tempered Jack Russell, Benjy, the love of her life.

Benjy trotted across the lawn now to snap at Miss King's feet. Then he made a sudden swoop into the heaving chrysanthemums to be extricated by a triumphant Miss King who bore him, struggling and snarling, indoors.

But when Cathy went down for her evening meal of cold meat and salad he was nowhere to be seen. Both ladies were sorting china at one end of the large dining table.

'Take no notice of us, dear, Miss King said,

busily engrossed in laying out rows of pink saucers. 'We're having one of our little parties this evening as you'll be out. You wouldn't enjoy it being young. We'll just spread all this out at one end and we won't disturb you at all.'

'I'm going along to the church to see if I'd like to learn how to ring the bells,' Cathy said.

Miss Buckley knelt down to reach inside the deep cupboard for more pink cups. 'A fine old English tradition,' she mumbled.

'There!' Miss King said in triumph as she placed the last saucer in place. 'Now all we have to do is to match them up.'

She examined each cup passed to her so that each self-patterned one could be placed in the correct saucer. For a few tense moments they matched in silence.

'There seem too many of this sort,' said Miss King at last. 'Are you sure, dear, that you got all the saucers out of the cupboard?'

Once more Miss Buckley grovelled on the floor and fished out a chipped saucer from deep inside.

Miss King eyed it in dismay. 'How very freak!'

Cathy smiled at her choice of expression and then poured herself another cup of tea wanting to ask if the chipped cups were to be paired with the chipped saucers but didn't quite like to. This was a serious matter.

'You've missed some of them,' Miss Buckley accused. 'Or broken some and not mentioned it. It's pretty pathetic if we can't offer our guests decent china.' She banged down an offending cup and charged from the room.

Miss King looked about to burst into tears.

Cathy leapt up. 'I'll help you match them, Miss King. We'll do the best we can. No one will notice anyway.'

'You're such a kind girl,' said Miss King.

Cathy smiled. Miss King was kind too.

She set out for the church far too early and wandered about the overgrown churchyard thinking of Jenny Finlay who had come here on that fateful windy day but couldn't explain what made her do it.

Perhaps the wind had excited her to such a degree that she couldn't stay indoors a moment longer and the churchyard seemed like a secret refuge?

'Why so sad?'

She spun round at the sound of Arnold's voice.

Amazingly she had almost forgotten his features in the time since they met in the farm kitchen and was surprised to note his moustache and the way he held himself so straight. His wavy brown hair was receding slightly though he could only be a few years older than her.

'Regretting coming along this evening?' he said.

'No, oh no. I was just thinking about the accident.'

61

'The tree? It's been rotten for years if you ask me.' He seemed supremely confident as he shrugged the subject away. 'Come on. The others'll be waiting.'

Several people were going inside the church.

'Evening Arnold,' said one of them whom Cathy recognised from his rugged features as Tom Barnet, the Tower Captain. 'Nice to meet you again, Miss Mellor. We'll go on up, shall we?'

They followed him up a spiral staircase to the ringing chamber, a small room with benches along two of the walls and narrow slits for windows. Through small holes in the ceiling hung eight ropes. The ends of the ropes were attached to a pulley and Cathy watched as Tom let it down and separated each rope and let it dangle on the floor.

'I'll get the tenor up and then take you up to the belfry, Miss Mellor,' Tom said as he removed his jacket and rolled up his shirt sleeves.

Cathy heard slow footsteps approaching and as Arnold pulled open the door she saw a shadow appear on the wall looking for a moment like a grey apparition disappearing in to the stonework as someone came into the chamber.

'Evening, Bill,' Tom said. 'We got a visitor tonight.'

'Evening, Tom,' Bill Gedge said as he sank down gasping on the nearest bench and shot

Cathy a suspicious glance. 'Them steps'll be the death of me.'

Cathy went with Tom further up the spiral staircase. He opened a small door and shone his torch into the belfry that smelt cold and dank. All the bells hung downwards except for the largest which was balanced, upright, on such a narrow piece of wood it seemed as if the merest touch would send the bell toppling.

'You can see why the rope ends must be tied up out of the way when the bells are ready for ringing,' said Tom. 'I've seen a man all but throttled with a rope lashing round his neck. He'd have been a goner if he'd moved.'

Cathy shuddered. 'What happened?'

'He kept still until it untangled itself.'

A sudden tremendous crashing made her jump.

'Someone's pulling up the treble,' Tom shouted in her ear.

The smallest bell swung from side to side in ever increasing arcs. Then it slid silently upright onto its stay and the silence was stunning.

Back in the ringing chamber Arnold was getting things organised so that they were ready to start ringing as soon as Tom got hold of his rope. Cathy's eyes were on Arnold who was ringing the fourth bell. The tip of his tongue showed between his lips. The sleeves of his green jersey were rolled up above his elbows and the muscles rippled in his strong arms. He was the most handsome man there.

Afterwards as they went out into the darkening churchyard Arnold caught hold of Cathy's arm. 'Shall we walk a bit?' he said.

She caught her breath. 'But don't you want to join the others?'

'And leave you on your own?'

'Well . . .'

'I wouldn't be happy about that.'

There was a chorus of goodnights and she marvelled that Arnold chose to be with her. As they walked down the path to the gate she struggled to think of something interesting to say to make it worth his while. But there was no need because he talked of the bad day he'd had trying to persuade his uncle that covering his land with conifers was the way to go in the future.

'Uncle Perry's as stubborn as they come,' he said. 'He thinks he knows best but I'm not having it. But enough of that. We'll go along by the brook for a bit. The moon will soon be up.'

She thrilled as he took her hand in his and switched off his torch.

* * *

On Sunday morning with the smell of late autumn in the air Elisabeth set out for church with Jenny. Mr Moore had been so kind, offering his support when she so badly needed

64

it that it was only fair that she should do something for him in return. Even though it was Sunday and a day of rest she would work hard for the rest of the day planning more oil paintings and making a start on one of them.

Jenny skipped along beside her, slowing to a walking pace as they caught up with Miss Lewis from the shop and two people Elisabeth didn't know.

As they went through the lych gate the bells quickened until they sounded paranoiac in their urgency. Ringing them down it was called, Elisabeth thought, proud of her newly-found knowledge. Mrs Cameron had told her that one bellringing practice night when she had run outside in alarm to find out what all the jangling noise was about. It made the bells safe apparently but she hadn't asked safe from what.

They seated themselves behind the rest of the congregation. The bells were silent now. A small door scraped open and figures emerged. Among them Elisabeth saw the young school teacher, Cathy Mellor, and the young man she knew was a forestry student staying on his uncle's farm. She was reminded of a painting she'd seen in an exhibition in Bournemouth that had intrigued her with its air of mystery surrounding the young man who was obviously leaving his beloved for exciting adventures elsewhere.

Afterwards in the porch the vicar shook her

hand with a warmth she found encouraging. 'Indeed it's good to see you, Miss Turner,' he said. 'I'm pleased you came along this morning and Jenny too.'

Elisabeth smiled. A job well done, she thought. As she turned hurriedly to follow Jenny she knocked her wrist against the stone doorway. Her gasp was unheard in the surge of words from behind as the vicar spoke to the two ladies from Lynch Cottage.

Jenny took hold of Elisabeth's hand as they emerged into the sunlight but the pain was so great she cried out.

Jenny looked at her in alarm.

'I've done something to my wrist,' Elisabeth said. 'It hurts. It'll be all right in a minute.'

But when she pulled her sleeve back it was obvious from the swelling that it would take longer than that. 'I'll get a cold water bandage on it when we get home,' she said. 'It's all right, Jenny, I've bruised it, that's all. She pulled her sleeve down over her wrist and they moved on.

Jean Varley caught up with them as they reached the gate and her calm face broke into a smile. 'How about coming along to us this evening, both of you?' She looked down at Jenny. 'My word, don't you look smart in that lovely coat?'

Jenny blushed with pleasure. 'It's new.'

Elisabeth felt pleased too. Jenny had taken such delight in its purchase on their visit to

Hilbury yesterday. She had put on a spurt of growth and now was the time to do something about it before winter set in. Since the proprietor of the art shop had agreed to take three of her paintings to frame and display in his gallery Elisabeth felt the need to celebrate.

She had to work even harder than ever now of course, even on a Sunday. Jenny understood this and also the need to keep it a secret between the two of them in case it offended sensibilities and caused comment.

'My young niece and nephew are with us at the moment and need some company,' Jean Varley said. 'Do come.'

Elisabeth hesitated. It was clear what Jenny felt about the invitation. 'Thank you,' she said. 'We'd love to.'

By the afternoon there were splatters of rain against the windows when Elisabeth opened her studio door and went inside but that didn't bother her. There were paints to sort out and her brushes to check. Even with her painful wrist she had plenty to do to keep her occupied. Jenny was busy in the living-room at her plasticine board fashioning all sorts of shapes and sizes of pots for the model flower shop she was constructing from an empty Cornflakes box. She would be absorbed for hours.

She winced in pain as she tried to twist her wrist. She had injured her it because she had tried to do something good to please the vicar.

How unfair was that? But it had happened, however unfortunate. What she found really disquieting was the feeling she was not alone in her studio when there was obviously no one here but herself.

She gazed out of the window at the thatched roof of the cottage and the branches of the elm tree against the leaden sky. The leaves would soon be all gone now. There was nothing tangibly wrong just a feeling of brooding malevolence she found hard to throw off.

Faint scraping against the back wall made her heart beat faster until she realised that it must be an animal . . . the black cat perhaps that sometimes came into the garden. Or was it someone who had climbed over from the school playground next door? But the school was closed today because was Sunday.

She shook herself mentally. She had no time for these silly fancies. She was here to work, wrist or no wrist.

CHAPTER FIVE

John Ellis heaved up a box of apples and staggered up the path to the door of Ivy Cottage. It had been a disastrous season this year with poor pollination because of the wet May. As if that wasn't enough the gale had brought down fruit before it could be picked.

A good twenty per cent of it was lost but at least Aunt Ruth would be glad of the windfalls for her innumerable jars of apple jelly.

Beaming, she came to the doorway and started to speak so fast that beads of perspiration glistened on her forehead. His uncle was slumped as usual in his armchair wearing large grey carpet slippers. On the shelf above his head copper pots glittered in the firelight and there was a warm scent of tobacco and burning coal from the fireplace.

'Hello there, John,' he said, as welcoming as his wife but in his deadpan way.

Mrs Cameron untied her apron. 'I was just saying to Donald that I promised Jean Varley I'd pop along and see her tonight. I won't be the only one there. You can come too, John. Martin's sure to be home.'

John shrugged his shoulders as he placed the box of apples by the wall. He caught a sardonic gleam from Donald Cameron's eyes.

'Best go with her, boy,' he advised. 'You know your aunt. You'll get no peace till you do.'

John thought of his own peaceful room and the few hours of leisure he had promised himself with the book on coastal navigation that had arrived for him yesterday morning.

He smiled. 'Get your coat on then, Aunt Ruth,' he said.

As she reached up to the nail on the door John caught a whiff of perfume that reminded

69

him of hiding beneath the lavender bushes as a small boy in his grandparents' garden over the road. Aunt Ruth had been slender then. She had worn her fair hair in soft waves round her head but her eyes had seemed sad.

As the years passed she had created a strict routine for herself no doubt in compensation for the children that never came. Now there was comfort and warmth about her and the sadness was gone. She made jam and marmalade in season and dried the mint and parsley from the garden. What she did with it all he didn't know. She probably gave most of it away and gained a great deal of pleasure from doing so.

'My shoes, John,' she said. 'Over by the fender.'

The shoes sat side by side, black and highly polished.

Grunting a little, she sat down and put them on and then picked up her fluffy mauve hat and placed it firmly on her head. She was ready.

A babble of voices greeted them when they were ushered through the kitchen at the farmhouse where he saw three children, Jenny among them, involved in a game of the board game Ludo at the table. In the large, rather dim sitting room only the crackling of the log fire gave it a feeling of life. John seated himself in the empty chair near Elisabeth and accepted a glass of sherry. In her brown long-sleeved

70

dress she seemed part of the background until she smiled and her eyes lit up in such a way that set her face glowing. Around them the other guests chatted as they began to talk of the countryside round Mellstone, inevitably getting back to the Tidings Tree.

'I had a word with the Highways Department,' John said, leaning forward a little. 'They're not admitting that the branch was rotten.'

'So why did they hack the rest of them off?'

'They had no sensible answer to that, I'm afraid.'

Elisabeth shivered. 'The tree was so beautiful and now it's an ugly stump. I'll never paint it again, even from memory.'

'But no doubt there are plenty of other suitable subjects. Tell me, how do you set about selling your work?'

Her eyes shone. 'There's a shop in Hilbury, the art shop in the main street. They have a gallery at the back and have taken three of my paintings. They like to do the framing themselves and I'm happy with that. I'm hoping to make other contacts too. Once I get known it may be easier.'

'I suppose at the moment it's a case of churning them out and getting a lot done in a short time to get yourself started?'

She looked shocked. 'Oh no, I'd never do that. Each painting is unique and portraying its own mood to satisfy myself.'

71

'But surely there's a difference between expressing yourself in paint and painting commercially?'

'Not in my case,' she said with a firmness that surprised him.

'Do you ever paint seascapes like your famous ancestor?'

She smiled. 'Turner, the English landscape and seascape painter? I'd claim him if I could. Sadly he was no relation of mine or some of his talent might have rubbed off on me.'

'I have a print of Turner's *Mouth of the River Humber* on my wall,' he said. 'D'you know it? The original hangs in the British Museum, I believe. Or it did.'

She gave a small sigh. 'He achieved such brilliant lighting with all that swirling brushwork.'

John was silent for a moment, thinking how very much he would like to own an original painting of the sea. 'You'll have to be hard on yourself if you're going to make a living.' he said. 'You'll have to concentrate on the selling aspect and take commissions whether you want to paint to order or not. You'll go under otherwise.'

She sighed. 'I can see I'll have to be really tough.'

'It's bound to change you.'

She leaned forward in her seat. The firelight cast flickering light across her face and heightened the auburn lights in her soft hair.

72

John knew, suddenly, that he didn't want her to change.

*   *   *

Jean Varley, trying to pass round a plate of sandwiches, gave up and placed them on the sideboard instead. 'My word, what a crush. I'm not complaining though. I like nothing better than to see so many here.'

Elisabeth smiled at her and received a warm smile and a shrug of the shoulders in return. It was good to feel this sense of well-being because she felt part of the scene in Mellstone. There was inspiration in it that took her by surprise. Perhaps she should get out in to company more. It wasn't wasting time as she had thought. She was shaken with the knowledge that being here in Mellstone was the right thing for her in spite of occasional misgivings. She must hold on to that.

Elisabeth leaned back in her chair, feeling her earlier fatigue seep out of her. She rested her right hand in her lap, making sure that the bandage round her wrist was hidden. Talking to John was pleasant even though his opinion that she wasn't going to make a go of it was disturbing.

But maybe she needed this challenge? Maybe it was enough to strengthen her resolve and prove to him and to Mellstone that the decision she had made was the right one. She knew this now just as Cathy knew that Mellstone was the right place for her. Tomorrow her wrist would be less painful and she could set to work with confidence.

*   *   *

As soon as the bus children had gone home next day Karen heard Cathy return to her classroom. She pushed open the intervening door and went in. Cathy was sitting at her desk but sprang up on seeing her.

'All that noise in your classroom this afternoon, Miss Mellor! What on earth were you doing?' Karen demanded.

'We . . . we were having a story. I let them act it.'

'The storming of the Bastille?'

The faint glimmer of something in the younger woman's eyes vanished immediately. Karen pressed her lips tightly together, the way they always seemed to be when the two of them were alone.

'I'm sorry,' Cathy said.

'You're supposed to be able to cope better than that, for goodness sake,' she said. 'Did they teach you nothing at your training college?'

Cathy let out a sigh which she tried, unsuccessfully to turn into a cough. 'I thought . . .'

'Well, don't think. Concentrate on keeping

74

the children under control. And if you need help ask for it. You can't go on like this and the sooner you realise it the better.'

Cathy bit her lip.

Now it was Karen's turn to sigh as she turned on her heel and returned to her own room. Next door the sounds of a cupboard being locked and of exercise books being scraped off a shelf soon ceased and there was silence. Cathy had escaped the other way instead of coming through the main classroom and wishing her goodnight as she left.

Well, she couldn't blame her. She knew she was unfair to the girl but couldn't seem to stop herself. One look at that submissive expression and she was off. Oh to be young again! Cathy made her feel so old.

Karen picked up her keys from her desk to lock the glass-fronted cupboard behind her. Then she paused to glance at her reflection.

Just look at all those lines, she thought in disgust. Only yesterday she had found the first grey hair in her dark head and that had been a shock. She was twelve years older than Cathy and felt every one of them like a burden.

In another year of two there would be nothing to stop the girl moving on to wherever she chose while she had nothing left to look forward to than growing older and crabbier and watching her mother suffer more and more with arthritis.

John was good calling in on Mother every

now and again and allowing her to reminisce about the old days when his own mother was alive. Just lately he had been coming when he knew she wouldn't be at home and the thought had occurred to Karen that he was avoiding her deliberately. Once he wouldn't have done that.

She sighed as she began to pack up, wanting the old days back when they had done so much together.

* * *

Elisabeth left her studio and came round the side of the cottage and into the front garden feeling exhausted and exhilarated at the same time. Completing a painting usually left her feeling drained but not today. Her wrist was less painful now and she had finished something she knew was good and she needed to celebrate. Jenny had gone to play with Judith Wintle and she was free. But free to do what?

She snapped off the dead head of an orange calendula and then heard the clatter of the school gate closing behind Cathy.

'I'm so glad to see you.' she called. 'Have you a minute?'

Cathy's pale face lit up into a smile. 'Of course.'

'I've got something to show you.' Elisabeth tried to suppress the excitement in her voice

76

but somehow couldn't help it. 'It's only a painting,' she added hurriedly.

'I'd love to see it,' Cathy said, obviously pleased. 'And to see where you work too.'

She was as admiring of the studio as Elisabeth could wish and looked at the painting on the easel with awe.

'I can see it's the downs as the sun's rising,' she said. 'And Larksbury Rings in the distance. It's beautiful. I love the misty effect of the fields in the foreground and the way you've caught the early morning atmosphere. I can almost feel how wet the dew is on the grass. You're so clever.'

'I'm pleased with it,' Elisabeth admitted.

'I'm not surprised. And you've done others too?' Cathy looked round as if expecting them to leap up on the easel for her perusal.

'Over here,' said Elisabeth. She pulled aside a piece of brown paper covering four canvases and Cathy exclaimed in delight as she saw them.

'Mostly of the Tidings Tree.' Elisabeth said. 'But there's another of the downs from a different angle.'

'And you'll sell them?'

'I hope so. I need to. This one will take a few days to dry, of course. I'll have to discover where I can exhibit them and I'll start on Monday now I've got a few in hand. I should have done it before but . . .'

'I know. Jenny's accident.' Cathy was

77

sympathetic. 'It's good to see her back at school again. You'll be able to get on with things now, won't you?'

Elisabeth nodded. 'And you, Cathy, how are things with you?'

She could see by the sudden droop of her slim shoulders and the worried expression in her eyes that something was not right.

Cathy hesitated for a moment and then said with a rush, 'My class was too noisy this afternoon. Miss Bryer didn't like it.'

'You've got the little ones. You can't keep them silent all the time.'

'Well, no, I can't can I?' She looked relieved to have this confirmed.

'Let's have a cup of tea and talk about it,' said Elisabeth. 'It's so warm out there in the garden. I'll bring it up here and we'll sit on the grass.'

'Lovely.'

When she got back with the tray Cathy was sniffing the late roses over on the trellis but came to help lay out the blanket Elisabeth had brought with her. It was pleasant sitting here in the sunshine and they talked a little of how Cathy had noted the times that the junior class would be out of their classroom having PE in the playground.

'I'll have my noisy activities then,' she said.

'Good idea. And there'll be no complaints.'

'No. Well, not many anyway.'

Elisabeth smiled. 'So I'm not the only clever

78

one then?'

Cathy looked gratified. 'It's good to talk about it. Things don't seem so bad now. And I do love living in Mellstone. I always wanted to live in the country.'

'Me too,' said Elisabeth. 'More tea? No? A biscuit then?'

Cathy took it and thanked her. There was curve to her lips now and Elisabeth was glad to see it.

'I've got a date with Arnold on Saturday.' Now the excitement was in Cathy's voice and her eyes shone.

When she got up to go she was still smiling and Elisabeth was glad for her. She had been happy too in seeing for herself the reaction to her work. When, if ever, she found a market for her paintings she wouldn't have that because she wouldn't meet any of the purchasers. Oh well, she couldn't expect everything. Making the sales should be enough.

*   *   *

When at last Saturday arrived and it was time to meet Arnold down on the main road Cathy felt as limp with longing as the waterweed in the brook that flowed beneath the bridge where she waited for him.

She was glad Arnold was late because she needed time on her own to get used to the idea

79

that she, Catherine Mary Mellor, had a date with someone as wonderful as Arnold. This exquisite knowledge was something to savour for the few precious moments before he came.

When at last she saw him something made her turn her head away in pretended interest in Mellstone Brook. She waited until he was close before she looked up and gave a start of surprise.

He stood close and looked at her in silence for a few moments with a smile in his eyes. She gave a little gasp of delight a he took her hand.

'I've been to look at the tree,' he said. 'What a mess! And all because a stupid child got in the way. You should hear what the other kids say about it. My young cousins . . .'

'The Wintle twins,' said Cathy.

Arnold grimaced. 'Young devils, the pair of them. They bug me no end. They could almost drive me away from Downend Farm if it wasn't useful to be there for a while. However . . .' He smiled at her. 'We'll leave the tree to take care of itself, what's left of it. The afternoon's ours, Cathy. We'll walk up to the farm and collect the car. Uncle Perry should have it back there by now.'

'Your cousins won't really make you leave, Mellstone, will they?' Cathy asked as they began to walk along by the brook.

He gave her a sideways look. 'It's useful Uncle Perry going in for conifers even if he did set about it the wrong way. I need a year's experience and I might as well get it here. I'll take you up to his plantation at the head of the valley one day, if you like.'

'What made you go in for forestry, Arnold?'

'Love of the open air. Trees. Trees are nicer than people.'

He was joking, of course. She laughed and he laughed too. A ray of sunshine set the brook glittering as it burbled beside them.

'Tell me some of the things you have to do, Arnold,' she said.

He shrugged. 'It wouldn't really interest you.'

Her eyes shone. 'Try me.'

'This morning I've been fencing against rabbits. You wouldn't believe the damage they do. Uncle Perry would do something more drastic about it if he listened to me but he's too stubborn for his own good. I've no patience with him. About six years ago he planted conifers only of all the fool things to do. Didn't know any better, I suppose, but I've put him right now for when he needs to plant again. Much better to have a mixture of conifer and deciduous. More firm for a start and better for the soil.'

Cathy glanced at him as he strode along with his head thrown back. She envied his sureness in everything he did, his complete lack of uncertainty. It even seemed to rub off on her a little.

'What would you have done about the

81

Tidings Tree, Arnold?' she said.

'Someone should have had more sense than to hack it to pieces like that. Fools!'

'I suppose they were afraid of another accident.'

'It was only one branch. They could have examined the rest, tidied it up a bit and left it. Now it's just a mess.'

'They say it will grow again.'

'It could start sprouting in parts but it'll be all misshapen. Better to have the whole thing out and start again with a young sapling.'

'And to think it was growing there all those years,' said Cathy, her voice full of sadness.

'I haven't brought you out here to talk about the tree,' Arnold said. 'We've better things to do, my girl.'

They were nearing Downend Farm now and Cathy could see Mr Wintle's green car parked ready for their use. As they got nearer the farmhouse door opened and a short rotund figure burst out.

'Aunt Delphine,' Arnold muttered, letting go of Cathy's hand. 'I'll soon get rid of her, the old bat.'

Cathy held back as he marched forward. 'Uncle's lending me the car for the afternoon,' he called. 'Didn't he tell you?'

'He did not,' his aunt snapped. She rammed her sturdy body against the green paintwork of the vehicle and looked as if she intended staying there for the afternoon. 'You won't bully me so easily, Arnold, my lad. I've got your measure even if your uncle hasn't.'

Arnold hesitated.

Seeing him at a disadvantage was strange, Cathy thought. She didn't like feeling sorry for him.

But then Mr Wintle appeared, rubbing his hands on some sacking and with a smile creasing his face as he saw his nephew and Cathy. 'It's all right, Delph, love,' he boomed. 'Arnold's got my permission. He's done a lot for me this morning. He deserves an afternoon off with the car.' He winked. 'And with the young lady.'

Cathy's face felt hot.

'Phew!' Arnold said, turning to her. 'I thought I'd have a battle on my hands. All set then? Where d'you want to go? We could take in a flick if you like. There's a new Western on at the Odeon in Stourford.'

Cathy hesitated. 'I'd rather go for a drive.'

'You deserve only the best and I'm going to see that you get it.' He let out a shout of laughter and caught hold of her hand.

Cathy smiled. She didn't know where they were going but anywhere with Arnold would be heaven.

Her cheeks glowed with pleasure.

*   *   *

Elisabeth's efforts to find somewhere else to

83

show her paintings met with little success. The best was a suggestion of the loan of a rented room between Poole and Bournemouth, a good two-hour bus journey away. Definitely out of the question and not only because of the expenses involved in getting there daily but also in valuable working time lost.

She alighted from the bus in Mellstone, glad to be back in spite of her disappointment. She paused on seeing the vicar emerge from the vicarage drive.

'Ah Miss Turner,' he said with pleasure, bending a little towards her.

'I've been looking for outlets for selling my paintings,' she told him as they continued to walk together the short distance to Marigold Cottage. 'No luck, I'm afraid.'

He drew his dark eyebrows together. 'Indeed I'm sorry to hear that.'

She indicated her parcel of paintings wrapped in their sheets of brown paper. 'At least they had an outing. I'll try other places, of course.'

'I wish you well.' He looked at her searchingly and she gazed back. She wasn't going to burden him with her problems since he couldn't help.

He left her at her garden gate. Her short encounter had cheered her a little and she was grateful.

*   *   *

As Karen drove along lanes damp with dripping hedgerows and parked her car by the playground wall her spirits lifted. And now even thinking of Cathy Mellor couldn't change her mood this morning.

Cathy was pleasant enough but she wished she had more go about her. That first day of term when Cathy changed the desks around because she wanted her classroom to be less formal had made her think there might be something in the girl after all. She had started a nature table too over by the window, now laden with hips and haws and the brown conkers that soon lost their lovely shine and looked dull and uninteresting. But the children loved it and came each morning clutching something they had found such as colourful leaves and acorns smelling of moist earth.

She wished Cathy would discuss things more and ask advice when she needed it. She wasn't the kind of person you could help easily with those anxious grey eyes staring at you every time you tried. Not for the first time she wished Cathy Mellor had not been the only candidate.

At her own interview for the headship the obvious calibre of her fellow interviewees had made her own success unbelievable especially as at twenty-nine she was by far the youngest candidate.

Now, three years later, she already felt a

fixture here.

A smile curved Karen's lips as she entered her classroom. Not even Mrs Pengold's glare as she gathered up her cleaning things could annoy her today. Wednesday was her favourite day of the week because Robert came to take the service and the religious instruction lesson with her own class afterwards.

This was the only time she saw him apart from an occasional chance to join his congregation at Mellstone church when she was reduced to slinking out of the house and turning her car in the direction she favoured and hope this wasn't noticed. Having been a member of the church at Hope Magna before she became housebound Mother insisted that their loyalty should remain there and so to avoid continuous arguments Karen had agreed.

And she had the nerve to criticise Cathy for not having more backbone! In this instance she was just as much a wet-rag, showing no backbone at all.

She heard footsteps outside and checked that her stocking seams were straight. The door opened and Robert came in. There was always this slight lurch of her heart each time they met. She marvelled that he should have no idea of the effect he had on her.

'He smiled. 'Good morning, Karen.'

'Good morning.'

His dark hair looked damp. He shrugged his

shoulders out of his raincoat.

She took it from him to hang on a peg on the door. 'Not a very good one, Robert. Or has it stopped raining now?'

'More or less.' His smile faded as he moved towards her desk. 'The post hasn't come yet? I saw Bob Horlock as I came along so it won't be long. You must expect a communication from the education office.'

She felt a stir of premonition. 'About the accident?'

'I'm afraid so.'

She saw the concern in his eyes and knew it was for the good name of the school and not for her.

'There's to be another visit from the powers to be.'

'Why can't they leave me alone?' she cried. 'The child's back at school and Miss Turner made no fuss. Why can't they leave it at that?'

He seemed to withdraw from her slightly. 'They will be in time. Just be patient with them and don't make things worse than they are.' A smile touched his lips. 'We must be grateful to Miss Turner.'

She looked at him in suspicion. So he had been talking about it with Miss Turner? She winced with the pain of suspecting he had spent time with her, offering sympathy.

He seemed not to notice her silence but to her it echoed between them. It was a relief to hear the postman at the door.

'You'll want to look at your post,' he said. 'I'll just have a word with Miss Mellor.'

'It can wait . . .' she began but what was the use? All too soon he would be gone for another week and that would be that.

But soon it would be Harvest Festival in church with the school children there bearing gifts and she would see him again. The church was always full, scented by chrysanthemums and Michaelmas daisies and the fruit and vegetables dominating every available space. She must be sure to talk to the children about it beforehand so that Jenny Finlay would carry the message home. Otherwise she might arrive without suitable produce to add to the profusion of gifts because Miss Turner had been too involved with her own concerns to realise what was expected.

* * *

Already the day was darkening and dark shadows lay on the ground. John, with Fly at his heels, made his way up the track through the trees at the back of the house. This might well be the last evening he would venture out for a walk after his late dinner now that the days were drawing in. Fly was rustling among the fallen leaves but was back at his side by the time John reached the top.

He paused to savour the quiet air and wondered what work Elisabeth was engaged on at the moment. He knew she liked to paint scenes in oils in her studio from the sketches she made of anything that took her fancy. Soon, though, winter would be here. Not so good for working outside then.

As they reached the top John was surprised to see someone coming up towards him and moving so slowly she hardly appeared to move.

'Karen!'

'She looked up as she got near. 'John.'

'It's good to see you again, Karen. It's been some time.'

In fact it must have been weeks even though Nether End and Haymesgarth were on different sides of the same hill. She was dressed in old clothes, ones he recognised from long ago, a grey jersey and brown skirt that made her seem hardly older than the wild young girl who liked to ride his pony about the place because she wasn't allowed one of her own.

'How are you then, Karen, and your mother?'

She bent to pat Fly and then shrugged. 'Mother's so-so. You know how it is, up one day and down the next. She's not interested in much outside the house now and doesn't want to go out. It's good of you to call and see her, John.'

'Not often enough I'm afraid these last few weeks.'

At once Karen's bright smile faded and he

89

saw how worn she looked.

'I've been gardening and took the chance to slip up here for a bit of a walk but I can't be long,' she said. 'Thank goodness for Marjorie who comes in during the day to look after her or things would be difficult.'

He knew they were difficult enough for her even with Marjorie Lunt's help. Karen was looking older too.

She seemed to throw off her sadness with an effort. 'And you, John, how are you? You've been having your difficulties this last year or two.'

He nodded, moving his feet slightly so that Fly looked at him in enquiry with bright button eyes. 'A bad business the foot and mouth last year. Never ending it seemed at the time.'

He didn't want to talk about it even to Karen. It was over and done with now apart from the worry that it would come again.'

'And you managed to sell the cottage.'

He nodded. 'It had to be done.'

And of course she knew the reason. He was grateful that she didn't allude to it. All that was past and done with now too. He wouldn't be caught again. 'Change is inevitable, I suppose. You can see that the Varleys are pleased that Elisabeth Turner has come to live in Mellstone.'

Karen was silent and he could see that something displeased her. Perhaps the thought of Jenny's accident and worry about the child.

'I hope all is well at school?' he said. 'I hear Miss Mellor is settling in well with the two ladies at Lynch Cottage. They're fond of her in their own strange ways according to Aunt Ruth. But tell me, Karen, how are things really with you?'

She shrugged. 'I can't complain.'

'And Miss Turner's little girl?'

She hesitated for a moment. 'Well . . .' she said at last and then hesitated. 'No, it would be unprofessional, John. I really can't say.'

'You can't? We've known each other a long time, Karen.'

He felt a sudden stillness in the air and thought of Elisabeth bringing up young Jenny on her own while struggling to make ends meet.

Karen rustled some fallen leaves with her foot. 'It's nothing you need to worry about, John. It's only . . . But no, I really mustn't.'

'Then I'll say goodbye, Karen. Don't work too hard.'

She nodded. 'Yes, I'd better get back.'

'It's getting late.'

She smiled as they parted but he could see it was an effort. With concern he watched her retreat down the path on her side of the hill until she disappeared among the trees. She had a hard time of it at home these days but there was something else, he felt sure, that gave that droop to her shoulders. But there was nothing he could do about it if she wished to keep her own counsel.

Whistling to Fly he set off homewards.

*   *   *

As Karen turned away and went swiftly down the stony track on her side of the hill she felt ashamed of herself for implying something about the child that wasn't there. But John's sudden stillness as he asked her about Jenny had alerted her to his interest in Jenny's mother and that had brought out the worst in her. His reaction to her deliberately misleading words had given her a glow of gratification that lasted only a few seconds.

Her short escape from Haymesgarth had lost all pleasure for her now. She slowed down as she reached the bottom and took several long breaths to calm herself. She had school work to do and she must focus on that and try to forget John's interest in someone she had disliked from the first moment she met her.

CHAPTER SIX

Grey clouds loomed over Larksbury Rings and Cathy, hand-in-hand with Arnold, looked at it doubtfully.

'Of course we'll make it,' he said. 'Clouds move on.'

A sheet of black moved across the sky towards them, changed direction and swooped and plunged again in a wide arc. Fascinated, Cathy clutched Arnold's hand harder at the unexpectedness of it.

'Starlings,' he said. 'Just look at them.'

The sky was dark with birds and she marvelled at the aerial display put on, it seemed, for their sole benefit. There didn't seem any reason in the sudden dives in different directions, all moving as one.

'How do they know when to swing round like that at the same time? It's amazing. I've never seen anything like it.'

She could see that even Arnold was impressed. 'They do that sort of thing often at this time of year.'

'There must be thousands.'

And then they were gone. The empty sky stretched above them.

'That's amazing,' she said. 'D'you suppose starlings put on that sort of show two and a half thousand years ago?

'What?'

'When Larksbury Rings was an Iron Age hillfort.'

'How should I know?'

'I wish we knew more about the people who built it apart from the tools they used and that sort of thing. It must have taken years.'

'Who cares?'

'The banks would have been higher then.'

'I suppose.

'And the area around would have been covered in trees, silver birch and alder. Not your sort of trees, Arnold.'

'You're right there.'

'But of course Larksbury Rings wasn't as important as Maiden Castle. Did you know that archaeologists found piles of huge round pebbles there that must have come all the way from Chesil Beach? A weapon store for when the Romans came? It didn't do much good though and they were over-run.'

'Now you're being boring.'

It started to feel chilly and she shivered.

'Cold, Cathy? Come on then.'

Their way led now across a yard near a haystack, only a low crumbling wall hinting that once there may have been more buildings nearby by. Suddenly, on the other side, she was knee-deep in thick smelly liquid. Arnold, safely at one edge of it, looked on in dismay as she floundered through the disgusting stuff.

'Slurry,' he said, pulling her free.

She giggled at the disgusted expression on his face and then looked down at her legs encased in an evil brown mess.

'Now what?' he said.

'Ugh! I'll have to take my stockings off.'

'Over here then.' He pulled her towards the haystack where on one side loose hay was available for scrubbing at her legs and getting most of the slurry off.

They climbed up into it the stack and sank down. Her stocking-less legs felt red and sore but at least they were cleaner now.

'I love you for that, Cathy,' he said. 'Laughing at your predicament. Most girls I know would have gone slamming off in a temper blaming me for it and vowing never to see me again.'

'I'd never do that,' she said.

He took her in his arms and kissed her. They lay back in the soft sweet-smelling hay and it was the most marvellous moment of her life.

'What's wrong?' he said after a while as she stirred and sat up.

She looked round anxiously. 'People might see us.'

'People . . .what people? And what does it matter anyway?'

But it did matter. Others beside themselves might come this way and report back that the school teacher and a man were up to something in a haystack. The parents of her children, even the children themselves . . . It was a public footpath to Larksbury Rings and people used it. Being discovered like this was humiliating for anyone but for herself who was in a position of authority, it was unthinkable.

She tried to explain this to Arnold but he was uncomprehending. 'Come here, Cathy. Don't fuss.'

'No, Arnold, please . . .'

As he kissed her again she tried to burrow

deeper in the hay but it was no use. She couldn't relax and at last he gave up.

'You're no fun now, Cathy,' he grumbled. 'This is a perfect place and you're spoiling it. I thought you had more pluck than this.'

She felt a spot of rain. Not so perfect after all, she thought as it began to come down heavier now.

'That's it then,' he said as he got to his feet and pulled her up. 'One last kiss and we'll go. Happy now?'

Not happy at all. In fact already regretting her reaction.

She looked towards Larksbury Rings but couldn't see the hillfort now because it had disappeared behind a bank of clouds. In her case the cloud was of her own making.

But she had laughed and Arnold had loved her for that.

*   *   *

Mellstone was an easy parish, if it was possible to have such a thing, Robert thought. He let himself into the vicarage one day in early December and pondered on the way his life had turned out and that he, still a relatively young man, should have been sent to this quiet backwater two years ago at the age of thirty three.

He pushed shut the door behind him, waiting to hear the click to show that it was really closed before removing his black overcoat and hanging it on the hall stand.

Mrs Froud, who came in daily to look after him, had left a paraffin stove alight to take the chill off the vast hall. It smelt rather badly today. He must get Bob Lunt to take a look at it.

Sighing, he warmed his hands by it for a moment before going into his study and switching on the electric fire. Because he had been out earlier Mrs Froud hadn't lit the fire laid ready in the grate. He stood with his back to the electric one, enjoying the warmth that gradually crept upwards to his shoulders, and contemplated the photograph on the wall opposite. It showed his university rugby team of which he was proud to have been a member. There he stood in the back row, young, dark-haired, fully confident that life was good and that he was all set for eventual work in the East End of London. He had felt eminently suitable for this because he had already done some work during the vacation in his uncle's parish of St Windhelm's and found it worthwhile.

He was nineteen when war broke out. The discovery of a heart condition that made acceptance into the services impossible had been a shock. He had always felt deep regret, too, being deprived of the work he had been so confident was for him. To say that he thought of himself as a failure in this area had not gone to the root of the matter. In fact, to his everlasting shame, his faith had been badly shaken. Some months had passed before he could accept fully that his life was meant to go in another direction.

A curacy in Swindon and then priest-in-charge on the outskirts of Salisbury had been his lot and eventually being installed as incumbent of St Mary's, Mellstone. He knew that there was important work to be done here in a different way that would not strain him to the same extent. With reasonable care, the doctors told him, he could live to a ripe old age but he knew he could never contemplate sharing his life and inflicting this on another person.

He moved to the window and stood looking out at the wintry garden. Not a twig stirred in the frosty air. He wondered how Elisabeth Turner was faring in these wintry conditions when sketching and painting out of doors would be difficult. Her studio would be cold too and need a lot of expensive heating. She had chosen a hard way of earning a living and although he admired her for it he wondered if it were wise.

Soon he would collect the cold lunch left ready for him in the dining room and bring it in here to eat. Then afterwards he would look in at the shop and remind Miss Lewis of the altered time of the P.C.C meeting this evening. His plans for a youth club in Mellstone would be discussed and voted on. Maybe even a few suggestions for suitable leaders would be forthcoming. He had hopes that Martin Varley and perhaps Jim Perry's young nephew, Arnold Bronson, might be interested.

Thoughtfully he fetched the tray, cleared a space on his desk and set it down carefully among the scattered papers.

*　　*　　*

Elisabeth closed the back door of Marigold Cottage behind her and crossed the lawn in the frosty dark. What was that? Alarmed she listened and heard it again . . . a sharp clatter of a pebble sounding on the studio roof. Her heart pounded at the sound of voices in the school playground beyond the wall, the scuffle of footsteps and then silence.

Her hands shook as she opened the studio door and switched on the light, remembering the furtive glances from the group by the Tidings Tree when she had passed in John's car on her way to visit Jenny in hospital. She was hurt at John's obvious opinion that she was imagining this but he hadn't seen the old man waving his arms or the scowl on the face of the stout woman she now knew as Mrs Barden.

'Why should they blame you?' he had asked, reasonably enough.

Why indeed? But they did. Someone had

thrown a stone over the wall. It was proof enough that someone wished her ill.

She stood there for some time, thinking about it and feeling the deepest loneliness of spirit she had yet experienced. She and Jenny were aliens here. They didn't belong. It wasn't coincidence that the pebble had landed on the studio roof. It was easy enough for anyone to climb over the wall into her garden. This was a disturbing thought. Now, after a quick look round she went out and locked the door behind her. From now on she would never leave it unlocked even for a short time.

There was no sound from the playground now. The intruders, whoever they were, had faded away into the chilly air.

*   *   *

When the first carol singers began their rounds none of them called at Marigold Cottage. Elisabeth hoped they weren't being avoided deliberately. A pebble on her studio roof, no carol singers . . . no connection surely? She tried not to think about it but the question was there at the back of her mind continuously even when she heard that the gallery had sold two of her paintings and wanted more. One of the paintings that had been sold was from the sketch of the black cat skulking in the garden on the Tidings Tree's last blustery afternoon.

But as she and Jenny walked to church for

the crib service on Christmas Eve Elisabeth felt a lightening of her niggling worry and hoped that it was permanent.

The soft murmuring and scraping of feet was not quite drowned by the soft cadence of Christmas music flowing from the organ. There was an air of expectancy here in the dim building, a hush of waiting for something exciting to happen.

The church was full. Ahead of her she could see Arnold Bronson from Downend Farm with some of the other bellringers. Martin Varley was there too and Jean. Some more people were pushing into their own pew now and Elisabeth moved closer to Jenny to let them pass. She recognised Mrs Barden with her faint cooked-cabbage smell that always seemed to hang about her. One of the boys trod on Jenny's foot and then looked furtively round. She heard Jenny's gasp but could do nothing about it.

Afterwards Jenny hung about near the crib and Elisabeth stood quietly in the shadows and watched the congregation leave. The vicar looking large and benevolent in his white surplice, stood near the door. The echo of his words as he wished each person a happy Christmas came faintly to her.

Surely, Elisabeth thought, she could ignore the sidelong glances and mutterings of the few? She must make a real effort to forget her feeling of blame that John was sure she had imagined.

Here in this quiet place it was easy to do so but once out in the world again what then?

'Come Jenny, 'she said. 'Time to go now.'

'Just one more minute?' Jenny begged.

The light illuminating the stable shone on her face and the wonder in her expression brought tears to Elisabeth's eyes. She blinked them away, remembering her own joy as a child looking on a scene that resembled this but only in the figures within it. Someone had made a good job on the building here with its roof that looked newly-thatched.

*   *   *

Robert felt saddened to see Elisabeth's smile as he took her hand in his at the church door because nowadays it was all too rare. She was finding life hard after her first enthusiastic weeks in Mellstone and he was sorry for it. He felt such a stirring of concern for her that he was loath to relinquish her hand but there were others pressing behind and they were his parishioners too.

He watched as Elisabeth and Jenny walked away down the church path and hoped that a happier time for them lay ahead. Jenny seemed so much better now and he hoped the accident wouldn't leave a permanent mark. It was a good thing he'd had a word with Bill Gedge on the matter of the tree. At first Bill had been difficult but had agreed eventually to say no more about whose fault it was that the tree was lost to Mellstone, if indeed it was.

Now, watching the last of the congregation leave, Robert permitted himself a brief smile. It wasn't often anyone got the better of Bill Gedge. He had done it by allowing the old rascal to think he was getting his own way about ringing in the New Year on Mellstone's bells.

'We'm always done it, vicar,' Bill had croaked. His lined face was so indignant at the upstart of a vicar unused to Mellstone's traditional ways that it didn't occur to him that there wouldn't be any objection. From the belligerent expression in the old man's eyes it had been clear that not only had this been done on Mellstone's bells from time immemorial but that it always would be, vicar or no vicar. Whose bells were they anyway?

'Well Bill,' he had said, deliberately frowning. 'If I agree I shall want something from you in return.'

'Ah, Vicar, what's that then?'

He had let a moment of time pass to add emphasis to what he had to say. 'I want to hear no more of this business of you laying blame on Miss Turner or anyone for the loss of the tree. Is that completely clear?'

The old man had gazed at him in silence before saying, 'It's clear, Vicar.'

'And you promise, Bill?'

'Aye, if you say so?'

It was unthinkable that the high feelings about Elisabeth's part in the tree's fate should continue to grow. If the old man kept his side of the bargain a great deal of unhappiness would be avoided.

*　　*　　*

Elisabeth picked up the envelope from the doormat, looked at it in dismay and then carried it into the living-room. Being careful not to disturb the cotton wool snow that Jenny had hung so carefully on the latticed window, she sat down on the window seat and ripped the letter from the envelope.

The Inland Revenue had made a mistake. She stared at the words, willing them to keep still. She would have to convince them they were wrong by producing her bank statement. In spite of the two sales she had made her account was much lower now than when they had come to Mellstone. But what did a bank statement prove? The tax people probably thought that she was selling her work secretly and amassing a huge fortune she kept under the mattress.

A gurgle of laughter welled up and she swallowed it back. No need to get hysterical however ludicrous the situation. This could be serious.

She glanced round the room. Coloured

paper chains hung from the beams and the branches of fir she and Jenny had brought back from Hodman's Hollow looked well in the earthenware jar with the baubles and tinsel almost disguising the fact that it was a makeshift Christmas tree.

This had been a good Christmas, made specially so by their being invited to Varley's Farm on Christmas Day to enjoy Jean's superb Christmas dinner. On Boxing Day afternoon she and Jenny had gone for a brisk walk to the top of Hodman's Hollow and then returned to read their new books that Bella had sent. Jenny had been delighted with Paddington Bear while she enjoyed the doings of the Larkin family in *The Darling Buds of May*.

Now she vowed that there should be no more social occasions until she had straightened out her financial position because the only way she could do so was to work every hour of every day. She would write to the Inland Revenue at once to say a mistake had been made and that should end the matter.

* * *

New Year's Eve was a solemn time, Elisabeth thought as she sat on the hearth rug with her chin in her hands and gazed into the dying fire. For a moment time seemed to hang in the balance.

Jenny had been in bed for hours. She had

intended to go early herself after her busy day but had lingered by the fireside. The pictures in it had held her spellbound until gradually they died away. Now it seemed too much trouble to stir.

A piece of charred wood fell in disintegrating sparks. She picked up the poker and knocked at the ash, scraping it away from the wood. Now it began to show signs of life again with little mutterings and cracklings. Her face glowed in the heat as she reached forward to throw on a handful of fir cones. They leapt to life, spitting and hissing. The wood joined in too with blue-tinged flames.

Life she thought, from small beginnings. A handful of fir cones and there was fire again. Two paintings sold must give her hope for the New Year. A glow of optimism swept through her. What would the New Year hold for them all . . . Mrs Cameron and Alice Pengold, Cathy Mellor whose eyes shone when she and Arnold were together, Tom Barnet and his band of bellringers? They would be up in the tower now preparing to ring in the New Year.

It was nearly midnight. Elisabeth got up and went to the front door. The air was frosty, the sky clear. Millions of stars hung above the village.

A sudden jangling rent the air like a wild giant bellowing in pain. She gasped in horror. Others had heard it too and were coming out of their cottages. Opposite, Alice Pengold stood motionless in her lighted doorway and it seemed to Elisabeth that she stared straight at her, blaming her . . .

She banged shut the door and ran, trembling, to the living-room. The fire had almost gone out now and there was just a heap of greyish-white ash in the grate.

*   *   *

Hanging upside down with the end of a bell rope in each hand, Ralph Varley surveyed the ringing chamber and the other bellringers. From this unique position they looked decidedly off, especially Bill Gedge who was pulling his New Year's Eve contribution from his pocket.

'What's it this time, Bill?' Ralph asked, his fair hair brushing the worn matting on the floor.

'Good stuff, this rice wine, boy. Aye, t'would draw the ducks across the pond, this would.'

'You look like the trunk of the tree stuck up in the air like that, Ralph,' Tom Barnet said as he removed his jacket and rolled up his shirt sleeves.

'Ah,' said Bill, glowering.

'Give him a drink for goodness sake,' said Arnold, leaning against the wall and looking at the young girl near the door with interest.

Tom reached for one of the bottles stacked on the seat. 'Don't forget the trebles up already,' he warned. 'No larking about on the treble, mind.'

'And we'd better lay off the booze till afterwards,' someone said.

Tom, his face even ruddier than usual, put up an arm and hung on a bell rope.

'Watch this!' Ralph yelled and made a flying leap at a rope which he missed. He grabbed it again, caught it awkwardly and reached for the next rope to steady himself. Too late he realised he had grabbed the treble.

The rope lashed round the ringing chamber while the treble bell, overhead, clanged madly. The others, cringing back against the wall with their hands over their heads, were safely out of the way but the rope caught Ralph and knocked him flying. He lay face downwards on the floor until the mad racket subsided and the rope was still. Then he got up, dazed.

'It's nigh on midnight,' said Bill shakily

The colour had drained from Tom's face. 'Better get six of them up and start ringing,' he said. 'You sit this one out, Ralph.'

Ralph's head was still spinning. As he did as he was told he felt a draught on the back of his neck and knew without turning round that the vicar was standing in the open doorway. But he was too confused to care. It was someone else's problem, not his.

At last Tom gave the signal and the bells were lowered once more. Robert came right into the ringing chamber. He looked at them

108

all under his bushy eyebrows, a red tinge in his cheeks and his eyes blazing.

'What's the meaning of that disgraceful racket?'

'I'm sorry, sir,' said Tom. 'There was a bit of an accident like with the treble's rope when the bell was already up. Ralph here was . . . I say, are you all right, vicar?'

Robert seemed to lurch forward before sitting down hurriedly on the bench by the door, his face ashen. He leaned forward. 'Yes indeed. I'm all right, Tom, thank you.' He reached inside his pocket for his phial of tablets and extracted one which he placed beneath his tongue.

They all looked at him, keeping as still as if carved from stone. After a while Robert stood up and Tom made a move forward to help him.

Robert waved him away. 'I can manage,' he said through white lips. 'Are you injured, Ralph? No?' He eyed the bottles. 'Later I'll want to know exactly what's been going on and what part you all played.'

It was obvious that he found it difficult to cope with the knowledge that he had been duped. Shamed, Ralph struggled to think of something to say to improve matters but could only stare at him, bemused.

'Don't expect permission again, Bill. You know me better than that.'

'But we'm allus . . .'

'Never again.'

Bill muttered something no one could catch and Tom cleared his throat. The rest had still not moved.

'My car's outside,' Robert said. 'I'll take Ralph home.'

'Happy New Year, vicar,' Bill croaked.

'Happy New Year,' they all chorused.

Down in the church Arnold flicked his torch on and off, moving closer to the young girl visitor whom he now knew was staying with her aunt, Miss Lewis. Maisie had asked to watch the Mellstone band ringing in the New Year because she was thinking of learning to ring when she got home.

'It's dark out there,' he said. 'I'll walk you home.'

Robert put his car into gear and they moved slowly up the lane past the Tidings Tree. The light in the front upstairs window of the farmhouse went out as he drove into the yard and pulled up by the back door.

Ralph laughed rather shakily. 'So there won't be a reception committee to greet me after all.'

'You'll need help to get out. Sit tight and I'll get your father.'

But Martin Varley was already at the door, yawning and rubbing his eyes. The light behind him lit a golden path to the car.

Robert got out and went to the other side of the car to help Ralph. 'Happy New Year,

Martin. I hope it will be good to you.'

'You too, Vicar.' The farmer's voice was slurred with sleep.

Robert glanced at Ralph who took a step forward but was looking none too confident.

'Your son's had a bit of a knock,' he said.

'How's that, then?'

'There's been a slight accident in the ringing chamber.'

To his dismay he heard Jean Varley's brisk voice. She pushed past her husband and emerged into the yard, pulling her thick dressing gown more tightly round her.

For Ralph's sake Robert hoped that no fuss would be made. By the look of him Ralph had been taught a lesson already he wouldn't forget.

'What happened up in the tower?' his mother demanded. 'You haven't been fooling around up there, have you, Ralph?'

'Let the lad alone,' said Martin, yawning. 'Time enough to discuss it in the morning.' He nodded to Robert. 'Happy New Year to you, Vicar, and thanks.'

'Happy New Year to you all,' said Robert.

CHAPTER SEVEN

The frosty weather was still with them in the first week of January, crisping the grass outside Marigold Cottage. Their faces tingled as Elisabeth and Jenny walked to the bus stop on the main road.

With her purse containing her Christmas money clutched in her gloved hand Jenny skipped along. Her excitement was infectious and Elisabeth began to lose her slight guilt that she wasn't working this morning even though she was taking two more paintings to the art shop gallery in Hilbury.

It was a morning to feel optimistic but suddenly Jenny gasped and clutched her arm as Alice Pengold pedalled past on her old-fashioned bicycle, sitting upright and looking neither to left nor right.

'Where's she going?' Jenny whispered.

Elisabeth laughed. 'You're not worried are you, Jenny? I've often seen her riding about the village like that. We used to call them sit-up-and-beg bikes when I was young.'

Jenny shivered and Elisabeth began to feel slight apprehension herself at the thought of leaving her studio unguarded when she was out of reach in town especially as it seemed the bus was going to be late.

When it finally came it looked full but they

found seats one behind the other, breathing in warm petrol fumes. Views of the downs appeared frustratingly dim through the steamed-up window as it crawled up the hills. It seemed as if it would never get there. It was a relief to get out into the chill air as the bus pulled up in Hilbury High Street. Jenny was off before Elisabeth, dancing with impatience. She stopped suddenly, her face changing. 'There's Mrs Pengold. How did she get here?' she said

Elisabeth watched Alice park her bicycle outside the haberdasher's and then march inside. 'It's all right, Jenny. She came on her bike,' she said. 'She had plenty of time. Don't forget we were at the bus stop far too early and then the bus was nearly half an hour late.'

Jenny looked unconvinced. 'I suppose.'

'Come on, Jenny, don't look like that. Where shall we go first? Why don't I leave you in the toy shop while I deliver my paintings? I'll join you there.'

The art shop a few doors away was larger than it looked from the outside and as usual took Elisabeth by surprise although she should have got used to it by now. Its deep interior was large enough to house collections of original paintings and was becoming well known in the area and beyond.

The proprietor came forward to greet Elisabeth with a smile. His tightly-fitting green cardigan was buttoned to the neck and gave him an elfish look. 'So what have you got for me today, Miss Turner?'

It was a pleasure to show her work to Mr Evans because she knew he appreciated her style. He had placed her previous work in an advantageous position and she was grateful for that.

'I have hopes for these,' he said. 'I have someone coming in next week who might well be interested. Our usual terms?'

'Of course. And thank you.'

He lifted them off the counter where Elisabeth had unwrapped them and placed them carefully alongside a pile of others. 'I've taken a commission from a pet owner to find someone to do a portrait in oils of her dog. I wondered if you would you be interested in taking it, Miss Turner. If so . . .' He broke off on seeing Elisabeth's frown and added apologetically, 'Yes, I know. Difficult, isn't it?'

'I'm not sure I could do it.'

'Would you be willing to try? You'd be doing me a favour.'

Elisabeth was doubtful. 'It's such a responsibility.'

'He's called Pixie. A black Labrador. Yes, I know, an inappropriate name.' His eyes twinkled at her. 'Let me show you the photograph Mrs Wentworth left with me.'

The photo was decidedly grainy and Elisabeth looked at it in dismay.

'The owner's such a dear lady and so fond of her dog. He's just been diagnosed with some incurable disease.'

'Oh dear. Now you're piling it on.'

'She'll pay well.'

Elisabeth hesitated. 'Isn't there anyone else good at animal portraits? I've never done one before.'

His eyes lit up. 'The black cat in the windy garden?'

'An image, not a portrait.' She looked at the photo again. The dog gazed back at her with soulful eyes as if he already knew his fate. She would have to agree. How could she let poor Pixie's owner down at a time like this? 'I'll try,' she said.

'That's good of you. I'll phone Mrs Wentworth straight away. Perhaps you'd write to her and confirm? I'll give you her name and address.'

'And I'm to bring it to you when it's done?'

'Thank you, my dear. It's a load off my mind.'

But not off hers, Elisabeth thought as she joined Jenny in the toy shop. Pixie was not unlike the Varleys' dog. Perhaps she could sketch Bruno as practice. This might certainly be useful in capturing the sheen of his black body not obvious in the photograph. Even though Pixie's coat might be dulled by illness now he would have had a healthy-looking one once.

Jenny's purchase made they had time for some grocery shopping in Home & Colonial before crossing the road to the bus stop.

They found Cathy Mellor there with two large suitcases at her feet. Her face brightened when she saw them. 'I'm so glad to see you. Are you waiting for the bus?'

Elisabeth placed her heavy shopping bags on the ground. 'Phew, that's better. And you've got those heavy cases.'

'I thought someone was meeting my coach but he hasn't come. I don't know whether to wait or get the bus.'

'Look, Miss,' said Jenny. She unwrapped her parcel to reveal a work basket in the shape of a thatched cottage. 'I've just bought it. Isn't it lovely? You lift the roof to get the cotton out and the needles and scissors too.'

Cathy admired it and then looked anxiously at her watch. 'I can't think where he is.'

'Did you hear about the incident in the tower on New Year's Eve, Cathy?' Elisabeth asked.

'Incident?' Cathy looked alarmed.

'No harm done but the vicar's displeased.'

'What happened?'

'Ralph tried to swing on one of the ropes when he shouldn't have. The bell made a terrible din.'

Cathy's face paled. 'Was he hurt?'

'Luckily only bruised. He's looked very subdued since, I must say. His mother says he's grown up at last.'

The bus came then and they got on. As they

116

arrived in Mellstone Elisabeth saw Arnold Bronson leaning against the stone bridge looking as if he had been there for hours and was annoyed by the wait.

Cathy sprang up, her face a mask of delight. 'He's here, he's at the bus stop!'

Pleased for her, Elisabeth stood back for Cathy to get herself off the bus first with her bulky suitcases. Then she ushered Jenny ahead of her, relieved to be back in Mellstone, soon to be in her studio checking that all was well.

Her rush of relief made Cathy stumble as she heaved her suitcases off the bus and placed them on the ground.

Arnold caught her to him and held her tight.

'Not now,' she muttered. 'Not here.'

He looked surprised. 'What's wrong, Cathy love? Aren't you pleased to see me?'

Of course she was pleased to see him. Hadn't she been sick with worry when he wasn't there at the coach station in Hilbury as he had promised?

'What happened?' she whispered.

'I knew you'd get the bus,' he said. 'Uncle Perry needed the car and there didn't seem much point me getting the bus in.'

She thought about it. Of course it was more suitable for Arnold to wait for her here and was sensible really. And she didn't mind a bit.

His eyes twinkled at her. 'Am I forgiven?'

Beneath his jacket he was wearing the blue cable-knit jumper she had made him for Christmas. She smiled at him rather tremulously as he heaved up her cases and they walked up the lane past the stump of the Tidings Tree set and the school. Even the thought of the first day of term tomorrow was exhilarating to her now she knew Arnold was safe.

They arrived at Lynch Cottage and it felt like coming home.

'Why haven't you got your own key?' Arnold muttered as Cathy knocked on the front door.

It was flung open immediately. Miss Buckley and Miss King stood on the threshold, one in her usual tweeds, and the other in stained slacks.

Miss Buckley thrust a key at Cathy. 'For you,' she said, her voice gruff.

Miss King wiped her hands down her side and gave a high-pitched laugh. Cathy felt Arnold blench behind her as they went inside. The dog, Benjy, emerged from some private occupation and gave a loud bark. Startled, Arnold backed into the hallstand and several umbrellas slithered to the floor.

'Pretty pathetic,' Miss Buckley growled as she bent to retrieve them.

'Your new room is all ready for you, dear,' Miss King said. 'Your young man can carry your suitcases up. So lucky the sink came in time.'

Cathy gave a sigh of pleasure as they went

into the room that was her new bed-sitting room. The cream and crimson cretonne on the bed and sofa stood out against the plain walls and the dark beams gave a feeling of cosiness to the large airy room that surprised her. The sink and cooker in the alcove at one end fitted in well.

'We've got some basics in for you, dear' said Miss King. 'The milk's quite fresh.'

Miss Buckley prowled round the room, poking at the sink each time she passed it as if she expected it to leap off the wall.

'Aren't they ever going to leave us on our own?' Arnold murmured. He yawned.

All Cathy wanted was to be allowed to be make a pot of tea for them both, the moment she had dreamed of all the way back to Mellstone. Would the ladies never go?'

Then she felt a stab of shame. It was all so perfect and they must have spent hours arranging it all for her. She repeated her thanks, enthusing about everything once again. She glanced at Arnold and saw that his eyes were glazed.

Miss Buckley rushed to the window and leaned out. Her tweed skirt ruffled up and her legs, encased in brown woollen stockings, stuck out behind her. 'Benjy, Benjy,' she called.

'What's she on about now?' Arnold muttered.

'They're quite intelligent really,' Cathy said as at last the two ladies got themselves out of the door. She gave a sigh of relief as she removed her coat. 'This perfect room! They've been so kind.'

'You're paying good money for it,' Arnold said as he yawned again. 'Stop fussing.' He took his jacket off and threw it on the sofa.

His jumper fitted perfectly. Cathy ran her hands across the cable pattern. 'D'you like it, Arnold?'

He nodded. 'We'll have a house-warming party,' he said, his eyes shining. 'We'll get the crowd in. And Maisie too.'

'Maisie?'

Miss Lewis' niece here in Mellstone for a few months. She wants to learn to ring and I said I'd teach her. She's been up to the tower a few times. You'll like her, Cathy. Yes, we'll invite Maisie.'

'But I don't think the ladies . . .'

Arnold grabbed her and held her tightly. 'Stop fussing, Cathy. I've waited a long time for this.'

It was impossible to say anything at all now with Arnold's lips pressing down on hers. Not that she wanted to. It was enough for the moment that he was here with her and to know that his feelings for her hadn't changed.

But, deep down she felt a niggle of something that wouldn't go away however hard she tried to suppress it. She gave a small sigh as she relaxed against him.

Cathy entered the shining school building next morning determined to make a fresh start. No more the ineffectual bungling of her first few weeks in September. It was January now and this term things would go well from the beginning. She even felt different now that her hair had been permed and her new cardigan and skirt were in plain green that matched perfectly.

Early as she was Karen was before her and stood at her desk in her dark suit slitting open the post with the penknife she kept at the front of her top drawer.

She looked up and smiled as Cathy came into the room. 'Hello there. Did you have a good holiday?'

She sounded friendlier than Cathy remembered. Her pink blouse gave colour to her cheeks and her eyes were bright.

'Everything looks so fresh and clean,' Cathy said, looking round the neat classroom with pleasure.

Mrs Pengold always gives it a good going over in the school holidays. We must try to keep it this way.'

Karen finished opening the envelopes and placed them in a pile in front of her. 'I must warn you. There's been a bit of trouble with Joe Barden. PC Peter Hallen's been in to see

121

me. We'll have to watch the boy. But don't look like that, Cathy. Joe won't eat you. He's harmless really if a bit dim. Pete wants us to keep an eye on him, that's all.'

Cathy smiled and nodded and as she went to her own room she managed to shake off her feeling of disquiet.

On the threshold she stopped still in astonishment to see low blue Formica-topped tables placed together in groups instead of the old-fashioned desks with their fixed seats.

'Surprised?' said Karen from behind her.

'Where did they come from?'

'Surplus to requirement at Hope Magna. Luckily the powers-that-be thought of us. They arrived yesterday morning.'

'The room looks so much bigger.'

'I thought you'd be pleased.'

Cathy's smile left no doubt of that. It was exciting to unlock her cupboards and get out the boxes of crayons and to arrange the new reading books on the shelves. It all smelt so evocative of happy contented children.

A sudden clash of milk bottles sent her flying to the outside door at the same time as Karen. Someone had kicked one of the crates against the wall.

'Joe Barden!' Karen cried. 'Come here at once.'

Cathy tried not to cringe at the ugly expression on the boy's face. He stood still with his head thrown back and stared at Karen through narrowed eyes. His dark hair was tousled and his bare knees grimed with dirt. He looked as if he hadn't been in bed for a week.

'Get the crate back in place at once,' Karen ordered. 'You're lucky none of the bottles broke.'

'Yes, Miss,' Joe muttered as he kicked at it.

'Not like that!'

He looked at her for a silent brooding moment and then heaved up the crate of small milk bottles and placed it by the side of the other.

'That's better,' said Karen. 'Now behave yourself until the whistle goes.'

He slouched off, whistling between his teeth. Cathy hoped that none of her infants would get in his way. Should she stay and make sure? She looked after his departing back and saw him join a group of bigger boys by the gate. There was something about the way he strutted among them that made her shiver.

Karen had gone inside now and with a last backward glance Cathy went into her classroom to get ready for the day ahead.

*   *   *

The portrait of Pixie was proving as difficult as Elisabeth had feared. She tried sketch after sketch but none of them pleased her.

At last she gave up and set out for Varley's Farm.

'You're in luck,' Jean Varley said when Elisabeth explained to her why she had come. 'Ralph's out at the back with Bruno somewhere putting him through his paces. Ah, here they are now.'

Bruno came loping towards Elisabeth across the yard and greeted her like an old friend.

'I need a model for an animal painting and I thought of Bruno,' she said when she had patted his sleek black body.

Ralph grinned at her, flicking back his unruly hair. 'Take him and welcome. Or do you want him to pose somewhere here?'

'It'll be easier at my place if he'll come with me.'

'I'll see he does,' said Ralph. He pulled a piece of binder twine from his pocket, attached it to the affable Bruno's collar and handed him over. 'And the best of luck.'

Bruno came with Elisabeth willingly enough. Outside in the lane they met Cathy who looked at Bruno in surprise.

'I'm not kidnapping him,' Elisabeth said. 'He's my new model.'

Cathy smiled. 'You're going to paint him?'

'A new venture. A commission. I'm needing a bit of inspiration.'

Cathy moved her bag from one hand to the other. 'I'd love to see you do it.'

She sounded so downcast that Elisabeth

looked at her in concern. 'Is something wrong?'

'Not really. We had a bit of fuss with Joe Barden this morning and I let it get to me, that's all. There's something about that boy I don't like. And school teachers are not supposed to dislike any child.'

'Who said that?'

Cathy looked at her solemnly. 'That was the rule at college.'

'Did they tell you how to avoid it?'

'They said we must do our very best to understand them, to show them sympathy . . .'

Elisabeth laughed. 'And to hide our true feelings. You need to practise that and you'll be all right. But Joe's not in your class, Cathy. It's not your problem. Come and have a cup of tea with me while I sketch our friend here. Jenny will make it for us.'

The living room was a mess but it didn't matter. Elisabeth applied a match to the kindling in the grate and while the flames were taking hold switched on the electric fire.

Bruno was the perfect model and stayed completely still while Elisabeth did two or three lightning sketches that would be invaluable when she started the painting in oils. The afternoon light was beginning to fade as she lay down her charcoal and accepted the cup of tea Jenny poured for her.

As a reward for his good behaviour Jenny held out a biscuit to Bruno and laughed as he took it eagerly and gulped it down. Cathy looked happier now and the firelight shone on Jenny's auburn hair as she stroked Bruno's glossy coat.

'I'll have to go,' Cathy said at last. 'Look how dark it's getting. Shall I take Bruno back for you?'

Jenny looked wistful as Elisabeth shut the door behind them. 'I wish we had a dog like Bruno,' she said.

Elisabeth smiled. 'Maybe one day,' she said.

*   *   *

The winter aconites in the front garden took Elisabeth by surprise. They seemed to have come from nowhere, one day there was merely a hint of green leaves in the corner by the hedge and the next shining golden flowers among the groups of snowdrops that had delighted her when they first appeared in the second week of January.

She was on her way out now to the downs, hoping to work outside for the first time for ages because it was her birthday. Now she paused to admire the brave show of flowers that proved the year was moving slowly towards spring and felt an upsurge of optimism. The post had come early today and in it were a card and a long letter from someone who hadn't written to her for ages, since Jenny's birthday in June in fact before they had moved to Mellstone.

She had written back to Bella at the time, telling of the new life they were soon to start in Mellstone but hearing nothing in return until the parcel came at Christmas with just the label to say who sent it.

Bella, her cousin's cousin, had good news of her own to impart. Happy for her, Elisabeth imagined her settling into the huge house near St Ives that she was well on the way to converting into a Centre for the Arts. The alterations would take months but no matter, the financial side had been sorted out at last.

The air still had a bite to it Elisabeth discovered as she set out with her sketch book in her canvas bag swinging at her side. Bella's exuberant personality was infectious when they were together and now she felt some of it filling her too.

Once out of the village in the lane leading to Downend farm and Nether End she saw that there were rims of frost on the fence posts and the tractor wheel marks across Mr Perry's field were rimed with white. She wondered if St Ives had woken to a frosty morning like this.

She and Bella had met first on the day Jenny was born and liked each other from the moment they had held the small bundle in turn, exclaiming over the baby's beauty with her fuzz of dark hair that would eventually turn auburn. At the time of the fatal accident three years later Bella had been in New

Zealand intending a long stay but she had come home as soon as her father's estate had been wound up to give what help she could, mainly financial, until the man she had met there and fallen in love with issued an ultimatum and Bella had returned.

Elisabeth smiled now, remembering Bella's distressed expression as she tried to justify her decision to go back to New Zealand. And now, widowed, Bella was back in this country again with this ambitious scheme in St Ives she had wanted Elisabeth and Jenny to become involved with. Possibly a lingering sense of guilt that she hadn't been able to help more had prompted the invitation.

Bella had always approved of her landscapes, urging her on to bigger and better things. What would she think of her latest venture, Pixie's portrait? Elisabeth smiled as she imagined Bella's scorn that she had allowed herself to be duped into doing something not worthy of her talent. But was that really so? If she managed a good likeness the painting would give untold pleasure and comfort to her client and that was surely worth a good deal?

Once started on the painting, she had found a pleasure in it that took her by surprise. Perhaps it was because she knew how much the dog, under sentence of death, meant to his owner. She hoped that some of that love transferred itself through her to the canvas and

Pixie's portrait miraculously became a perfect likeness.

The painting was on her easel now needing to dry completely before she took it to the art shop next week. Now she was glad to be out today enjoying the fresh air on her face. Birds chirped in the hedgerows and overhead a group of starlings swooped. Long green waterweed swung gently in the water of the brook and the muddy smell from the banks pleased her. She hadn't been along here for some time and now she saw that the hazel catkins were long and loose and already the tiny red flowers were showing on the stems.

It had been her intention to walk up through the young conifer plantation to the top of Uckdown Hill from where she would get a view of Larksbury Rings from a different angle. But now she saw that the swinging hazel catkins made interesting patterns against the wintry sky and that the roof of Downend farmhouse showed clear and bright between them.

She got out her charcoal and sketchbook and was immediately engrossed.

She wasn't aware of anyone approaching until they were upon her. Arnold Bronson hesitated, obviously startled to see someone half-hidden by the hedge sketching branches and twigs. Then he strode on, the girl with him running to keep up. Elisabeth had a glimpse of fair hair and long legs.

But he had gone out of sight now, intent on escape it seemed. Elisabeth gazed after him, wondering. It was none of her business, of course, who Arnold Bronson chose to walk along the lane with but she had Cathy's interests at heart.

Concerned for her, she began to pack away.

CHAPTER EIGHT

A few days later the door of Elisabeth's studio burst open and Jenny, in her blue pyjamas, collapsed in a heap on the floor.

Instantly Elisabeth was down beside her, a now-familiar dread clutching at her. But Jenny leapt to her feet at once. 'It's Mrs Cameron,' she cried. 'She said to get you. She knocked on the door and now she's waiting.'

They ran out of the studio and across the lawn. Mrs Cameron sat huddled on the hall chair, her face stone-white. She struggled to her feet as they came in. 'It's Donald,' she gasped. 'He won't wake up. I thought he was asleep but I can't make him stir.'

Elisabeth pulled off her painting apron and dropped it on the floor. 'Come into the living room, Mrs Cameron. Here, let me help you. I'll run and phone the doctor. I'll be as quick as I can. Jenny will stay with you.'

Jenny, wide-eyed, clutched Elisabeth's hand.

130

'Let me come too.'

'No, stay here. I won't be long.'

'It's too late,' Mrs Cameron said, her voice breaking on a sob. 'It's too late for the doctor but I must get back home to Donald.' She moved to the front door, knocking against the table near the wall.

'If you really feel you must.' Elisabeth gave her a quick hug and propelled her gently outside. 'I'll be over as soon as I can, Mrs Cameron. Don't do anything until I come. And Jenny, I won't be long. Get ready for school and have something to eat.'

Elisabeth ran down the lane and found Jean Varley in the farm kitchen. The smell of frying bacon and tomatoes rushing out to greet her made her eyes water.

Explaining what had happened took only a few moments.

'You get back to her,' said Jean, whipping off her apron. 'I'll do the telephoning to the doctor and her nephew. John will come at once, I expect.'

After checking that Jenny was coping well Elisabeth sat with Mrs Cameron in her tidy kitchen and waited for someone to come.

In one corner of the room a pile of clothes was placed ready on a table with an electric iron in its box by the side. Only the grey ashes in the grate showed that things weren't normal for this time of day.

As she sipped the cup of tea Elisabeth made

for her Mrs Cameron began to talk, not about Donald as Elisabeth expected but about her sister's son.

'John's always been a good boy,' she said as she held both hands round her cup and stared into it. She sighed and her lips trembled a little. 'Always. He was so young when his father died, an old head on young shoulders looking after the farm and all. And now look at him with a farm manager to look after things for him at Nether End while he branches out advising people. There was a time when we thought he'd turn his back on farming. Always keen on the sea, John was, right from a little boy but he was his father's son in the long run. Madge, my sister, was pleased about that. I can see her now. . . John's so like her with that way of looking at you without saying a word while he thinks things through. It used to annoy Stephanie so much. I never thought that marriage would work out. And now they're divorced.'

Elisabeth was surprised. 'John was married?'

'Far too young. And Stephanie was no saint. We always thought Miss Bryer would be the one but no, it was Stephanie he wanted.'

Elisabeth leaned forward and filled Mrs Cameron's empty cup from the big pot on the table. She seemed not to want her to say anything, just to listen.

'Stephanie never liked the farm,' Mrs Cameron confessed. 'Couldn't stand the quiet.

They met when John was down in Weymouth in his friends' boat. Loved the sea, she did. That's what attracted him. He'd have more sense now.'

Mrs Cameron struggled to her feet as she heard a sound at the door. Her nephew came in and immediately her face crumpled. He was at her side at once, his arm round her. Gently he lowered her into her chair then turned to nod briefly at Elisabeth.

Outside the early morning air was fresh, the sun a red ball in the sky. She took deep strengthening breaths as she ran across the lane to Marigold Cottage where Jenny had her coat on and was ready to leave for school.

'Good girl,' Elisabeth said, bending to kiss her. 'Poor Mrs Cameron needed me but Mr Ellis is with her now.'

The expression in Jenny eyes was anxious. 'I didn't wash up. Did you want me to?'

For answer Elisabeth kissed her again and sent her on her way.

*   *   *

Elisabeth moved restlessly about the living-room. She had washed the breakfast things but that was all. Normally she would have been working in her studio by now but there was no question of that today. Mrs Cameron might need her at any moment.

She threw herself down on the window seat

and thought of Donald Cameron whom she hadn't known very well, in fact hardly at all. It was his wife who had been so kind to them as soon as they moved in. Now, staring out at the yellow aconites in the front garden, Elisabeth waited. The ringing of the door bell made her leap up instantly. She blinked in the blaze of light from the open door after the dimness of the hall and then saw John.

He looked strained and sad and so different in his working clothes. She stood aside to let him enter

'How is she now, John? What can I do to help?'

He looked at her without speaking for a moment and then ran a hand across his forehead as if to smooth away some of the worry. 'She's calmer now, thanks to you, Elisabeth. It was good of you to sit with her until I could get here. I wonder if she could come over here with you while the funeral people are at Ivy Cottage? I'd rather she was out of the place.'

'Of course.'

His face lightened. 'You're very kind.' He smiled at her briefly and was gone.

The electric fire, Elisabeth thought. She must have some warmth for Mrs Cameron. Hastily she tidied a few things off the table and piled them on the floor. She only just had time to leap upstairs and change out of her old clothes she kept for painting before the door bell rang again.

Mrs Cameron held out her hands to the heat as soon as she was seated. 'I'm stopping you painting,' she said. 'You ought to be up in your studio now, dear. You don't need to waste your time with me. Such lovely paintings . . .'

Elisabeth smiled. 'Shall I make some tea? It would warm you and me too.'

Mrs Cameron shook her head, looking suddenly bleak. 'In a minute perhaps. Sit down, dear.'

Then she began to talk, letting it all out about finding Donald asleep at her side when she woke. Or so she had thought at first.

As Elisabeth listened to Mrs Cameron she felt her own sick horror when news came of her cousins' accidents, the young Jenny's parents. The family, and especially her grandfather, had needed her to cope and to take on the three-year-old child left orphaned. At first she had been rigidly calm as she made decisions. It had been her grandfather's own death two years later that had at last cracked her armour and by then, of course, Jenny had become an important part of her life.

And so John found them when he returned, Elisabeth sitting on the hearth rug and his aunt with a glowing face.

'Elisabeth has been so good to me,' Mrs Cameron said, looking up at him as he helped her to her feet. 'I've been rambling on when by rights she should be painting.'

John turned to Elisabeth with a smile. 'Thank you,' he said quietly.

Feeling a little confused, she got to her feet, conscious of the untidy room with books and papers strewn everywhere and dust on the shelves and mantelpiece. She hardly gave housework a thought these days until she saw the rooms through the eyes of someone else. No one who didn't know what it was like to try to earn so precarious a living could possibly understand the urgency she felt to make the most of every daylight hour.

When they had left Elisabeth thought briefly of Bella down there in Cornwall where she could be too if she had to chosen to take up her offer of tutoring art courses there. For a few minutes she allowed herself to imagine what life would be like without the continuous worry about making ends meet. There, the meals would be provided, the housework done. It sounded like a dream and yet she had had no difficulty turning it down because she had felt the need to be on her own with Jenny doing something she had long wished to do.

Later that morning Elisabeth returned to the studio she had left in such a hurry but, frustratingly she could not work. Her mind was full of Mrs Cameron's anguish and her own remembered pain. And something else, too, a swift vision of John as he comforted his aunt. It disturbed her, this knowledge that his life hadn't been as uneventful as she had imagined.

136

Sighing, she picked up a piece of charcoal and in a few deft strokes sketched Mrs Cameron sitting bowed on the hall chair. She stared at it for a moment as if wondering what she was doing. Then she tore it to pieces and dropped it all in the waste paper basket.

*   *   *

Jenny scuttled down the lane away from the village, the wintry sunshine glinting on her bright hair. It was the dinner hour and Miss Bryer thought she was going to Marigold Cottage for dinner today because her mother wouldn't be working as it was Mr Cameron's funeral this afternoon. But she had been wrong about her going home and Jenny hadn't corrected her. Instead she had set off along the lane in the opposite direction and no one had seen her.

What would it feel like, she wondered with a spasm of fear, not to wake up in the morning? Just last week Mr Cameron was in his front garden when she came out of school. Mrs Pengold was in hers too, cutting cabbages with a knife and looking as if she knew something bad was going to happen.

Mrs Pengold had made it happen . . .

Jenny started to run and only stopped when she came to the gate that led into a sloping field with the overgrown brook at the bottom. There was a bridge made of thick wooden planks spanning the water. Jenny squelched her way through the marshy overgrown bit that smelt of wet grass and wild mint to reach it. It was lovely here, all wild and beautiful.

She stood on the bridge for a long time, listening to the invisible brook beneath the brambles. She would call this lovely place Brooklands and come here again.

Then she remembered that afternoon school started at half past one. She turned and ran. She heard the whistle as she reached the council houses and arrived breathlessly in the deserted playground as Miss Mellor was about to go into school.

'Jenny!' she cried in alarm. 'Where have you been? You'll get into trouble.'

Jenny trembled and Cathy looked down with sudden pity at the small grubby face. It was obvious that Jenny had been doing something she shouldn't but surely here was no harm done and she wasn't very late. She had been on the end of Miss Bryer's tongue more than once herself and wouldn't wish it on this poor child.

'Let me pull those burrs off your skirt,' she said, her voice full of sympathy. 'And your hair, Jenny. It's a mess. You'd better get cleaned up as fast as you can. Look, here's my comb.'

'Thank you, Miss,' Jenny whispered.

Cathy smiled and gave Jenny a friendly push and watched her slip into school

Donald Cameron's funeral was taking place on such a bright day that it was hard to remember it was still January. After the service Elisabeth walked slowly down the path in the churchyard and hesitated outside the gate. John, seeing her, left his aunt's side to make sure a seat in a car was at her disposal so that she, too, could come with the family to Nether End. The solemn sounds of half-muffled bells followed them as they drove away from the village and she wondered if Cathy was among the bellringers up in the tower. But she had caught a glimpse of Karen Bryer at the service so it was unlikely that both would have been away from school at the same time. Cathy's young man would be there though. She thought suddenly of seeing him with Miss Lewis' niece but Cathy had seemed so happy lately that it obviously hadn't been important.

John's housekeeper welcomed them to Nether End with glasses of sherry. Elisabeth sipped hers standing a little apart from the others in the long low sitting room and trying not to feel out of place. Mrs Cameron, of course, would have hated her to feel like this. She was seated near the French windows looking a little better now, pleased to see so many friends and acquaintances come to show their respects.

A hum of conversation rose and fell. Jean

139

and Martin Varley joined Elisabeth and talked quietly until it was time to partake of the sandwiches and sausage rolls being handed round.

Jean Varley indicated the person sitting next to Mrs Cameron. 'That's Donald's sister,' she said. 'She's been involved in looking after an invalid friend and unable to get away much until recently.'

'Has she come far?'

'From Weymouth. I haven't seen her for some time. I'll just go and have a word.'

'This is a sad business,' Martin Varley said. 'We've been fond of them both for years. I wonder how poor Ruth is going to cope.'

Jean was back with them now smiling a little sadly as she took a sandwich from the plate offered to her. John came to join them then and with an apology carried Martin off to his study. Elisabeth looked about her, liking the muted colours of the room and the view of the garden and hill from the windows.

Mrs Cameron beckoned to her. 'Elisabeth, my dear, this is Muriel, my sister-in-law. She wants me to go back home with her but John seems to think I should be here.'

Elisabeth smiled and shook hands. 'Donald was such a good, quiet man and a kind friend,' she said.

His sister looked pleased. 'I'm glad that Ruth has someone like you to help her.'

She spoke so simply that Elisabeth felt tears

of sympathy spring to her eyes.

'We lived here at Nether End as children, you know, Donald and me,' Muriel said in her soft voice. 'Dad was head cowman and we had one of the tied cottages.' She sounded forlorn now obviously struggling hard to keep her composure. 'Donald was so happy living in Mellstone and I don't wonder.'

Afterwards Elisabeth couldn't forget Muriel's quiet sorrow for her brother. From the number of people at the service Donald Cameron had been truly loved and respected. That was success in life, Elisabeth thought, inspiring selfless love in others.

*   *   *

Karen returned to school after the funeral service with a feeling of deep weariness. She had hung back a little as the rest of the congregation left in the hope of a word or two with Robert but apart from a nod of recognition at seeing her there he had seemed as if his mind was miles away from Mellstone instead of here mourning a man whom he had come to know well. No doubt he would be on his way to Nether End now with the others. She wished she could have been there too.

As she walked up the slope toward the Tidings Tree she felt strangely detached. The bells sounded odd, muted as they were, and cast gloom over the whole place. No one was about now but the church had been full. No sign of the bellringers though. Obviously they had been in readiness up in the tower and had enough people to perform without the help of her assistant teacher. Cathy was needed at school to look after the two classes while she was attending the funeral of someone she had known all her life.

Karen crossed the silent playground and entered her room by the main door. The gloom seemed to have pervaded here too and her class were all apparently engrossed by the writing exercises she had set them. A pile of arithmetic books was on her desk ready for marking.

Joe Barden looked up, glowering. 'I got to be excused, Miss.'

'And?'

'Please Miss, can I be excused?'

Karen nodded her permission and then turned to Cathy in the doorway between the two rooms. 'Everything all right?'

'I think so.'

It certainly seemed like it but then she hadn't yet seen the results of the work she had set for her children.

'And the little ones?'

'Colouring in,' Cathy said with a rush. 'I thought it wouldn't matter for once.'

'I see,' said Karen. She wondered what that training college of hers would have said about that activity but didn't care. Cathy had done a good job keeping both classes quiet even if Joe Barden had obviously been banned from leaving the room while she was away.

* * *

A day or two later Elisabeth stood in the hall of Marigold Cottage and stared at the letter in her hand. Another tax demand, another letter wanting money she didn't have. Who would believe that she didn't owe this money they kept wanting her to pay? Tears gathered in her throat. It was all too much after Donald Cameron's death and her worry over Jenny's health since the accident. She couldn't cope with demands such as these arriving constantly.

The ringing of the door bell made her jump. She was surprised to see John outside in his jacket the colour of autumn leaves and his face glowing. The warmth from him was strangely comforting.

'Aunt Ruth sent me to tell you. . .'

'Come in,' Elisabeth said, struggling to gain control. What a fool he must think her with red eyes and trembling lips.

He bent his head as he stepped across the threshold and looked down at her with a concern she found unnerving, 'Can I help at all?'

'This letter caught me at a bad moment,' she said. 'It's a mistake but still . . .'

'May I see?'

It was a relief to hand it over to him, to have someone else take over. And yet she was strong, able to cope with anything that came up. Or so she had thought. 'It's all right really,' she said with a firmness she hoped was convincing. 'I expect I'll get it sorted out in time. It was just . . .'

The tiny lines at the corners of his eyes deepened as he frowned over the words that had worried her. 'It seems a lot. You say you don't owe this money?'

He looked at her sharply as she nodded her head. 'Then surely you've no need to worry.'

'I've written to them but they don't seem to accept it. This is the second letter in a few weeks.'

'They'll have to believe you. Please don't upset yourself, Elisabeth. It's not worth it. You've kept accounts and receipts for your expenses? Would you like me to have a look at them for you? I may be able to help.'

'Come into the living-room. I'm sorry there's no fire but I'm trying to economise.' She rummaged in the bureau drawer for her account book and looked up in time to see his expression as he glanced at the fire laid ready to light and the jar of hazel catkins in an earthenware jug on the table. She had moved all the odds and ends away now and dusted everything she could.

He raised his eyebrows as he took the book from her. 'You've been tidying instead of painting?'

She smiled. 'After what happened . . . I couldn't concentrate on my work. And the place was a mess. It needed doing.'

He opened the book and flipped to the current page. 'But there's hardly anything here,' he said in disbelief.

'I've made two sales so far. And I've been working on a commission which should bring in more.'

'You live on this?'

'I hope to make more sales when the summer visitors arrive.'

'Summer's a long way off. Surely there's something more lucrative you could do in the meantime that would provide a regular income?'

She bit her lip.

'I'm sorry,' he said, his voice gentle. 'It's none of my business. I'm merely trying to help. It seems such a haphazard way to go about things.'

She went to the window and gazed out at the cottages opposite. A silvery silence hung over Mellstone. A sense of urgency bit into her worry over the letter and she longed to capture the scene in the only way she knew.

She swung round. 'It's the whole point of our coming to Mellstone.'

John looked unconvinced as he glanced at the letter again.

'Five months is no time at all to build up a

large body of work and to find suitable outlets for the paintings to be sold,' she said more quietly. 'For that I need time which I wouldn't have if I was working outside the home. It's true I didn't know quite what I was letting myself in for when I began but I'm learning.'

'With letters such as this?' His expression as he looked at her was quizzical. 'I can see it's upset you, Elisabeth. I don't believe you're as hard as you like to pretend. You need to be ruthless both with yourself and others. I'm not sure you can be.'

She pulled out her handkerchief and blew her nose hard. 'You caught me at a bad moment, that's all.'

'And the other bad moments that will come?'

'I'll have grown a few more skins by then.'

'A pity,' he said gently.

She held out her hand. 'The letter. Can I have it please?'

She took it from him and folded it to hide away in the pocket of her skirt. 'I can't give up now,' she said. 'We'll manage. I'm used to going without things.' She felt herself flush as she saw him look at the cold grate.

'And Jenny?'

She made no reply because this was sore point. How could she explain to him what her painting meant to her without sounding incredibly selfish? Was she sacrificing Jenny's happiness as so many people seemed to think?

She hoped and believed not but she was always on the defensive now where Jenny was concerned. She must give herself a year, two years . . .

'Aunt Ruth was telling me you used to teach,' he said. 'Wouldn't it be sensible for you to do that and paint in your spare time?'

'Sensible, yes,' she cried with such passion that he took a step back. 'Of course it would be sensible. But that's not what I want. I'm no spare time artist. It's my whole life.'

He looked down at the account book still open in his hand. 'You'll land yourself in real trouble if you're not careful. It's madness to exist like this.' He snapped the book shut and placed it on the bureau. 'Being sensible and finding some other paid occupation makes sense.'

She glared at him. What he was saying could be true but she wouldn't give up under any circumstances.

Suddenly he smiled. 'I wish you luck, Elisabeth, though I think you're wrong. If you have any more trouble let me know and I'll get my accountant to deal with it.'

He was halfway out of the door before he remembered why he had come. He turned with a swiftness that almost seemed to tie his legs in knots. He returned Elisabeth's smile with one of his own that seemed to remove twenty years from him. She could see how he had looked as a boy, with the eagerness to get with something he loved shining out of him. That he was unable to understand her own yearning was something she found it hard to accept.

'My aunt's coming back with me to Nether End,' he said. 'I was to ask if you'd help with some packing.'

'Of course. Tell her I'll be over as soon as I can.'

There was a sparkle of amusement in his eyes. 'A fine example of being hard and single-minded.'

She flushed and he was immediately serious. 'I'm sorry, Elisabeth. That wasn't fair. Don't let that wretched tax demand get you down. It will be sorted out in time.'

As soon as he had gone she pulled out the offending letter and went straight to the bureau. But instead of settling down to write her reply she sat with it in her hand and wondered why she had allowed John to criticise her way of life. She didn't care what others thought, the vicar, Miss Bryer or even Mrs Cameron who had championed her more than once. But she had tried hard to gain John's understanding. Now she felt deflated because she hadn't got it. He was kind, yes, but unconvinced.

No longer conscious of the bureau in front of her, she gazed into space. She saw John's lean figure and bent head as he offered her advice she wasn't prepared to take. He had said she should be sensible and that had hurt. Well, she would prove to him that she was right to do things her way. She would make a complete success of it.

CHAPTER NINE

Alice Pengold looked askance at the paper littering the floor of the Infants' Room. She sniffed. More arty-crafty work, she thought in disgust, and that old stove had been smoking again.

She gave a deep throaty cough as she got hold of the broom to start work and then a groan as she bent to pick up the dustpan and brush. She'd have to go to the doctor again and he'd only tell her the same old thing, to take things easy. And what good was that when a body had a living to make?

She snorted in derision as she tipped the contents of the dustpan into the waste paper basket. Then, hearing a sound in the next room, she paused. Normally both teachers had gone home by the time she came over school. She banged the broom against the skirting board, hoping whoever was still here would take the hint and go.

She finished sweeping the floor, gave another cough, opened the door into the Junior Room with her elbow and backed in clutching her cleaning things to her.

She looked round and saw Miss Bryer. No call for she to be looking as if she'd lost a bob and found sixpence.

'Have you seen the *Hilbury News*, Mrs Pengold?' Karen asked, her voice more clipped than usual.

Alice dropped her cargo against one of the desks and prepared for action. 'That I haven't.'

'Just a minute then. This concerns you. Look, here on the front page. I was informed of this by County Hall this morning and now here it is in the paper. 'Shock Proposal. Mellstone School might close in September."

Alice stared at her. 'So what do they want to go and do that for? It don't make no sense.'

'I'm afraid it does. Numbers are dropping here. A larger unit is more economical. Wernely School is going to be enlarged to take the children from here.'

But what about her money? No one cared about that, Alice thought. Aloud she said, 'Mellstone won't be the same without no school. It'll be the pub next and the church.' She yanked up her broom against the table legs. 'What's going to happen to me . . . and to you too I'd like to know? Shipped off somewhere else I shouldn't wonder and Mellstone left for dead.'

Alice, muttering to herself, swept with such vigour that dust flew into the air. She wondered that the headmistress didn't seem stunned. Did that mean she wanted to see the place closed down so she could get on and marry the vicar and have done with it?

*   *   *

As she drove through the twisting lanes to Haymesgarth Karen sighed. Perhaps it would be possible to apply for another headship within travelling distance of home, just supposing there were any vacant. The alternative was shunting round from school to school when needed. Not much fun in that.

It was all so totally unexpected. So impersonal, so uncaring. . . the proposed closure of a small village school. Not very important in the great scheme of things but the very life to her. She had enjoyed her time here working out her ideas and seeing most of them come to fruition. She had always demanded a high standard and usually got it. Now it was to be thrown away.

As she accelerated on one of the few straight stretches of lane she thought of Joe Barden who was easily the worst young devil in her class. What chance would he have away from Mellstone where three generations of his family were known and understood?

She removed her foot as she reached the next bend, realised too late that she should have braked, and swerved. She felt the back of the car swing round and hit the opposite bank.

151

Shaken, she sat still as the driver of the vehicle coming in the opposite direction pulled up and came towards her.

'What the. . .' she began as she wound down her window and saw John. Shaken, she didn't at first recognise him.

'Your own fault, Karen,' said John Ellis. 'You were driving far too fast.'

'Oh, it's you,' she said as she got out gingerly and looked to see if any damage had been done.

'You're lucky,' said John, his voice like steel. 'Whatever possessed you to drive like that? You could have been killed.'

She shrugged. 'Problems. My mind on other things.'

'Nothing's more important than your life, Karen. Mine too.'

'I'm sorry.' She struggled not to tremble with the shock of it all.

He hesitated. Then he put his hand in his pocket and drew out his pipe which he stared at for a moment before replacing it. He stood there as if he had all the time in the world. 'Why not come back to my place for a while until you feel better?' he said. 'You're in no fit state to drive the rest of the way home.'

'But I must,' she said in calm desperation. 'Mother will worry.'

'You could phone.'

'It's kind of you, John, but I'd rather not.'

'Then I'll drive you.'

'No, John, don't fuss. It's not far and I can't leave my car in the lane.'

To prove how well she could cope Karen got back into her car and hoped he didn't see how her hands were shaking as she put it into gear. She set off, inched forward until she was clear of the bank and then drove at a low speed even when John's Land Rover appeared in the driving mirror. At the entrance of Haymesgarth she waved her thanks and drove across the gravel to the garage door.

She turned off the engine. The silence was beautiful. For a moment she leaned her arms on the steering wheel and bent her head, savouring it. She needed a little time on her own to try to convince herself that the proposed closure of the school was not her fault and had nothing to do with Jenny's accident. And of course it was going to mean that working closely with Robert would come to an end.

After a while she looked up and got out of the car. Indoors the sun shone through the coloured glass of the front door and illuminated the plain hall carpet into mosaics of rippled splendour. Karen trod through them to enter the sitting room that smelt faintly of camphorated oil. Huge green plants filled every available space. She looked at them with loathing as she sank into a low chair.

'How are you, Mother?' she said. 'Marjorie been gone long?'

Mrs Bryer, struggling awake, spoke from the depths of a massive arm chair. 'A hard day, was it?'

'Nothing I can't cope with. Now let me make you a cup of tea.'

Her mother's air of frailty was enhanced by her fluffy white hair and pale face. Even her thin lips were colourless. Hating herself, Karen felt the familiar surge of impatience. 'I'll tell you all about my day, Mother, while we drink our tea.'

She wouldn't, of course. She would prattle on as usual about some trivial thing and keep the heart-aching worry about the school closure to herself. If she didn't her mother would assume immediately that this was all her daughter's fault and give her no chance to air her own point of view. It would all be quashed beneath a veneer of knowing best that was so hard to bear from someone who knew so little about it.

But surely she had got over all that years ago? Karen stifled a sigh as she went out into the kitchen and, shivering, busied herself with tea preparations. But to have someone to discuss it with who had her interests at heart would be sheer heaven.

As she removed the boiling kettle from the stove she began to whistle and found that it was the hymn tune she had chosen for tomorrow morning when Robert was due to come into school to take his weekly service.

John parked his vehicle opposite his aunt's cottage, shut the door and looked down at Jenny who was lying half-hidden in the long grass by the front fence of Marigold Cottage. 'What are you doing there, you silly girl?' he said. 'I could have run you over.'

Jenny jumped to her feet, glowering. 'It's my fence. I can lie where I like. I was hiding. Something bad's going to happen.'

John noted her unkempt hair that stood out round her tear-stained face like a red bush. Her grey skirt had green patches on it and a button had pulled off her coat leaving a jagged tear.

'What bad thing is that?'

'The school's going to close.'

He was surprised. 'The school? I hadn't heard that.'

Jenny gazed up at him, two spots of high colour on her cheeks. 'It's my fault. Everybody says so.'

John put his hand in his pocket for a pipe. Thinking better of it, he left it where it was. 'How can it be your fault, Jenny?'

'Because of the Tidings Tree. I got Miss Bryer into trouble and so they'll close the school.'

'But that's nonsense.'

Jenny lips trembled. 'It's not nonsense. It's

155

true.'

'Who says it's true?'

'Everybody. Joe Barden . . .'

'Then he doesn't know what he's talking about.'

'He does,' Jenny cried passionately. 'He says so all the time.'

'Believe me, Jenny, if it's true to school is going to close it will have nothing to do with the tree.'

She gazed at him with unhappy blue eyes that said quite plainly that she didn't believe him. Unsure of how to handle it he saw, with relief, the door of Marigold Cottage open. Elisabeth came out with her shopping basket and ran lightly down the path. 'Is anything wrong, Jenny?'

As she heard the faltering explanation Elisabeth looked troubled. 'You don't really think, John, that . . .'

'That it's the result of the accident? Of course not. How could it be?'

Elisabeth bit her lip and didn't answer. Instead she looked down the lane to where the stump of the once-beautiful tree stood stunted and bare on its triangle of grass. Her vulnerability touched him.

She tapped Jenny lightly on the shoulder. 'Run indoors, Jenny. I won't be long.'

John cleared his throat. 'It's ridiculous,' he said. 'Sheer superstitious nonsense and I'd like to get hold of the young thug who taunted

156

Jenny.'

'I'm not superstitious,' Elisabeth said quietly. 'But there's something about that tree. It has queer effects on people.'

'And you still think you're being blamed?'

She looked directly at him. 'I'm sure of it.'

'That sort of nonsense is communicating itself to Jenny and it's not doing her any good. Something should be done about the odd notions that fill her head.'

The colour flew to Elisabeth's face and her eyes blazed. 'What exactly do you mean by that?'

He took a step towards her and saw her stiffen. 'I was concerned about Jenny being so much on her own, that's all.'

She snapped the gate shut behind her. 'I'm going down to the shop,' she said. 'I must hurry.'

And she was off before he had the chance to tell her why he was here. He had shown concern for Jenny, that was all, but it was clear that it was considered none of his business. And it wasn't, of course. He gave a deep sigh as he fished in his pocket for the key to Ivy Cottage. Too much to expect that Elisabeth would be back by time he had collected a few bits and pieces for Aunt Ruth. The invitation to Elisabeth and Jenny to visit his aunt at Nether End would have to be made another time.

By the time Elisabeth pushed open the shop door she was breathless. The bell jangled somewhere in the back regions. At first, in the gloom, she didn't see the two customers deep in conversation with Miss Lewis in her usual place behind the counter. They had their backs to her and were examining something closely. Elisabeth glanced towards them and as she did so Miss Lewis held something up for her to see. It was a delicate arrangement of dried grass and flower heads.

'Hand-done,' Miss Lewis said with pride. 'And made locally.'

Elisabeth would have liked a closer look but the other two blocked her view. Closed ranks, she thought as she made her purchases. She shivered. The atmosphere was decidedly chilly. She was aware that as soon as the door clanged shut behind her they would spring apart and resume their conversation. It was not difficult to guess what it was about. And John believed all this was imagination!

She packed her bread and marmalade and Cornflakes into her bag and looked up. 'Oh, and the *Hilbury News* if you still have one, please.'

It seemed that even Miss Lewis felt the disapproval in the air now. She hesitated, glanced at her other two customers and then hastily pushed a copy of the paper across the counter.

Elisabeth paid what she owed and left. Her bag felt heavy as she walked up the hill to the Tidings Tree and she was relieved to get to Marigold Cottage without meeting anyone. She made a restorative cup of tea and carried it into the living-room to drink while discovering what the paper had to say about the latest rumour.

Nothing was definite of course but there was enough there for it to be worrying. It was thought that a public meeting would be called in Mellstone in the near future to consider the implications of the possible school closure. She would have to attend, of course, although her instincts were to stay away. She must expect bitter accusations thrown at Jenny and herself because certain members of the community would consider the loss of the tree Jenny's fault and because of it the decision to close the school.

Elisabeth stared at the article for some time. Then she flicked through the rest of the paper, her eye caught by a familiar name in the announcements column, *Pixie Wentworth*.

She read the notice of the Labrador's death with sadness. *Peacefully at home leaving behind his grieving Mother*.

Elisabeth was astonished. He had a *mother*? Oh of course, his owner, Mrs Wentworth. She bit back a giggle and was immediately ashamed of herself. She read the announcement again and then sprang up. In her studio she gazed at Pixie's portrait and knew that here was some of her best work because it had been done with compassion. The dog looked back at her with soulful brown eyes just as he must have looked back at his loving owner so many times. Tomorrow she would take it to the art shop proprietor and with it a letter of condolence for Mrs Wentworth.

* * *

'Ellis is far too cautious,' Arnold said, his voice scornful. 'His land is perfect for forestry. Far better than this.' He waved his hand at his uncle's plantation that covered the hillside at the top of the valley.

Cathy stopped and breathed deeply. She had expected to be climbing Larksbury Rings for the first time as Arnold had promised and the change of plan had been a surprise. The trees ahead of them, head-high, were a dark patch on the hillside. 'Wait, Arnold,' she called, 'Don't stride along so fast.'

'Come on, Cathy, for goodness sake. We won't have time to get to the top if you dawdle. Ellis should be getting on with planting while he's got the chance. I've no patience with him.'

Or with her sometimes, she thought. She must make more effort. This last day or two the proposed closure of the school had been on her mind constantly. Moving away from

Mellstone and leaving Arnold didn't bear thinking about. When she'd raised the subject as they set out he had brushed it aside even though she had voiced her concern about the strong feelings likely to erupt against Elisabeth.

'It hasn't happened yet Cathy. It might not anyway so stop fussing about something that may not come about,' he had said.

Sensible advice if only she could take it.

He paused to wait for her, shading his eyes as he looked around him.

'It's a big decision for your uncle to make,' she said. She spurted forward to catch him up and sniffed at the pine-scented air with pleasure. An invisible bird squawked from somewhere near and made her jump.

'A jay,' said Arnold. He pushed aside an overhanging branch. 'Ellis is afraid to grasp what life offers. I prefer people who know what they want and go for it. Like that artist woman.'

'Elisabeth Turner?'

'You never get anywhere in this world if you allow people to trample you down. That's why Maisie's all right.' He laughed, sounding happy and carefree.

Cathy frowned. The last person she wanted to talk about this afternoon was the girl Maisie who had come to work temporarily in the village shop after Christmas and was still there, off and on.

They were nearly at the top of the plantation now. The rows of dark trees had their own beauty. She hadn't noticed it before but they seemed to still the air and cut off time so that for a moment her deep worry about the school closure and the meeting arranged to discuss the implications receded.

'Look, Cathy,' Arnold said in triumph. 'I've planted things differently on this side of the hill. Can you see what I've done?'

She stood at his side and looked uncomprehendingly at the rows of tiny trees. 'They're planted close together,' she said at last.

'Exactly. I'd like to have seen more hardwood among them though. Uncle Perry won't wear it. I had to make do with alternative rows of larch.'

'Why is that important?'

His confident smile turned to a frown. 'Larch are deciduous. Light gets to the Norway spruce now, in the winter. I should have thought that was obvious. The spruce will be marketed as Christmas trees as soon as they're about three feet high for a quick return. And the larch will have more room to grow,'

Cathy smiled. 'That's clever.'

He threw his head back in the gesture she had come to know so well. 'That's what Maisie thinks.'

'Maisie? You've told her about it?'

'Why not? It's important to me.'

162

'I'm surprised that's all.'

'Don't you trust me?'

She bit her lip. 'It's not that.'

'You're not jealous?'

'Of course not.' Cathy pressed her lips tightly together and then took a deep breath. It was nothing so why make a fuss? 'Do we have to talk about her?' she said, a rough tone to her voice she couldn't control.

'If you're going to be silly we'd better go back.'

Tears sprang to her eyes. 'If that's the way you really want it, Arnold, I suppose we'd better.'

She started to run down through the trees. It seemed to take ages yet no time at all. At the bottom she stopped, wondering what to do. As she brushed her loose hair away from her eyes she heard him coming after her but wouldn't look round. Instead she started to walk along the track that led to the road, pulling out her handkerchief to wipe her face without letting him see.

Something at the edge of the track made her pause, a dead rabbit with its fur matted and rough.

'Don't touch it,' Arnold ordered as he reached her.

But she had already turned it over with her foot. The bulbous eyes stared up at nothing. She moved swiftly back and at once Arnold's arms were round her.

'Oh the poor thing!' she said. 'It's that disease everybody's talking about.'

'Myxomatosis. Poor thing nothing. The sooner the rabbit population is wiped out the better. But there are more interesting things to talk about. Come here, Cathy, and stop being stupid.'

He looked his old self again now, the Arnold she had fallen in love with. The same clear-cut features and high forehead. The same look of firmness about him that had attracted her in the beginning. Up on the hill he had seemed different but not down here. His air of casualness had gone. There was nothing to worry about.

She smiled as he pulled her close to kiss her. Today was their own. It was enough.

CHAPTER TEN

Elisabeth was just in time to slip into the last seat in the front row before the vicar stood up to open the meeting. An air of expectancy filled the place as he stood up and gazed at the audience. On the desk in front of him was a neat pile of papers topped with his fountain pen. He looked ready for business.

At first everything was orderly. Martin Varley wanted the alternative arrangements for Mellstone children made clear if the decision to close the school went ahead. It was while Karen was on her feet that Bill Gedge started to growl out loud.

At once Mrs Barden joined in. 'We don't want no bus taking our children away,' she shouted.

Hastily Karen sat down as several others joined in. Robert lifted his hand for silence and apart from indistinct muttering he was obeyed. 'May we first have a show of hands for all those against the school closing?' he said. 'Indeed, unanimous as I thought. Now I'd like to hear your reasons. One at a time, if you please.'

Martin Varley got to his feet again and Elisabeth's apprehensions subsided a little. He spoke with an air of assurance that convinced her that everything that could be done to change the decision would be taken care of. She began to think, too, that it was sheer nonsense that Jenny's accident had anything to do with it.

'For years the school has taken an important part in village life,' he said in measured tones. 'Without it Mellstone is in danger of losing its identity.'

Several others stood up and said more or less the same thing, Miss Buckley muttering about it being a pretty pathetic state of affairs.

'These reasons will have been thought about already,' Robert pointed out. 'I have been assured that the decision was not taken lightly.'

'We haven't got a village hall,' someone shouted from across the room. 'How can we manage if we can't use the school for meeting and such like?'

'A good point, Mrs Harvey.'

Karen moved slightly in the seat next to Elisabeth. 'Not good enough,' she murmured. 'The building will still be here. They won't remove it brick by brick and cart it to the scrappers' yard.'

Elisabeth gave a gurgling laugh that she suppressed hastily.

Bill Gedge began to struggle to his feet. He glared round at the audience. 'Look at the Tidings Tree,' he cried, his voice hoarse. 'They cut that down without asking we. Now they're going to take the school.'

'The tree is another matter . . .' Robert began, on his feet again, but an ugly murmur cut him short.

Elisabeth felt herself flush. Now there would be trouble.

Robert seemed to think so too as he shuffled the papers on his desk. At the same time he glanced around the room beneath his heavy brows as if summing up the deep emotions so obviously running beneath the surface.

Elisabeth glanced at Karen and saw spots of high colour in her cheeks.

'It's the Tidings Tree that's shutting our school,' Bill shouted above the increasing noise.

'Nonsense,' Robert said, raising his voice. 'Anyone with any sense knows it had nothing to do with it.'

'We've no sense then,' cried Mrs Barden. 'Is that what you'm saying, Vicar? Children wandering about all over the shop when they ought by rights to be in school! No wonder they wants to shut the school.'

Karen leapt to her feet. 'Wait a minute.' The ring of authority in her voice silenced everyone. 'Have you no confidence in Miss Mellor or myself to keep your children safe in school?' She glared in scorn around the room. 'I'll tell you this. There'll be no school bus taking the children in my class to Wernely. We're just under the mileage limit for the seven year-olds and upwards.'

'Thank you, Miss Bryer,' said Robert.

But Karen was in full flow now. 'Your children will be in far more danger from traffic along the main road than they would ever be from the Tidings Tree or anything at Mellstone school.'

'You've made your point, Miss Bryer.'

' Just because one child . . .'

'*Sit down*, Miss Bryer.'

Among uproar she obeyed, cheeks aflame. For a few moments Robert gave up any attempt to keep control.

Elisabeth looked uneasily at the chairs blocking her way of escape. She had had enough. Even though Jenny was being looked after at the farm by Jean Varley she had a desperate urge to get away.

Karen was breathing deeply, her eyes bright. 'I see red every time that wretched tree is mentioned,' she muttered.

'They're laying the blame on me as well as you,' said Elisabeth.

'I know that.'

A faint hint of understanding passed between them but was instantly gone.

Gradually the noise in the room subsided until Robert, looking rather strained, was able to make himself heard. After some more lengthy discussion it was decided to draft a petition setting out the reasons for wanting the school to remain open. The meeting then closed with prayer.

Elisabeth made her escape at last and hurried out of the building, glad to feel the fresh air on her face.

*   *   *

'We'll leave the room till the morning,' Karen said as Alice Pengold starting collecting chairs together.

'Some folk like to get on mornings without clearing up first,' Alice said without pausing.

'Very well,' side Karen wearily. 'Have it your own way.'

They worked together, one stacking the chairs and the other moving them to the side

168

of the room ready for the desks to be replaced in their correct positions. Karen then helped Cathy pull the partition back into place so that Ms Pengold could help her set the Infant Room to rights.

On her own side Karen glanced at Robert who was still standing by her desk after bidding the last of the villagers goodnight.

How pale he looked, she thought with a stab of sympathy. She wished she could comfort him in some way and take that look of strain away from him.

He smiled at her. 'And now you'll want your desk moved back to its rightful place,' he said.

'It'll be good to get things back to normal,' she said. 'If it's ever possible after all this. What a waste of time.'

'The meeting had to be held,' he said. 'Indeed it was expected. Now all we can do is put our views to the authorities.'

Karen nodded but before they could do anything about moving her desk he made a little stumbling movement and then remained quite still as he rested his weight on it.

'What is it?' she gasped. 'What's the matter?'

She pulled a chair forward and he sank down on it, his face chalk-white.

'Some water,' he breathed.

At once she was in the cloakroom filling a cup at the tap. She bent over him anxiously as he swallowed some tablets. Gradually the

169

bluish tinge vanished from his lips.

She let out a shaky breath of relief. 'You feel better now, Robert?'

He nodded. 'I'll sit here quietly for a few minutes. Thank you for not making a fuss. Naturally I'd rather this wasn't generally known.'

'But what's wrong? Why does it happen?'

'There's no need to worry. My heart's a little uncertain, that's all. I'm supposed to take things quietly.'

'Then you're really ill?' Karen couldn't quite control the panicky element in her voice and hoped he hadn't noticed.

'No, not really. This doesn't happen often. It rather restrains what I'm able to do, that's all. Indeed, I have to accept that my life isn't quite normal nowadays and abide by that knowledge.'

Unable to go on, he turned his head away.

She saw the movement away from her and felt it as a criticism of her. But perhaps she deserved it for her fiery reaction to what was being said by people like Mrs Barden. She was silent, struggling to hide her feelings.

He took another sip of water and put the cup down on the desk. 'Thank you, Karen.'

'Why didn't you get someone else to chair the meeting for you, Robert? You must have known how rowdy it would be.'

'It was my place to do so as Chairman of the Governors. I couldn't shirk that duty. I hoped

170

the meeting might have done some good for your sake, Karen. We've known each other how long? Indeed over three years and in all that time I've seen the improvements you have made here. I've appreciated your dedication and know you have more to give. It's a difficult time for you.'

Her heart leapt because he sounded as if he cared for her sake. Going away from Mellstone meant going away from Robert too and she would have to face that. He was rarely more than friendly but occasionally, like now, she felt the faintest glimmer of something more. Then he would clamp down again for no apparent reason and leave her feeling lost and depressed.

'The meeting was rowdier that I expected,' he said. 'I wish you hadn't felt the need to stir things up to such a pitch. Unnecessary, I would have thought.'

'Yes, well . . .' She broke off, unable to explain the sudden blaze of fury that had swept over her at the mention the Tidings Tree. All they could think of was the child's accident and yet the school had been here educating Mellstone's children for generations and doing a good job of it on the whole.

'I didn't intend to apologise to you, Robert, but . . .'

'Please don't if it's not a genuine feeling from the heart. I don't wish to be treated as someone in desperate need of protection.'

'No, I can see that.'

She almost offered him a lift back to the vicarage but could see that it wouldn't do. He would get home on his own two feet if the effort killed him. At least he was looking better now.

He stood up. 'I see Miss Turner came to the meeting. I hope she wasn't upset about what was said. I noticed she left early.'

Karen's throat felt tight. 'Perhaps you'd better go and find out.'

He looked at her with an expression she found hard to fathom. 'I hope I have enough sense not to call on Miss Turner at this hour even if I have none where you are concerned. Good night, Miss Bryer.'

He went and she felt bereft. Why did she have to goad him like that and spoil everything?

She jumped as the door burst open. She knew that Cathy Mellor had gone but had forgotten Mrs Pengold was still in the next room.

'Ticked you off, did he?'

Karen sighed. 'I expect everyone will consider themselves well rid of me when the time comes.'

Alice looked round the room with a critical eye. 'They said a lot of things they don't mean though half of them's afraid of you.'

Karen laughed shortly. 'You're a comfort, Mrs Pengold. I don't know what I'd do without you.'

'No more do I.' Alice agreed. 'Come on now. It's time we was off home.'

*   *   *

Robert let himself into the vicarage and felt for the light switch. In his study the fire had been banked down. Now all he had to do was to give it a poke to bring it to life. For a moment he stood and watched the flames leap up to provide the warmth he so badly needed.

Soon he would bring in the tray Mrs Froud had left ready in the kitchen but now he needed to relax a little after the rowdy scene in the school room. Small wonder that Karen had lost the grip on her temper. Her flashing eyes and heightened colour had lent her dark attractiveness a beauty he hadn't seen in her often but when he did he found his thoughts dwelling on her far more than he should for his peace of mind. There was something about her that had drawn him to her from the first moment of meeting when he, too, had been settling in to his position in Mellstone.

He smiled now, remembering how she had looked this evening . . .

He had always admired her clear thinking and her understanding of the needs of the children in her care. But that sort of emotion had a price and she had looked pale after her outburst. The longing to comfort her had

173

been strong but as usual when they were alone together a purely innocent remark on his part had led to a certain coldness that was difficult to penetrate. No doubt this was for the best.

Her first reaction to his slight attack had been instant . . . a cup of water and no fuss, just calmly standing at his side until it passed.

Afterwards he had seen in her eyes a wish to offer him a lift home but she had resisted because of her understanding that he prefered to be independent.

There was no doubt in his mind that his secret was safe with her.

*　　　*　　　*

Cathy unlocked the front door of Lynch Cottage and took the stairs two at a time. As usual she felt a sense of excitement as she reached the door of her room, even tonight after the exhausting meeting that had been such a waste of time.

'What sort of hour do you call this?' Arnold demanded as she went in.

She looked at him in astonishment as he got to his feet and stretched. He smoothed his moustache and looking at her critically.

Cathy flushed. 'How did you get in Arnold?'

'Let in by one of the ladies, of course. She said you wouldn't be long.'

She gasped as he caught her to him and then let her knees sag as she relaxed against

174

him. He felt warm and solid and smelt faintly of musk. His lips were gentle at first and then pressed down on hers with a hardness that hurt her teeth.

As he released her she glanced at the pink cups and saucers on the table.

He grinned as he seated himself again. 'I've not been having a party in your absence, my love. Miss King fancies me, I swear. It's true I accepted the cup of tea she insisted on bringing me.'

'That was kind of her,' Cathy said as she unbuttoned her coat.

'It helped to pass the time anyway.'

'I'm sorry I've been such a long time, Arnold.'

'She's been in and out like nobody's business. She can't leave me alone.'

'The meeting was awful. Mrs Barden was yelling her head off and very abusive. It was embarrassing. The vicar looked ill.'

Arnold yawned. 'Forget it, Cathy.'

'I thought . . .'

'There's no need to go on about it. I'd have been there if I'd been interested. It's bad enough Miss King doing her Mother Hen act.'

Cathy hesitated, aware she was being boring. It wasn't fair to Arnold to think about the school closure when they were together because it made her miserable. She couldn't blame him for not wanting that. 'Tea?' she said. 'I'm parched.'

There was a tap on the door.

'Not that woman again?' said Arnold in disbelief.

The door was pushed slightly open and Miss King sidled in. Her baggy corduroy slacks had muddy patches on the knees from earlier gardening activities. 'Oh, you're back, dear,' she said. 'I was just a bit concerned. Miss Buckley has been home for some time.'

'I stayed behind to help clear up,' said Cathy.

'You poor dear,' Miss King's voice was hushed. 'Such a difficult time for you.'

'You're very kind,' said Cathy. She bit her lip to stop it trembling. She wished Miss King would go away before she dissolved into weak laughter. She couldn't remember feeling quite so tired and dispirited before.

Arnold cleared his throat.

'So that's why I popped up, dear. Are you sure you're all right?'

Cathy nodded. 'Thank you, Miss King. I'm sure.'

'Keeps a check on you, does she?' Arnold said when she had gone. 'I wonder you stand for it.'

Cathy sighed. The evening had got off to a bad start and wasn't improving. She picked up the kettle.

'Not for me,' said Arnold. 'Come and sit down, Cathy. You're as bad as old Baggy Pants with all this pottering about.'

Cathy put the kettle down. There was a

rustling outside the door.

Arnold raised his head. 'I could swear the wretched woman is out there listening. What does she think I am, a white slave trader?' He got up in fury and leapt towards the door. 'In falls King,' he cried and wrenched open the door with a suddenness that nearly had Miss King sprawling on the floor.

Cathy hardly knew whether to laugh or cry.

Miss King's face was pink. 'I just wanted to make sure you're not still upset about the school,' she said, almost in a whisper.

Arnold made a choking sound as she withdrew. Then with a shout of laughter, he caught hold of Cathy. They fell back on the sofa, giggling.

Now the evening was transformed. Arnold was smiling, his disgruntled feelings forgotten. Cathy wished he were always like this with his eyes sparkling and a little quirky lift to his lips.

*　　　*　　　*

The chilly air in the hall of Marigold Cottage made Elisabeth shiver. How easy it would be to switch on the fire in the living-room and settle down in front of it with a book until bedtime. But in the studio were three paintings waiting to be finished. She had left them ready before taking Jenny along to spend the night at Varley's Farm so that she could attend the meeting and now she was free to work as late

177

as she liked.

For a moment she hesitated and then she picked up her torch, went out of the back door and locked it. Inside the icy studio she blinked in the sudden glare from the unshaded light and tried to stop shivering as she removed her painting apron from its hook on the door. She put it on and tied it round her waist with chilly fingers.

Perhaps, this once, she would switch on one bar of the electric fire for ten minutes to take the chill off the place. After that she would be too engrossed in what she was doing to notice the cold.

As she set to work she thought of what Robert had once said, that we must always believe that things would get better. Perhaps when the cold weather passed and the spring brought visitors to Mellstone someone might like her paintings enough to purchase one. It was a comforting thought anyway.

Time now to switch off the fire. As she did so there came a soft scraping sound. She stood upright and heard it again. Her heart quickened as she glanced at the curtained window. Someone was out there!

A bang on the glass shattered the silence. She rushed to the door, threw it open and heard the sound of running footsteps. Then silence again.

She closed the door, tempted to run across the lawn herself and lock the cottage door behind her. But she had work to do here and no one was going to drive her away from Mellstone with these tricks.

She reached for her brush and set to work again. She must forget how easy it was for someone to get into the garden from over the school wall.

It had been her dream to move here just as it was Bella's to set up a centre for the arts near St Ives. Bella wouldn't let a thing like this stop her from fulfilling what she set out to do. And neither would she.

As she worked she thought of Mrs Cameron and her invitation for them to visit her at Nether End. Soon Jenny would have the two-day holiday from school for Half Term. It would be good to spend one of them with their friend. In her company she could forget for a short while the worries and troubles here at Marigold Cottage and work extra hard when she got back to make up for it.

Another letter had arrived in the post this morning at the same time that had given her pleasure too. Elisabeth smiled, thinking of the extravagant phrases as Pixie's owner poured out her heartfelt thanks both for the wonderful portrait of her pet that was so lifelike and which gave her such comfort. Elisabeth hadn't expected a reply from Mrs Wentworth to her letter of condolence and hearing of her reaction to Pixie's portrait was heart-warming.

CHAPTER ELEVEN

Elisabeth, sitting with Mrs Cameron in the elegant sitting room, gazed out through the French windows to the wide expanse of lawn that stretched to where the wooded hill began.

'How peaceful it is here,' she said. 'So quiet.'

'This is what John likes,' said Mrs Cameron. 'Even as a little lad he liked the bare emptiness of it here with the downs and all. And Jenny too. I watched her go dancing off across the grass so happy.'

'She loves the freedom. And she wants to look for primroses. 'She won't go far. She makes sure I always know where she's going.'

'Such a good child.'

Mrs Cameron's plump hands lay idle in her lap. Her pale mauve cardigan suited her, Elisabeth thought. Stout as her friend was she could fade into any background of sweet pea colours.

'I told Jenny there's some sweets for her when she gets back,' Mrs Cameron said. 'Donald loved his sweets.' A vague expression filled her eyes for a moment.

'You spoil her, Mrs Cameron.'

'Do I, dear?'

Elisabeth smiled. 'And she loves you for it.'

'She deserves spoiling now and again.' Mrs

Cameron's chair creaked slightly as she leaned forward. 'And it's so nice to buy sweets again as many as we want. I can't get used to them being off the ration now, even after all this time. So I'm spoiling myself too.'

'And why not? You deserve it.'

Mrs Cameron smiled. She struggled to her feet and stood, panting slightly, with her hand on the back of Elisabeth's chair. 'Why don't you go up the hill after Jenny, dear, while I start to get the tea?'

Elisabeth sprang up. 'Oh no, I must help you.'

'No dear. I like to have something to do and it's a lovely afternoon even though we're still in February.'

'If you're sure?'

'You'll like it up there. I'll tell John where you are when he comes in.' Mrs Cameron moved to the door. 'She's been gone quite a long time, hasn't she? I'd go after her if I were you.'

The sun felt surprisingly warm as Elisabeth crossed the grass. How calm and unhurried it was at Nether End, she thought, and a completely different world from her own busy one. She felt wafted back to a gentler way of life that she had almost forgotten existed during her busy working days.

At the end of the lawn she paused and looked back at the old house that lay low and mellow in the afternoon sunlight. The peace

181

was so beautiful it hurt. She felt a sudden urge to return to a calmer life in which social occasions such as this could play a reasonable part. A regular job would ensure this for her.

Then she gave herself a mental shake, ashamed of swerving even for a moment from her determination to succeed in the life she had chosen.

As she started to walk up the track John joined her. She stopped, confused because of a softness about his expression that made her feel special. He had obviously come to find her.

He smiled. 'I saw you from over there,' he said. 'I didn't know if I should disturb you. You were deep in thought, Elisabeth.'

'I'm looking for Jenny.'

'She's up there somewhere picking primroses. They're always early in that sheltered spot. There's no need to worry.'

'I'm not worried.' She quickened her pace. 'I'd better find her.'

Amusement flickered in his eyes. 'I'll come with you if you don't object to my working attire.'

She smiled. 'It feels odd not to be in mine.'

She felt him glance at her as they set off together up the track.

'I prefer you like this, Elisabeth. That shade of green suits you.'

She flushed, ill at ease. After his criticism of her in Marigold Cottage she hadn't known what to expect of this visit to Nether End today. His kind friendliness surprised her. He looked comfortable in his old clothes with the sunlight glinting on his light hair. She wished that she, too, was wearing her old familiar things. She shrugged and smoothed her skirt with a sudden feeling of panic because she wasn't in the paint-smeared one she had left behind and her old blouse that had seen better days.

'You haven't heard any more about that tax demand, have you Elisabeth?

She shook her head.

'I'm sorry. I shouldn't have reminded you. Please, don't worry about it. Look, let me show you the view from here.'

How could she help worrying now that he had reminded her? But she was aware of how sorry he was that he'd raised the subject and did her best to push it to the back of her mind.

They paused by a field gate from which they could see the Iron Age hillfort that was Larksbury Rings. Sheep dotted the grassy ramparts and the hollows between were in shadow. John was silent for a moment as he filled his pipe and lit it.

'Any view that includes Larksbury Rings is a good view, as Bertram Russell once said,' he murmured.

'Bertram Russell said that?'

'Well, not quite. Chanctonbury Ring in his case.'

Elisabeth laughed. 'It's a beautiful view.'

'Remarkable, don't you think, that well over two thousand years ago there was so much activity over there?'

'It's so peaceful now it's hard to imagine.'

'Just think how many men it must have taken to build it and how glaringly white from the chalk it would have looked at first.'

'I suppose it would. I hadn't thought of that before.' She looked across the intervening fields and tried to imagine sunshine illuminating the stark white hillside. It would be seen from miles around especially on a day as clear as this.

'Larksbury Rings has never been excavated although there's talk it might be before long. They'll get some idea then, of course, if it was used merely for defence or if there was a settlement there too. If so they'll likely turn up pottery, jewels and coins. Post holes for rectangular granary huts too and pits for storage perhaps such as they've found on other Iron Age forts. There was a lot of hillfort mania, as they called it, in the thirties. That's when my father got interested. He was a fount of information as I was growing up.'

'And then the Romans came with their superior weapons and warfare skills and over-ran the country?'

John shrugged. 'The people couldn't hold out against them.'

'But the hillforts weren't all abandoned?'

'Certainly not the larger ones that had become more like towns by then. Others were destroyed, the local people evicted and the forts left derelict. Some were reoccupied and refortified after the Romans left.'

'So we don't really know yet what happened at Larksbury Rings except that there was change?'

He looked thoughtful. 'I think there's something in us that makes us curious about what has gone before. We will always need an understanding of the past to make sense of the present.'

'Yes, I see.' She stood at his side, leaning on the gate and gazing into the distance as if she couldn't see enough.

Then John began to talk in his quiet voice of some of his plans for the fields below.

'Small changes adding up into big ones as the years move on,' she said.

He nodded. 'The only constant is change, Elisabeth.'

She was silent, thinking about it. Her canvasses changed as she applied paint, creating something that hadn't been there before. She glanced at him, moved by his obvious love for the place.

'My family have been here for generations,' he said and then was silent for a moment. The smoke from his pipe rose in the still air. After a while he said, 'I don't think I could bear to lose it and I very nearly did because of someone I thought I loved as much as all this. If I hadn't had Marigold Cottage to sell . . .'

She was startled. 'You mean . . .'

'The cottage belonged to my grandparents.'

His closed expression didn't invite comment. She was afraid to move and his quiet words hung between them. She was fully aware of her own good fortune in finding the cottage on the market at the right time for her.

'Divorce is a kind of death,' he said at last. 'At the best it leaves a sense of deep failure.'

She leaned back against the bars of the gate and turned to look at him. 'I can see how much you care for all this, John, and you have it still. It's your life just as mine is painting. There's satisfaction in it.'

He gave a brief smile and looked down at the pipe in his hand as if he didn't know what he was doing with it. Then it was in his mouth again and he puffed hard once or twice.

'I wish I could convince you of how much my painting means to me,' she said.

He removed his pipe again. 'You could try.'

'Painting gives me a surging sense of release, of well-being, of completeness. Don't you feel the same when you look at your land, John? I think you must do. All I know is that I'm happy when I paint.'

'Happy?'

'Perhaps content is a better word.'

'I see.'

'When I'm not painting I feel a terrible urge

186

to be working again.'

'And everything else is a waste of time, like today?'

'I didn't mean that.'

'It sounded as if you did.'

He didn't really understand, she thought, saddened. She turned away and stared up at the track that disappeared among the trees.

A sudden weariness filled her and she needed action to dispel it. 'D'you mind if I sketch this?' she asked.

He looked surprised. 'The track? Not if you think it's worth it.' He leaned on the gate and watched her swift pencil strokes until she finished.

'May I see?'

'It's only a preliminary sketch to help me paint it later from memory.'

'You're able to do that? Wouldn't a photograph be better?'

'I shall hold it in my mind,' she said, smiling. 'I'd like to be chosen to stage my own exhibition at the art shop gallery in Hilbury during the summer. I applied the other day and I'm waiting to hear. If I'm lucky this could be one of the ones hanging there. Perhaps I'll show you the finished painting one day.'

'I hope you will.' He smiled too and moved slightly against the gate.

She wouldn't need the sketch to remind her of this moment, she thought because John's presence in this quiet place was suddenly important to her. In some intuitive way she suspected that he felt the same about her, too, and she wasn't sure she could cope with knowing that at the moment.

She put her pencil and pad into her pocket and started to climb up the track.

'Not so fast,' John said from behind her. 'Don't run away from me, Elisabeth.'

Running away . . . was that what this was?

'Elisabeth?'

'I must find Jenny now. I don't know where she is.'

'Listen,' he said. 'She's here somewhere. Can't you hear her?'

Jenny appeared on the track ahead of them, her red hair a mass of leaves and grass.

John smiled at her. 'Have you been picking flowers for your mother?'

She gave him a glare of withering scorn. Her was face was flushed and her eyes bright as she thrust her primroses behind her back.

'You look a mess, Jenny,' Elisabeth said. 'What on earth have you been doing?'

Jenny caught hold of her hand to pull her forward. 'There's a ditch full of leaves. Can we go further down the track on the other side of the hill?'

They paused at another gate that gave a view of a different valley. Down below was a large brick house in a rambling garden.

'That's Miss Bryer's house down there, Jenny,' John said.

She stared at him, wide-eyed. Then she pulled quickly at Elisabeth's hand. 'Can we go back now? I don't like it here.'

John began to speak of his aunt as they retraced their steps. 'Aunt Ruth's missing Mellstone,' he said. 'I thought a change of scenery might help but she doesn't seem to know what she wants. There was some talk of her going to stay with Uncle Donald's sister in Weymouth but I don't know . . .'

'I don't think she has enough to do here, John. Your housekeeper is so efficient. Mrs Cameron needs to be in her own place with her own things about her. Then she can think about what's best for her.'

'Reminding her of what she has lost?'

'I don't think anything really helps. Only time.'

'Well yes.'

The path narrowed as they reached the bottom and he stood aside for Elisabeth to go ahead of him.

She was asking me about the school,' he said. 'It worries her that she wasn't at the meeting.'

'The school?'

Elisabeth smiled at his incredulous expression. 'There's so much feeling about it and she wanted to know everything that happened the other night. She's concerned about it closing. We all are.'

'But what can she do about it?'

'She just wants to be there in Mellstone is case anything else happens she needs to know about.'

'You're sure about that?'

'As sure as I am about anything.'

John was deep in thought for the rest of the way. She hoped she had done a little good in giving her opinion. But only time would tell.

*   *   *

Elisabeth slipped into her studio for a few moments when at last Jenny had fallen asleep. As soon as they got home she had arranged some of her primroses in an empty paste pot that now stood on her bedroom window sill where she would see it when she awoke tomorrow morning.

The evening was calm without the slightest sound disturbing the quiet air, Elisabeth's favourite time of the day. From the light from the kitchen window a clump of white crocus by the steps was illuminated into pure gold. She hadn't known what time John would drive them home and hadn't planned to work now but something drew her up to the studio to check that all was well even though she could only stay here for a few minutes because of Jenny alone indoors.

She thought of Jenny's silence as they walked with John down the track to the house. He had tried to jolly her along but she would have none of it. Maybe she was just tired after clambering about on the hillside and it wasn't an instinctive reaction to something in the atmosphere of which she didn't approve?

Three of the canvasses were still wet and Elisabeth had placed them on the floor against the end wall to dry so that she saw them on first entering. This way she was able to pick up on anything that was not quite right and make mental note. This evening she was pleased with all three, two of the thatched cottages round the green, each from a different angle, and one of the downs with the afterglow from the setting sun misting them with faintest mauve.

The rattle of stones on the roof made her jump.

There was no other sound, just that. She stood motionless for a few anxious moments and then opened the door. As she expected she saw nothing unusual. Whoever it was had escaped from the school playground with speed. She closed the door and stood leaning on it until her heart stopped pounding, glad that she hadn't planned to work up here this evening and that returning indoors did not seem like running away.

Tomorrow she would report this to PC Pete Hallen, their local policeman, and see what he had to say about this worrying business. It had gone beyond a joke, even if she had ever considered it one.

*　　　*　　　*

Later that evening, when Fly had flopped exhausted into his basket in the kitchen after their evening walk, John sat alone in his sitting room and listened to Beethoven's Pastoral Sympathy. He lay back in his arm chair and let the freshness and cheerfulness of the opening movement sweep over him.

He had chosen to play this record instead of the sea symphonies that had been his favourites for many years because it reminded him of Elisabeth as she stood at the field gate this afternoon looking out over his fields to the hills beyond. One day he would take her to the top of Larksbury Rings to see the view across the Vale on a clear day when they could see for miles. Today Jenny had been with them casting antagonistic glances at him as if she knew what was in his mind.

He would like to talk to Elisabeth, too, about his thoughts on putting some of the land on the other side of the hill to forestry. He had been thinking of it for some time and reading all he could before discussing it with Perry Wintle over at Downend.

'Get my nephew over to your place,' Wintle had advised. 'Knows it all, or thinks he does. He'll soon put you right.'

It wasn't a bad idea. He would need to give it more thought. He couldn't expect Elisabeth to know much about what was involved but she would listen with sympathy as he outlined the pros and cons.

He had told her this afternoon that this place meant more to him than anything else but that wasn't true any longer. He was fully aware now that, love this place as he did, that there was something . . . someone . . . who was beginning to mean more to him.

As the music flowed he allowed his imagination to soar into realms of fancy and he found it easy to think of her with him now, relaxing and talking quietly. She would be wearing that pretty shade of green that highlighted her hair with auburn lights and made her eyes glow.

For once, as they walked on his land, Elisabeth's worried expression had vanished and he had been pleased to see it. He wished it could always be so and that he was the means of banishing it for good. Life here could be leisurely and carefree for her with no financial worries. No need for the continuous hard work that he could see was grinding her down. Jenny could enjoy her exploring in safe surroundings. Elisabeth would be free to go with her, spend more time with her.

Smiling slightly, he allowed his mind to dwell on the happiness Elisabeth would bring with her.

Never before had he been aware of the deep feelings beneath the musical description of the pastoral scenes. Now, leaning back in his chair, the delicate passion of the music engulfed him.

CHAPTER TWELVE

Elisabeth stood at the bus stop half way along the High Street in Hilbury unaware of the icy March wind tugging at her clothes. She held her precious canvasses tightly under her arm and almost laughed out loud.

A minimum of fifty paintings by the third week of May, she thought. Not impossible if she worked hard. And if the exhibition was a success and most of her work sold it could mean financial security for Jenny and herself for quite some time. It might well establish her name further afield if she were lucky. The thought of three busy months ahead was exhilarating.

With the light of determination in her eyes and her back held straight she stared across the road at the art shop. Her reception there earlier had been so full of appreciation that she blushed now with pleasure to think of it. It had been well worth the effort of packing up her three best oils and carrying them to the bus stop. The shivering wind had whistled round her as she waited in the bus shelter by the Swan Inn. The bus was almost full when it arrived ten minutes late and was off at once, swaying round the bend in the road, before she had time to find a seat downstairs.

But none of that mattered now.

The proprietor, Mr Evans, had come forward at once, his face shining with welcome and hands outstretched. 'Ah Miss Turner. A final judgement of your work, isn't it?' he had boomed. 'Let me see what you have to show me. Bring it all through here at once, my dear, if you will.'

In the large exhibition room at the back her paintings had looked good and she was proud of them. He stood back, smiling with approval. 'With work of this quality I can safely say that we can offer you a place in the exhibition, Miss Turner,' he said. 'Can you assure me that the required number will be delivered on time?'

In that instant she knew that she could do it and a contract had been produced and signed by both of them. She looked forward to telling Cathy, not knowing she would be delighted for her.

Now, at the bus stop, it was some moments before she became aware that a vehicle had slowed down and stopped nearby.

'John!' she cried.

He leaned across to open the door for her. She scrambled in with her parcel, clutching at the door before the wind slammed it out of reach.

'Not a good day to be standing by a bus

stop,' he said as they joined the stream of traffic leaving the town.

Elisabeth moved a little so that the canvasses on her lap were well away from the gear lever. She felt as if her excitement was bursting out of her and filling the car. They were ahead of the bus and she would have plenty of time to start a new painting before tea. Jenny would be happy enough in the living-room with the model shop she was making when she came in from school.

'Something important must have happened,' said John, amusement in his voice. 'You look radiant, Elisabeth, and you don't appear to have noticed that it's sheeting down with rain.'

She laughed. 'It's wonderful. I've been offered a part of an exhibition. They've just told me. I can hardly believe it.'

'A part of an exhibition?'

'I'm lucky to have been one of the two artists chosen for the month of June. Actually the exhibition opens in the last week of May, the day after Whit Monday. We submit at least fifty paintings each. With luck they'll take them all.'

John was silent as he concentrated on the traffic moving slowly in front. She wondered that he could drive so calmly when her elation was like a living thing.

'It seems a lot of hard work,' he said at last.

'It's my golden opportunity. I'm to portray Mellstone and the area round about in all its

196

moods and in different genres. Someone else will be doing Hilbury and Stourford. Then in due course they'll have someone else to do the Dorset coastline, the Purbecks, the heathlands and Poole Harbour. Other parts too. These exhibitions will continue until Christmas. Dealers come from far and wide. It's a wonderful chance to get known.'

'I see.'

The traffic was clearing now and John accelerated as they left the last houses of the town behind them. Low cloud hid the downs and a fine mist of rain hung over the fields. The car tyres swished through wide puddles on the road and seemed a cheerful sound to Elisabeth.

'I don't know much about painting,' John said. 'But it seems an extraordinary number. How long have you got?

'I have to deliver them in the third week in May,' she said, her voice vibrant. 'A challenge.'

'And you're sure it's not too big a one?'

'Of course I'm sure.'

'Forgive me, but I can't help feeling concerned.'

'Concerned?'

'That you'll find it too much for you. I hope you've given it enough thought before agreeing to this?'

She ignored the censure in his voice. 'I'm so lucky to be one of two artists chosen to open the exhibition. Mr Evans loved these paintings

I showed him.'

'I'm not so sure it's a good thing.'

'It's wonderful, believe me. The best thing that could happen.' She laughed, so enthralled with her good fortune that nothing that John said could touch her today.

There was a long silence she didn't attempt to break until they reached the first cottages in Mellstone. 'I haven't asked you how Mrs Cameron is,' she said.

'I'm about to call on Mrs Pengold now to ask her to light fires and tidy round a bit. Aunt Ruth's coming back on Saturday.

'That's good,' Elisabeth said. She was pleased, of course, but she found it hard to think of anything at the moment but the fire of creation in her veins. Even the matter of the stones thrown at her studio no longer seemed important. But perhaps that was because Pete Hallen had taken it seriously. He had hinted that he knew who the culprit was and would warn him in no uncertain terms to behave in future.

The stump of the Tidings Tree was hidden in waves of rain as they drove past. John slowed down and drew up outside Marigold Cottage.

'Better wait for a while, Elisabeth,' he said. 'It may ease off in a minute.'

She gazed at the soaked garden and the rain dripping off the thatch. As she moved slightly the sodden brown paper pulled away from the top canvas on her knee and revealed the

198

browns, greens and yellows she had used to portray the track leading up the hill at Nether End with Larksbury Rings in the distance.

John smiled as he looked down at it. 'You've captured it perfectly.

'I started work on it that same evening and it went well from the beginning. I'm glad Mrs Cameron is coming home.'

'Will the painting be part of the exhibition?'

She nodded as she looked down on it, knowing in her heart how precious it was to her and how much she would like to keep it in her possession. But at least she had it for the next few months. Mr Evans had asked for her whole body of work to be delivered in its entirety

But she had to be hardhearted about her work. There was no room for sentiment. This painting would go with the others and with luck would sell. All the same the restricted feeling in her throat she had felt at the time when she sketched the view was with her now.

'If your others are as good as this you'll be a success,' John said.

The gentle expression in his eyes unnerved her because it was unexpected and to her dismay her lips trembled. She crumpled the brown paper that had come loose and felt for the door handle.

'Thanks for the lift,' she mumbled.

She flung open the gate and stumbled up the path in the drenching rain.

To her surprise the door was unlocked. Water dripped from her clothes as she placed her canvasses against the hall chair. It was some moments before she saw Jenny's coat draped across it and pushed open the living-room door to see her lying on the sofa. Cathy Mellor was seated on the stool beside her.

She sprang to her feet on seeing Elisabeth and smoothed down her damp skirt. 'We think Jenny's sickening for flu. She was very hot one minute and shivering the next,' she said. 'Miss Bryer thought she'd be better at home. Jenny said you wouldn't be long.' Her hair looked limp, her eyes anxious.

Elisabeth threw herself down at Jenny's side and felt her warm forehead. 'Flu? I must get her to bed at once.'

Afterwards she thought she hadn't been grateful enough to Cathy for bringing Jenny home and staying with her. In fact she hadn't thanked her at all. Jenny was now asleep, her hair spread on the pillow like an auburn halo.

Elisabeth was reluctant to go downstairs and make a start on some work. It was hard to think about it at all with Jenny so flushed and restless. It seemed too much like the aftermath of the accident all over again.

Presently, though, she would have to make an effort. She was committed now.

But suppose she became ill too? She felt an upsurge of panic. It only needed something like that to throw her whole programme out of gear.

*   *   *

Rain lashed Cathy's hair into a clinging mess and water dripped down her face as she ran down the path and into the playground. She shook herself as she entered the cloakroom, wrinkling her nose at the damp atmosphere of wellingtons boots and wet coats.

Miss Bryer had the door in the partition open between the two classrooms so she could keep an eye on her own class while the little ones were busy with paper and crayons.

'I'm back,' Cathy said breathlessly.

Karen glanced at her watch and frowned. 'When I agreed to your taking the child home I didn't expect you to be all morning doing it.'

Cathy felt herself flush. 'Miss Turner was out. It seemed best to stay there with Jenny rather than bring her back.'

'Oh?'

'We don't want to start an epidemic.'

'I see.' Karen gave a dismissive nod. The girl was right, she thought, and had the gumption to say so. Once she would have let herself be reproached without saying a word in her own defence. This was an improvement. She smiled rather grimly as she told her own class to put their reading books away.

*   *   *

After school next day Cathy rang the bell hard on the front door of Marigold Cottage, prepared for a long wait. To her surprise the door was opened almost at once. 'Miss Turner, Elisabeth, I mean,' she said.

'You've got that right at long last,' Elisabeth said, smiling. 'Come in, Cathy.'

Cathy stepped into the hall. 'I thought you wouldn't mind if I called in to see how Jenny is now.'

'I'm glad you came.' Elisabeth opened the door into the living-room and ushered her inside. 'She's still in bed, of course, the best place for her. And I didn't even thank you for bringing her home yesterday.'

Cathy shrugged and offered the packet she had brought with her. 'It's a few little things she might like when she's feeling better, a crayoning book of wild flowers, some sweets and her school reading book so she doesn't get too far behind.'

'Oh Cathy, that's so thoughtful.' Elisabeth switched on the electric fire and indicated the chair nearby.

'I expect you're busy,' Cathy said as she sank into it. 'I won't stay long.'

'You can't think how glad I am to see you,' Elisabeth said as she pulled up a stool for herself.

Cathy looked at her with sympathy, noticing the dark shadows beneath her eyes and the way she held herself stiffly with her hands gripped together in her lap.

'If there's anything I can do to help I'd be glad to do it,' Cathy said.

Elisabeth smiled and then began to tell her about the work she had agreed to do for the exhibition in June and what an honour she felt it to be.

'But that's wonderful,' Cathy said, delighted for her.

'It's good to talk to you about it, Cathy. You see, several agents on the look-out for artists they can promote will be visiting the exhibition through the summer months and a lot might come of it. I have to be aware of that. Anyone else might criticise me for being selfish and thinking only about that when Jenny is ill. But it's not like that really.'

Cathy nodded. 'I know it isn't.'

Elisabeth smiled. 'It's such a relief to hear you say so. The work just has to be done, you see. I can't break the contract or I'll be in trouble.'

'And you can't leave Jenny on her own while you're working in your studio.'

'Well no.'

Cathy hesitated, considering. Elisabeth looked so drawn and worried but on Saturday she expected Arnold to suggest spending time

203

together although he hadn't said anything yet. And Sunday was bellringing and . . . 'I'll come here and be with Jenny at the weekend while you work if you like,' she said hurriedly before she had time to think more about it.

'Oh would you, Cathy?'

'Of course. Saturday morning?'

'That's so kind.'

Cathy could see the relief in Elisabeth's eyes and was glad she had offered. What good was offering to help out without making a definite commitment to do so? No good at all. All the same it was hard to look as if she was happy about it when she knew Arnold would complain.

She smiled and stood up to go. 'I'll be here directly after breakfast on Saturday then. See you then.'

*   *   *

John stood on the hillside with his dog, Fly, at his feet, and surveyed his land, deep in thought. Arnold Bronson was on slightly higher ground which brought their heads to the same height. The younger man's air of assurance as he looked about him with his head thrown back gave the impression that he was the taller of the two. In his neat brown jacket he was by far the smarter. His moustache looked freshly shaped and his hair was sleeked back from his forehead.

Fly stirred a little and John looked down at his dog with sympathy. Most likely he was as bored as he was beginning to feel with all the information thrown at him as if he were a five year old barely able to read for himself. The arrogance of the young man was astonishing but at least he had surprised him with his remark about the amount of rabbit netting required for a larger area being comparatively cheaper per acre because of bulk buying. Bronson obviously hadn't considered him intelligent enough to work that out.

'Of course there's another way of getting rid of rabbits that's a hundred per cent effective. You'll try that of course.'

'Definitely not,' said John, his voice stern. 'Pests as rabbit are I've no moral right to inflict this Myxomatosis on them.'

'Then you are your own worst enemy.'

'Have you any idea of the suffering, the length of time . . .'

Arnold shrugged, uncaring.

John turned away, regretting entering into the discussion with someone so scornful and impatient. He would consider at his leisure his options about planting trees, reading all he could and talking it over with men he could respect. Bronson had already been here for an hour expounding his views. It was a waste of time.

'Go in for it in a big way,' Arnold said. 'Make something of it. There's all the land this side. Get it all covered in conifers. Something for your children, your grandchildren to fall back on.'

John nodded. Children had never been part of Stephanie's plans and he had accepted that it was so. But now he found that his thoughts of the future and his lack of someone of his own to inherit often took him unawares.

He made a movement to go. 'Shall we return to the house?'

Arnold glanced at his watch. 'Not this time,' I'm afraid. My Saturday plans were changed so I'm off to Bournemouth on my own and should get going.'

John nodded and fingered his pipe in his pocket. They reached the broad track that led to the farmyard where the Wintle car was parked. With a feeling of relief John watched it drive off. Rarely had he met anyone so willing to knock obstacles aside with no thought of the consequences. The surprising thing was that the young man had gone in for forestry. It hardly provided immediate gratification for someone of his temperament. Forestry was long term. It needed a great deal of consideration on his part before he made any commitment.

*   *   *

Some days later Jenny sat on the window seat in the living-room and pressed her nose against the windowpane. She watched John Ellis reverse his vehicle and park it neatly on the spare ground in front of Marigold Cottage. She let out a gasp of relief as he walked purposely towards Mrs Cameron's cottage.

'What's wrong, Jenny?' Elisabeth asked, intent on her charcoal sketch of a bowl of daffodils.

'Nothing,' Jenny mumbled.

'A few more minutes and then it will be your bedtime.'

Pretending not to hear, Jenny moved her nose and watched the mist on the glass disperse. She wished Mr Ellis would get the flu because she didn't like seeing him in Mellstone. Joe Barden, too. Mrs Pengold could make things happen so why didn't she do a simple thing like that and make Joe die?

Jenny shuddered and then pressed her nose against the window again. She thought, suddenly, of the primroses she had picked at Nether End and seeing her mother and Mr Ellis walking up the track towards her. She had been jumping into the dead leaves before that to try to forget something disturbing, the way Mr Ellis looked at her mother that was the same way Mr Moore looked at Miss Bryer when he came in to school. But she couldn't forget.

'I don't want us to go away from here to live, ever,' she said.

Elisabeth replaced her charcoal in the box

207

and smiled. 'You can't stay on the window seat for ever. Come on, Jenny. It's time you were in bed. School tomorrow. What have you been staring at out there?'

'Nothing. I'm just looking.'

Elisabeth got up and felt Jenny's antagonism as she put her hand on her shoulder. Until now she hadn't noticed John's Land Rover out there this evening and had no wish to stand looking out at it now.

'Come,' she said gently. 'I'll help you get ready for bed. I haven't time to look out of windows.'

'We won't go away, will we?' Jenny said again when she was in bed. 'Promise?'

Elisabeth bent to kiss her and then smoothed the red hair on the pillow. 'You remember what we said when we decided to come to Mellstone, Jenny? Nothing's changed. Marigold Cottage is our home, for both of us. We'll both decide together if we ever want to move somewhere else.'

Jenny smiled and her eyelids drooped.

Elisabeth looked down at her for a few more moments. Then she rubbed her hand across her own forehead to check that it wasn't extra warm. She couldn't risk becoming ill now.

Downstairs the living-room was in a mess. She flung open the window and began to tidy up. It would take an hour or two to get everything ready to make an early start tomorrow. Tired as she was, there was pleasure in the prospect of the alarm clock going off at six o'clock and two hours solid work up in the studio before she called Jenny. Then back up there at nine. And peace.

*   *   *

Busy as she was during the next few days Elisabeth was only faintly aware of how others in Mellstone were coping with the flu bug that swept through the village. Backed up by John she had made Mrs Cameron promise to keep away from Marigold Cottage which she had done reluctantly. Several mornings Elisabeth had found packets of sweets on the doorstep and knew who had put them there. Cathy came, of course, on the Saturday and told her that other children as well as Jenny were off school with flu. She sat with Jenny for the time it took Elisabeth to make a quick visit to the shop and then do a couple of hours work in the studio . . . Jean Varley came with offers of help and went off with a shopping list for some of the more bulkier requirements.

Once or twice Elisabeth caught sight of the bustling figure of Alice Pengold vanishing up the lane. She gazed after her wistfully, wishing she had to time to take her sketching things up Hodman's Hollow to catch the inspiration of the moment, shadows across a chalky path perhaps or a lone kestrel hanging in the sky above Mellstone Hill.

It was now a period of strict routine. How John would approve, she thought, as she stood back to study the effect of light on dark in the foreground of a painting of sheep huddled by a greening hedgerow. Ruthless and single-minded, he had said she should be if she wanted to do well. Well, she could be both in spite of occasional set-backs. The canvasses were piling up, slowly it was true but given time she would produce the required number. Hard work, that's all it took. She had planned most of her subjects, the ideas coming thick and fast.

Now all she had to do was to carry them out.

*　　　*　　　*

'Please Miss, what must I do next?' Joe Barden asked. The expression on his sullen face was dogged and he looked anywhere but at Elisabeth.

How on earth had she allowed herself to be talked into being here in school when she should have been catching up with her own work? Next time Jean Varley came knocking on her door at eight thirty in the morning she would have more sense than to answer it.

'They need you at school,' Jean had said as if there wasn't the slightest doubt Elisabeth would drop everything. 'Cathy Mellor is at home with flu and Miss Bryer has to be at the hospital. Her mother's been taken ill. A stroke and serious, I understand.'

'I'm sorry,' Elisabeth said, taken aback. 'But I don't see . . .'

'There are no supply teachers available because of the flu so we thought of you. Just for today. A lot of children are away ill.'

'But I'm not on the official list.'

'No matter. Robert said it would be all right. The school bus will be arriving soon. We need someone qualified to be there. Will you do it?'

Reluctantly, Elisabeth agreed.

The morning was taken up with arithmetic for the Junior children with tables practice and silent reading afterwards while in one corner the five little ones who were all that were left of Cathy's class rolled out long worms of plasticine. Before that they had drawn pictures in their writing books and then copied the words she had written for them underneath.

This afternoon, ignoring the timetable, she decided they would all have painting.

To her surprise Joe Barden offered to help get things ready. He held his thick hands steady while he emptied powder paint into jam jars. Then, with his tongue protruding, he added water and pounded away with the mixing spoon with decided vigour. When he looked up at her there was a strange light in his eyes that she found disconcerting. Then it was gone and he gazed past her as if she didn't exist.

Later she wandered round the room and

211

paused by Joe's desk. His painting of the downs was startling. In the foreground the vivid reds and purples of the nearest ones stood out against the subdued background.

'You like painting?' she asked him.

He looked at her with scorn as he jammed his paint brush in his water jar. 'I got more important things to do than paint.'

His sense of colour was amazing. If the school closed what would happen to a young tough like Joe in a larger community? His mother feared this, of course. No wonder she tried to take her venom out on herself who was the cause, as she saw it, of their troubles.

Elisabeth sighed as she returned to the teachers' desk. She was aware of the knowing looks from Joe who no doubt despised her for a fool for not guessing who threw the stones at her studio.

She found a piece of plain paper and picked up a pencil, unable to resist making a lightning sketch of Joe's absorbed expression as he bent over his painting.

*   *   *

'Ah, Miss Turner, I've caught you before you go.' Robert came into the classroom and closed the door behind him. He brought with him an aura of concern that was comforting. His white collar stood out sharply against the black of his suit.

He smiled at her. 'Indeed, you look tired. How good of you to help out like this when you are so busy.'

In her exhaustion it was an effort to smile back. She longed for the peace of her sitting room and a cup of tea but knew she would get neither until she had done some work in her studio.

She caught a look of interest in his eyes before he glanced at the rows of paintings put to dry on the spare desks at the side of the room.

'Ah, I see you've been using your talents in a different way from usual,' he said in approval as he moved across to examine them. 'They're good, especially this one in bright colours.'

He picked it up to examine more closely.

Elisabeth moved to his side and stood looking down on it. 'That's Joe Barden's. I find it interesting.'

'Incredible,' Robert murmured. 'He's a strange boy. I hope he's been behaving himself?' He looked at her intently as he replaced the painting. 'I'm more grateful than I can say for your taking over at such short notice. Someone will be here to take over tomorrow and Miss Mellor will be back soon. Go home and rest now and get young Jenny to look after you. How is she now?'

'Back at school and not too pleased that I'm here too. But how is Miss Bryer's mother?'

'I've just been notified that she died this

213

morning.'

'Oh, I'm sorry.'

Robert moved away from the paintings. 'Indeed I'm on my way to see her daughter now.'

Afterwards Elisabeth wondered that she could feel so little sympathy. To her shame she was conscious only of a deep weariness and the need to return at once to her studio.

CHAPTER THIRTEEN

At Haymesgarth Karen walked from room to room. She should have been at home more, she thought, talked to Mother more. Now she couldn't bear the emptiness of the house, the silence. She stood hunched at the kitchen window and stared out at the cedar tree on the back lawn. Mother had often sat there when the shadows were deep on the summer grass. Today there were no shadows and a chilly breeze stirred the withered daffodil leaves in the neglected flower beds.

She moved back to the sitting room. The maidenhair fern in the shiny black pot on the bookshelf looked dusty and forlorn. She picked it up and hugged it to her and then put it down with a clatter as the front doorbell rang. She stood without moving for a moment and wondered who this could be.

She opened the door and saw, with a tremor of her heart, that Robert was outside.

We should have had more visitors, she thought, *friends dropping in.* But her mother didn't like casual callers and Haymesgarth was isolated.

She stared at him as if she didn't know who he was.

He smiled slightly and gazed at her beneath his bushy brows. 'I came as soon as I could, Karen.'

The sympathy in his eyes was hard to bear when she knew she didn't deserve it. 'Yes, well, come in,' she said.

The room was cold. She switched on the gas fire and applied a match. She knelt on the hearthrug far longer than was necessary, listening to the plop and then the roar as the flames took hold. When she got up he was standing by the door, looking like an explorer in a foreign land.

She waved her hand at the sofa. 'Please . . . sit down.'

He lowered himself gingerly and then cleared his throat. 'I'm so very sorry, Karen. If there's anything you would like me to do . . .'

He says this to everyone, she thought. *It's not me he's come to see, it's only me in my capacity as headmistress of the village school.*

'Thank you,' she said, her voice faint. 'Really, there's nothing. Our own vicar, Mr Lacey, I mean, has already been to see me.'

She sank down in the armchair opposite Robert, unable to look at him for the surge of tears in her throat.

He leaned forward and she could feel his concern. She really couldn't bear it. She needed to be strong, to be in control of the situation but now her hands trembled and she didn't know what to say.

He began to talk of death in a general way and then about her mother. How he could know so much about her when they had hardly met Karen couldn't understand. She dared a look at him and saw that the moisture near his hair line had dampened the dark wavy strands.

'The funeral will be at Hope Magna,' she said. 'Mother and Father were married there. And I was christened and confirmed there too.'

He nodded. 'I think many of your Mellstone friends will wish to be present.'

She wasn't too sure about that but let it go. 'I'm all right now,' she said. 'I'll be back at school tomorrow.'

For a moment he looked at her without speaking. His concern was like a soft blanket in which she longed to submerge herself, to cling to him for the solace she craved.

'My dear,' he said at last. 'Is returning so soon quite wise?'

She squeezed her hands together. 'Of course it is,' she said, her voice sharp. 'Why should you doubt it?'

'Please think seriously about this for your own sake, Karen. There are no problems at school. Indeed everything's functioning well. Someone is coming to take over tomorrow and Miss Mellor will be back . . .'

'Cathy wasn't there today? Then who . . ?'

'Elisabeth Turner very kindly stepped in.'

'*Elisabeth Turner?*'

'She's qualified to do so and there were no other teachers available. Please don't look like that. I assure you that everything went well. I've just been in to see her.'

Before he came to see me, she thought. She sank back against the cushions. Pain ran through her in icy streams and for a moment she couldn't speak.

'Miss Turner appeared to have everything under control. In fact she did rather well. I saw the paintings the children had been doing. Some of them were really good but indeed with her talent one would expect that.'

Karen clutched the arms of her chair and took a deep breath.

Robert smiled. 'The children seemed to have enjoyed themselves. Even the Barden boy was well-behaved.'

Well, yes, he would be, it seemed, with Elisabeth Turner in charge. Silently Karen willed Robert to go. He was a fool. Did he really think she would let anyone interfere in her school until it was forced on her? She would be back there tomorrow if it were the

217

last thing she did.

Unbidden came the memory of her young life here at Haymesgarth and she saw herself. Slim, rosy-cheeked and dark-haired astride John's pony, eager to show off her paces to her parents. Then, a fall, the pony on one side of the fence and she on the other. No more riding. No bicycle either and forbidden her dearest wish, the promise of a pony for Christmas.

She had been expected to get her first teaching post near home because Mother needed her. 'You should be grateful, Karen,' her father said at these times. For what? He had never specified. Now, all the money and this large house would be hers and she could do as she liked.

And all she wanted now was something no money could buy.

'Don't be too hard on yourself, Karen. Let others take over for a day or two.' Robert's brown eyes were pools of kindness and his voice gentle.

He was kind to everyone, she thought. He had plenty of practice but she no longer wanted him here in her room. She remained silent until at last she had the satisfaction of knowing that he could bear no more.

She closed the door behind him and then stared at it blankly. Programmed to believe that anything she wanted could never be hers she didn't know how to accept that it could ever be. She didn't know, either, how to curb her tongue from ruining everything before it had a chance to come to fruition.

She went into the garden and walked past the cedar tree and didn't pause until she got to the shrubbery. How often she had played here with John as a child. And now here they were practically middle-aged, John with a broken marriage behind him and she trapped in self-loathing.

*   *   *

Elisabeth settled herself in the churchyard, moving her easel a little so that the legs stood on firmer ground. She had brought her painting gear with her, intending to make the most of the early April warmth this afternoon. Her mind whirled with ideas that needed immediate action.

The handwriting on the envelope that had arrived in the post this morning had given her a strange feeling she couldn't quite account for at first. Mrs Wentworth's gratitude for the portrait of Pixie had warmed her because she liked the personal knowledge that her work had found a good home. But she had also been asked as a favour to paint two young kittens, playful and charming, who lived near Penzance with an old friend of Mrs Wentworth. A photograph would be forthcoming as soon as the subjects remained still enough to get a good likeness.

Elisabeth craved the personal feedback of knowing that what she had given out of herself was recognised and appreciated. By exhibiting and selling from exhibitions she didn't get this, of course, but it had to be done because of her financial situation. She hadn't realised until now how much the personal approach meant to her. It was a loss she was finding increasingly difficult to deal with and so refusing Mrs Wentworth's latest request was going to be difficult. But it had to be done and the sooner the better.

Meanwhile she must put it to the back of her mind and concentrate on the matter in hand.

The angle of the ancient tombstones was pleasing. Masses of mauve violets bloomed in the straggly grass at their feet. Beyond them the church tower was strong against the sky. Rooks cawed, incessantly whirling above their colony of nests high in the elm trees. There was more than enough here to keep her occupied for hours. She would come again another day to paint the church from a different angle and perhaps the lych gate with the downs in the background. She wished she could capture the delicious smell of growing things and the birdsong.

She began to mix some colours to create the subtle tones she wanted. A robin came to perch nearby, annoyed at the violation of its territory. Time had no meaning when she was working. She wasn't aware at first of Alice Pengold stumping round to her side of the church even though the noise on the gravel path had the robin fleeing for safety to the churchyard wall.

With a disproving sniff Alice obviously saw her but, thankfully, didn't stop to talk but emptied her bucket on a grave near the path and retreated. The next time she carried a dustpan to empty in the bin behind one of the buttresses.

Elisabeth, glancing at the church clock, heard the sound of voices that hadn't been there before. Although she felt happy and relaxed she couldn't welcome interruptions if she wanted to be finished in tine to get home in time for Jenny.

She dipped her brush in the paint and held it poised, hearing the vicar's vibrant voice as he spoke to Mrs Pengold. He saw Elisabeth and came across.

'A warm afternoon,' he greeted her.

She smiled and blinked.

'I'm sorry. I'm interrupting you.'

She painted a few last strokes. 'I think I've got it now. I have to go home for Jenny soon, I'm afraid.'

'Then I mustn't detain you.'

She hated to cut him short but time was pressing. It was already later than she had thought. She began to pack her things away with speed.

'Indeed, you might just like to know that I received an important communication this morning,' he said. 'It's likely that second thoughts have prevailed and the school may stay open for another year.'

Elisabeth was delighted. 'That's wonderful news.' She replaced the top on a tube of paint. 'Thank you for telling me.' Maybe now Jenny's suspected part in all this would be forgotten. She thought of Cathy and the worries she had confided in her. Such a kind girl who obviously had settled down in Mellstone and didn't want to leave. The young chap, Arnold Bronson, would have had a lot to do with that, of course.

'Yes, indeed,' said Robert. 'We can't do without our school. I hope they have the sense to drop the matter for good.'

He leaned forward to examine the painting Elisabeth had been working on. 'Such talent,' he said in admiration. 'If all your work is as good as this you should do well.'

She smiled, pleased at his appreciation.

*   *   *

The warmth in the sun surprised Karen as she crossed the school playground after school. The rooks were busy in the topmost branches with their usual racket. Soon the trees would all be in leaf. She closed her eyes for a moment, wishing she were miles away luxuriating on a palm-fringed exotic island.

But even if she had the chance of doing that she wouldn't willingly leave Mellstone while Robert was here.

She thought of the letter that had arrived from County Hall this morning, carried gingerly in by Alice Pengold who had met the postman at the gate. The proposed school closure was postponed. She felt warmth flood through her in her relief. However she didn't regret all the fuss and emotion because she had come to know Robert better because of it and now she would continue to see him every week and perhaps more.

Outside the gate a child lingered, the sunlight turning her red hair to fire.

Karen glanced to left and right along the empty lane. 'What are you doing here, Jenny? Everyone else has gone.'

'Nothing, Miss.'

'Is no one at home? Where's your mother?'

Jenny fidgeted one sandalled foot in the dust and gazed at her. 'She's in the churchyard, painting.'

Karen smiled. 'So why not go there too?'

'Yes, Miss.'

But of course that was where the child had been just before the branch fell off the Tidings Tree, Karen thought. No doubt she was frightened of going back there. 'I'm going down to the shop,' she said. 'You can walk down with me to find her.'

Jenny stared at her, round-eyed.

Karen opened her car door to reach inside for her shopping basket. 'Come on, then. What are you waiting for?'

Reluctantly, Jenny came. 'She's not late every day,' she muttered.

'I expect she forgot the time if she's painting.'

Jenny nodded. 'Yes, Miss.'

'It's such a beautiful day.'

They reached the church gate. Karen opened it and then stopped. 'There she is, talking to the vicar,' she said, her voice flat.

She wished she hadn't seen Robert bending over Elisabeth Turner and gazing at the painting on the easel. The way he stood sent a shaft of pain through her like a jet of cold water. Robert straightened as he noticed the two of them and a smile obviously meant for Elisabeth lingered on his lips. It was all Karen could do to acknowledge him with a swift nod and a grimace of a smile. It was surely enough that John was in Elisabeth Turners' thrall without Robert as well?

She turned away, sick at heart. Leaving the village might well be the best thing she could do after all. As soon as she got home she would examine the advertisements in *Teacher's World* for a suitable headship as far away as possible. There was still time to get her notice in to take effect from September.

* * *

'You must have been let out of school early today, Jenny,' Elisabeth said as she packed up her remaining things.

Jenny smiled. The churchyard felt safe now with Mr Moore here, a warm, sunny place. She took a deep breath of bruised grass scent and wondered what it would be like in Brooklands today down by the wooden bridge over the brook.

Robert looked at his watch in concern. 'Indeed the church clock is slow.'

'But Jenny knew where I was,' Elisabeth said.

'And Jenny's a sensible girl.' Robert gave her a warm smile as they walked together to the gate. He left them as they reached the stump of the Tidings Tree.

Jenny watched him go and then caught hold of Elisabeth's hand. 'What's that?' she said in alarm.

'What's what, Jenny? I can't see anything.'

'There's something . . . someone coming out of our place.'

'But there's no one there.'

And of course there wasn't but Jenny wasn't convinced. She hung back a little as Elisabeth flicked the gate open.

'I'll have to get all this painting stuff up to the studio,' Elisabeth said as she unlocked the front door.

Jenny followed her through the kitchen

225

and up the steps to the back lawn. The studio looked peaceful in the afternoon sun. Inside, Jenny looked in suspicion at the canvasses stacked against the wall.

'What's the matter, Jenny?' Elisabeth said as she put down her bag of equipment and prepared to leave.

Jenny bit her lip. 'Nothing,' she said but she was glad to be leaving the studio behind her. Inside the cottage was the security of tea and Children's Hour on the wireless. Afterwards she'd probably get out her new packet of plasticine and make some more flower pots to decorate her bedroom window sill.

Elisabeth lingered for a moment to glance at her unfinished painting of Joe Barden on her easel. She had made him deliberately unrecognisable and had let the idea simmer in her mind for several days before starting work on it. She wanted to capture the expression of deep concentration that gave a hint of a normal daily life that might well be transformed through his obvious love of art. Given a miracle in Joe's case, she thought, but how likely was that? She had recognised her own golden moment but she had known what she wanted and been given the opportunity to fulfil it. His watercolour painting of the downs in glorious Technicolor could be plainly seen in the background and so would fit the theme of the exhibition.

As she locked the studio door behind her

the doorbell rang on the extension. It rang again before she reached the back door of the cottage. Someone in a hurry. She moved swiftly to the front door and threw it open.

John's face was flushed and the lines deep on his forehead. 'My car tyres have been tampered with,' he said.

This was so unexpected that Elisabeth laughed. 'I'm sorry,' she gasped. 'I know it's not funny.'

'I wondered if you'd seen anything?'

'I've been in the studio since I got back from the churchyard.'

'And Jenny?'

'You're not suggesting . . .'

'Someone's let the tyres down while I've been at Aunt Ruth's.'

His eyes had a coldness in them but she couldn't help another bubble of amusement welling up in her. 'Take no notice of me, John. I've been working too hard. It's left me a bit weak-headed.'

He looked at her quizzically. 'I hear you've been teaching in the school?'

'Just for a day. I'm back to my real work now.'

'You're pushing yourself too hard, Elisabeth.'

'I think that's my business.'

He said nothing and she looked at his tense face in concern. Something had set this off surely but she couldn't imagine what it could be.

'Your tyres,' she said at last. 'What are you going to do?'

For a moment he looked as if he didn't know what she was talking about. Then the gentleness of his smile made her hesitate and feel awkward.

'This is no place for what I want to say, Elisabeth. In fact it's a damn silly place. But I think you know what it is. When you have finished working for this exhibition I'll . . . Please, Elisabeth, don't work too hard. Don't overdo it. I can't bear to see you like this with those dark shadows beneath your eyes. Is it all worth it?'

She knew her eyes flashed. 'I wouldn't be living like this if it wasn't important to me. I know you can't understand that, John, but it's true.'

Jenny came to the door and stared at him, round-eyed.

'Did you see anyone tampering with my car, Jenny?' he asked.

She flushed and rubbed her sandal along the floor.

'Well, Jenny, what d'you know about it?'

'I'm going to play with Judith Wintle,' she mumbled.

'Jenny?'

'Nothing. I never saw your car.'

'I'm not so sure it's nothing.

'For goodness sake,' Elisabeth cried. 'She

doesn't know anything about it. Of course she didn't do it. How can you think such a thing? Off you go then, Jenny, and don't be late back.'

John straightened and watched Jenny run off down the lane. 'You spoil that child,' he said.

Elisabeth gasped. How dare he assume he had the right to interfere!

'She could hardly look more guilty,' he pointed out. 'Be reasonable, Elisabeth. Why didn't you let her finish answering for herself?'

'Reasonable! She's no more capable of tampering with your car than I am.' She turned away and took a deep breath. Along the lane she saw the vicar standing near what was left of the tree, his dark hair bent as he spoke to someone. Robert understood her necessity for grinding hard work even if John couldn't. In any case she felt too weary to stay out here. She was sick with fatigue and there was an evening of work ahead of her.

She crashed shut the door behind her. It was clear she could expect no sympathy from John and what was any relationship worth without understanding and sympathy? And trust. She had been on the point of telling him about the stones thrown on her studio roof but was glad now that she had kept that to herself. Either he would have accused her of fantasising or another lecture would have been forthcoming.

Why should John think Jenny responsible

for letting down his tyres? It was true she had blushed a fiery red but so would anyone accused in that arrogant way. She would herself, she thought. Then a vision of herself crawling about beneath his vehicle shook her with its absurdity. She laughed and found it hard to stop.

At last she wiped the tears from her eyes. This was a waste of precious time.

*　　　*　　　*

'I've got no time for meetings,' Alice Pengold muttered as Robert approached the Tidings Tree where she had been stopped by the two ladies from Lynch Cottage.

'Just to put everyone in the picture,' he heard Miss King plead.

Alice moved her shopping bag from one hand to the other. 'I don't need to see no picture. I've got work to do.' She tried to move off but the Jack Russell, Benjy, was sniffing round her feet and somehow caught his lead round her legs. 'Dratted dog!'

There was so much commotion as Miss Buckley dived to extricate him that Robert tried to slip past unnoticed.

'I expect you're busy too, Vicar.' Miss King trilled after him in her high-pitched voice.

'Going into school again, more like,' Alice muttered.

He had some sick visiting to do in one of the

council houses past the school and intended to call in and see Karen for a few minutes. Ostensibly this was to check the dates of the start of the summer term and it provided an excellent excuse for satisfying himself that she wasn't overdoing things.

He smiled ruefully to himself as he turned in at the school gate. No doubt he would be greeted in the same brusque way as usual. All the same he needed to know how she was at this difficult time for her. That she seemed not to appreciate his concern was a matter for him to deal with in his own way.

* * *

Karen was at the open door in the partition talking to Cathy while the little ones got into their coats and stood waiting by the door. Her own class, silently reading, had ten more minutes before it was time for them to pack up and go.

She looked round in surprise as Robert came into her classroom. No head looked up but she was aware she was being watched surreptitiously by one and all.

He cleared his throat. 'I'm on my way to see Mrs Hill,' he said, as if that explained everything.

Cathy was busy ushering her own children outside and Karen closed the door between the classrooms.

A smile touched Robert's lips as he looked at the pictures on the wall painted by her class while she was away and which she had no excuse not to display. Was he remembering who had inspired such excellent work?

'I have an after-school meeting in Hilbury I must attend,' she said rather crisply. 'Miss Mellor is seeing the bus children away today and everyone off the premises. Would you like to lead our closing prayer for us, Mr Moore?'

He inclined his head. 'Indeed.'

'Books away, everyone.'

The clearing up took far longer than he had imagined. Once the prayer was said and the children gone off Karen locked her desk. The click of her key sounded final in the quiet room.

Then she removed her coat from the hook on the door, gave him a nod and was gone. Only then did he realise that he had asked her nothing about herself and was no wiser about how she was coping.

CHAPTER FOURTEEN

'So where are your primroses, Jenny?' Elisabeth asked.

Jenny scuffed her sandal against the pew in front. 'Nowhere,' she whispered.

'Nowhere? But you picked a large bunch

232

down the lane specially. Didn't you bring them into church?'

'They didn't want them.'

'What d'you mean?'

'They had too many already.'

Elisabeth glanced at the window sills where paste pots full of primroses stood among green foliage. Plenty of room for more she would have thought. 'But who told you that?'

'Rosie Wintle. She said her Mum said they had enough and to take them away.'

'Did anyone else hear her?'

Jenny shook her head and mumbled something Elisabeth couldn't hear, her words drowned by the organ's superb sound as the music rose to a crescendo.

The service was beginning now so there was no time for more but instead of concentrating Elisabeth dwelt on what Jenny had told her to such an extent that she heard little of it. She rose with the rest of the congregation for the hymns without being aware of the words she sang and then sat down again and stared straight in front of her. Jenny had been so pleased with the bunch she had picked. She had tied them with a piece of red wool and gone skipping off down the lane to the church to give her offering to the flower ladies to decorate the building because it was Easter. Knowing what had happened to them now gave Elisabeth a numbing little pain.

Suffer little children to come unto me, she

thought. Well hardly, in this case. And for supposedly the most important day in the church's calendar, too. What sort of message was that giving out? Jenny hadn't breathed a word about it to her so the rejection had obviously cut deeply. She wouldn't know about it now if she hadn't come to church and found out for herself.

The building, of course, was full. The Varley family sat in the front row with their son, Ralph, who was looking handsome with his mop of fair hair highlighted by the electric light. She couldn't see Mrs Pengold but Mrs Cameron was there, of course, seated next to her nephew and Karen Bryer too whom she hadn't seen here before. Others she didn't know because she didn't have time to join things and socialise.

'So what did you do with your primroses, Jenny?' she whispered as the service came to an end and Robert came down the aisle to stand by the door to greet his flock as they emerged into the spring sunshine.

'Nothing. I threw them in the ditch,' Jenny muttered.

This was too bad. Elisabeth held back behind the rest of the congregation and wondered if she should mention this to Robert even though it seemed like telling tales out of school. But Jenny had been hurt and Jenny mattered to her.

She caught hold of Elisabeth's hand. 'Don't

tell anyone,' she said urgently. 'Promise. Rosie will get at me. I know she will.'

'But Jenny . . .'

They had reached the door now. One or two groups were forming outside, obviously wishing to continue conversations begun earlier.

'Happy Easter to you both,' Robert said.

They shook hands and he looked at her in concern as if he realised that she had just discovered something that troubled her. 'I trust all is well with you?'

Elisabeth hesitated but Jenny was clutching her hand tightly and she knew what that meant. 'I . . . I. Well, yes, thank you,' she said.

She could see he didn't believe her because he was still looking at her intently. He cleared his throat.

'We're going for a walk this afternoon,' said Jenny.

He smiled. 'Indeed that's a good thing to do, my dear. I hope you enjoy it.'

Making an effort Elisabeth smiled too. One thing was certain. Robert would have had nothing to do with those unkind words and would be horrified if he knew about them. Jenny obviously realised this too and was anxious to leave things as they were.

*   *   *

Karen walked to the church door with John

and they stood outside to wait until Mrs Cameron had finished her chat and was ready to leave.

'How are you now, Karen?' he asked, his voice full of sympathy she badly needed at the moment.

'I'm coping. Just.' She turned to look at him and saw that he was gazing at Elisabeth as she talked with Robert at the church door. It was hard to take her eyes from them. 'I think Robert is rather fond of Elisabeth, don't you?' she said with a calmness she didn't feel. 'And she of him, of course. He's an attractive man. And so understanding. I know she appreciates his interest and support.'

John became still and she was pleased. But not by a flicker would she let him see her reaction.

'He's arranging to go to Marigold Cottage this afternoon for a private show of her paintings, most likely,' she said. 'Such as they are, of course. They make a lovely couple, don't you think?'

Karen smiled brilliantly as he turned away from her but her heart was sore. As she drove alone to Haymesgarth a few minutes later she despised herself for succumbing to the temptation to utter those stupid words with the intention of hurting him. She had succeeded in planting doubt in his mind but she could feel only despair.

Her manipulative words couldn't be taken

236

back now. It was too late.

*   *   *

Cathy knelt on her bedroom floor with her largest suitcase open before her. Soon she would be back in Mellstone again and seeing Arnold. Her heart quickened. Usually packing was a chore but today every garment she placed carefully into position seemed to sing with expectation.

He had told her he would be back too late to think of meeting her from the bus but that didn't matter. She knew he had spent the previous night in London on the way back to meet a school friend. Arnold didn't go home to Norfolk often and this was a good opportunity.

One day she would invite Arnold to come back with her for the weekend so he could meet her family. She had talked about him, of course, and they'd all seen the photo taken at his college reunion she kept on her bedside table when she was home. He looked so handsome, standing apart from his friends and not looking straight at the camera. A smile curved his lips and she could see by the line of his body that what he was looking at was far more interesting than the photographer.

She smiled. Yes, she would invite Arnold to Gloucester soon. One day. What would he think of them all? Both her sisters were pretty. Noreen would look at him in silence for a

237

moment and then smile in that devastating way of hers that everyone found so attractive. With luck she wouldn't be between boyfriends though or that wouldn't be good. Sonia would giggle a lot and marvel that Cathy had found someone so wonderful at last. She might even be a little jealous.

Feeling superior to them both was a new experience for Cathy and she liked it. For the first time since they had grown up she didn't mind being the tallest of the three because Arnold liked her.

She smiled as she placed her best dress on top of the rest and then shut the lid of the trunk and locked it. There, that was done. One more job finished and now she felt free to think of Arnold and remember with a surge of joy that he had promised to take her to Sandbanks for the day as soon as his uncle could let him have the car. Arnold worked so hard for Mr Wintle, often out all hours night after night on some business or other so he felt that he deserved it.

The summer term, a lovely thought . . . nature walks, lessons out of doors, long warm evenings . . .

She got up and went to the window and leaned out. A landmark from miles around, May Hill, in the distance looked slightly hazy, a good sign. With its group of trees on the top it was like a larger version of Mellstone Down. Soon she would be seeing that for herself and an hour or two later Arnold would be back in Mellstone too. The thought was like a golden beacon.

*   *   *

'A letter for you, dear,' said Miss King next morning. Her smile was bright as she held it out to Cathy, 'I found it on the doormat and have brought it up to you at once. So lucky Benjy didn't find it first.'

The unstamped envelope with her name on it in large flowing handwriting looked intriguing. Cathy took it from her, surprised to see that this morning Miss King was up and dressed in her old clothes as if she was going to burst out into the garden immediately and set to work. Usually there was no sound from either of the ladies when it was time to leave for school.

'So much to do at this time of year,' Miss King confided. 'Did you know that the onion is related to the lily of the valley?'

Cathy admitted that she didn't.'

Nothing daunted, Miss King seemed about to offer more horticultural gems but instead gave a startled gasp as Benjy streaked between her ankles. She rushed downstairs after him so quickly Cathy wondered that she didn't fall in a heap at the bottom.

Smiling, Cathy took her letter inside her room to read. She could see now that it was

239

from Arnold but had to look at the envelope closely to be quite sure. His writing seemed to have changed. Where before it had been neat and sloping now it was flamboyant and spread across the envelope. But still his, she was sure.

The flap wasn't quite stuck down and it opened easily. She spread out the sheet of paper inside and began to read. But the words made no sense! She stared at them and then read them again, willing them to keep still.

A slow feeling of dreadful disbelief crept over her.

'My dear Cathy,
As you know I've felt for some weeks that I've been wasting my time here in Mellstone workwise. Now I think it's time to get out. And of course, there's us. I expect it's clear to you as well as me that it couldn't last much longer. I'm putting it baldly, but do try to understand. There's no time to see you as I'm off tonight. Someone I know thinks he can land me a job on the Halland Forest Estate if I get up there right away, so keep your fingers crossed. I'll be in touch as soon as it's fixed.
   Yours ever
   Arnold.'

Her body was like stone, her mind too. She forced herself to read it again until the words sank in. He couldn't do it, not in this indifferent way as if his leaving Mellstone for good didn't matter one way or the other. And it didn't . . . to him. That was startlingly clear. He had written this last night and had come to Lynch Cottage to push it through the letter box so he didn't have to see her.

The clock downstairs struck half past eight.

Maisie, the girl who had joined the ringing band? Cathy's blood surged through her veins red hot. The thought of them together was too painful to contemplate and she put out a hand on the back of the sofa to steady herself. She mustn't think. She must hide Arnold's decision for a while at least and most certainly from the ladies downstairs until she got a grip on herself. It was time for school. She must go. She would think about it later.

She folded the letter and put it in her pocket. Then picking up her coat and bag she went downstairs. Even Benjy was silent as she let herself out of the front door and closed it softly behind her. She unlatched the front gate and saw that some of the early clematis flowers along the front fence had little tips of brown on their pink petals. Miss King would soon deal with them.

Outside the school Cathy met the vicar, there to take his weekly service. She braced herself as if the shattering news was written all over her face for him and everyone else to see.

He smiled and wished her good morning. His voice boomed out at her as if she were deaf. He seemed about to sprint across the playground but held himself back out of politeness.

She managed a tremulous smile that seemed to pull him up short. He looked at her closely. 'Is there something wrong, Miss Mellor?' he asked.

'No really, I . . .' she began but couldn't go on. She fought desperately to keep the tears back.

'It's your forestry student friend, isn't it?'

She nodded.

'He was saying something to Tom Barnet about leaving. Is it more than that, Cathy? Is he leaving you too?'

She nodded again, unable to speak.

'I won't sympathise,' he said, a firmness in his voice she found comforting. 'It won't help at the moment. You know where to come if you want to talk about it. We're all behind you, my dear. Remember that. And we are never alone.'

'You're kind . . .'

'Would you like me to mention this to Miss Bryer?'

'No,' she said, her voice desperate. 'No, not that. Please, I don't want people to know, especially . . . No, please not.'

'I see.' He paused for a moment, a frown creasing his forehead. 'Then of course I won't say anything more. But do keep busy, Cathy my dear. What have you planned for your little

242

ones today?'

She made a great effort to thrust aside the fog that clogged her mind. 'The usual things. Reading and writing. Some number work and then free activity. I've got a new story to read this afternoon about castles. And we might do something with the clay that came yesterday.'

He patted her on the arm. 'Good girl. Keep them at it. And yourself too. You'll get through this, my dear. You're not alone.'

With that he left her to go into the Junior Room through the main entrance. She waited a little while and then went in to her classroom by the other door. Some of her little ones followed her in and she let them stay. Nothing felt quite real and she wondered if it ever would again. She breathed deeply, willing herself to smile at their prattling and to pretend that today was just like any other.

*   *   *

Later, after tea, Jenny crept up the path that led to the top of Hodman's Hollow. The challenge she had set herself to follow Mrs Pengold to see where she went led her on. In spite of her thumping heart. A long way ahead of her the dark figure of the old lady plodded upwards as if she knew exactly where she was going and why. She was carrying a black shopping bag that jerked against her side with each step she took and she looked down as she walked.

Jenny looked down too but she could see nothing apart from the occasional clump of bluebell leaves in the long grass. Not once did Mrs Pengold stop to pick anything but kept marching upwards until she disappeared over the brow of the hill.

Jenny felt safe now. She hurried and arrived at the top out of breath. Her horror at seeing the old lady close by picking the cream feathery head of cow parsley was so great she could only stand and stare.

Mrs Pengold turned and the lines deepened in her cheeks as she smiled. 'I won't hurt 'ee,' she said.

Jenny tried to speak but couldn't.

'You didn't ought to be up here on your own.' Alice Pengold stuffed more cow parsley in her bag and reached out to pick more. 'Get along home wi' you before anyone misses you. It don't do to wander on your own.'

She moved further along the hedge and then turned to come back again.

Suddenly Jenny came to life. With a gasp she ran back the way she had come, saw a small gap in the hedge and shot through it.

There, in front of her, lay a body face downwards on the ground.

Jenny tried to scream but no sound came. The person on the grass sat up and was at once so familiar that the blood seemed to gush back into Jenny's veins.

244

'Jenny!' she cried. 'What are you doing here?'

That she was lying down up here near the top of Hodman's Hollow seemed to Jenny so reasonable that she was ashamed of her sudden fright.

'I thought you were dead, Miss,' she said.

*   *   *

Elisabeth moved a pile of finished paintings from one side of the studio to the other. These were dry now and ready to be packed up in due course. For the last few days before Delivery Day her work would be in watercolours because it dried quickly.

The latest oil painting to be completed was her painting of the good-looking dark-haired boy absorbed in his own work and inspired by Joe Barden. Her favourites was still of the track at Nether End that John had seen the day she found out that her application to take part in the exhibition was successful. She didn't want to include this in the exhibition but knew she had no choice.

For a few precious moments she allowed herself the luxury of standing still and doing nothing. Her work was very nearly complete and she would then have only to wait, with what patience she could muster, to see what became of it. Dwelling on failure was unthinkable but sometimes she woke

245

in the early hours and had lain shivering in apprehension. Their whole future depended on the success of the exhibition.

But now, gazing at a half-finished painting on her work bench she felt a surge of optimism, strong in the knowledge that she had very nearly finished what she set out to do. Here it was, the proof to John and everyone else that she was doing more than merely playing at being an artist.

She glanced at the alarm clock on the shelf and saw that it was later than she thought. Where was Jenny? She should be home soon.

The clatter of stones on the studio roof made Elisabeth jump although she should be used to this sort of thing by now. She refused to react. Whoever it was would soon get tired of it.

She waited another five minutes to prove her point and then left, locking the door carefully behind her.

*　　　*　　　*

Cathy had seen the bridle way that led up from the village was little used these days. The hedges of hazel had grown tall and almost met overhead so that it was now a silent forgotten place. Or so it seemed to her.

She had not intended to come as far as this, only to get away to somewhere private to keep her grief to herself. Soon she would have to turn back and pretend that she didn't care tuppence that Arnold had gone away from Mellstone because he wasn't only disillusioned with Downend Farm but with herself as well. She knew that was the true reason because she had seen Miss Lewis' niece, Maisie, by the bus stop earlier. She had never thought of herself good enough for Arnold and now she was proved right. And not good enough for anyone else either most likely. She was only too aware of the publicity in which she lived in Mellstone. Everyone would know about it.

A blackbird flew low across the path in front of her, uttering staccato cries of alarm. She came to a narrow gap in the hedge and paused to look through it. She could see Larksbury Rings drowsing in the late sunshine, its deep ledges filled with shadow. They had never climbed it as Arnold had promised. They never would now.

Tears streamed down her face and she longed to lie down and cry her misery into the ground. She pushed through the gap. Below her the thatched cottages of Mellstone slept in the evening air dominated by the church tower.

She would still have to help ring the bells on practice night and on Sundays but Arnold wouldn't be there. She didn't even know where he was ...

How was it possible to go on day after day not knowing that, she thought. And knowing that Arnold had stopped loving her, had perhaps never loved her in the way she had loved him. How could she face the knowing glances, the derision because he had deserted her? And waiting, always waiting, for the letter he might write which she suspected would never come.

She threw herself down and buried her face in the soft sweet-smelling grass. At last she sat up and, startled, saw she wasn't alone.

Jenny shuffled her feet a little, hesitated and then sat down too. 'Why are you unhappy, Miss?'

Cathy didn't answer at once. She looked down at her damp handkerchief, spread it out and studied the flower pattern on it. 'The man who said he . . . the man who wanted to . . . he's gone away.'

'And you won't see him anymore?'

Cathy shook her head. She found a dry handkerchief in another pocket and attacked her face with it.

Jenny stared at her with wide-open blue eyes. 'All the time the wrong things happen,' she said. 'The wrong people get flu, the wrong people go away. It's not fair. He used to ring the bells, didn't he? And you rang them too. Is that why?'

'Partly, Cathy admitted.

'Will you stop ringing them now?'

'I can't. I'm part of the band, you see. I can't let them down.'

'But he did.'

Cathy looked down at the village below half-hidden in the trees. Only the church tower showed up really clearly. 'He had to go away.'

'There are bluebells growing by the path,' Jenny said. 'They'll soon be out in flower. It would be a good place for a nature walk.'

Cathy nodded. 'I think it would.'

'But it's not my best place in Mellstone.'

'So where is that?'

'Brooklands.'

'Brooklands?'

'You go past the school and it's through a gate on the right and down the field to the brook. There's a wooden bridge but you don't go over that. You go over the rough bit of field in the corner, all overgrown. Right at the edge all covered in brambles there's a secret path by the brook. Where's your best place, Miss?'

Cathy gazed over towards Larksbury Rings. 'I haven't been there yet but that's my special place. Larksbury Rings.'

'Larksbury Rings,' said Jenny rather wistfully. 'We haven't been there either. I wish we could.'

'It's a bit far for a nature walk.'

'We nearly got there once when we went for a walk.'

'Does your mother know where you are now?'

Jenny got up and brushed the grass from her skirt. 'She knows I go for walks. I'm not supposed to leave the village, though,' she added in a burst of confidence. 'She's doing a lot of painting for the exhibition.'

'Then for goodness sake . . .'

'I've got to be home by six.'

'It's nearly that now,' Cathy said in alarm, leaping up. She propelled Jenny towards the gap in the hedge. To her surprise Jenny caught hold of her hand and squeezed it. Cathy felt a lump in her throat and swallowed hard.

They hurried down the Hollow and were walking through the village before she realised that the homeward walk through Mellstone she had been dreading was almost over. She was concerned for Jenny and for Elisabeth worrying where she was. At the same time she felt a sort of peace engulfing her. However much she wished it she knew in her heart that she couldn't change Arnold's decision. It was made and done with. She had to learn to live with it.

At the gate in the white fence Jenny let go of Cathy's hand. 'I'm glad you were there, Miss,' she said.

Cathy was too. She smiled down at her, grateful for the friendship of someone who was beginning to mean a lot to her. Then she looked up and saw Elisabeth coming down the path the meet them.

She looked anxious. 'I was wondering where Jenny was,' she said.

'I got late and Miss Mellor helped me,' she

said simply.

A lump rose in Cathy's throat and she couldn't speak.

'You're not well, Cathy?' Elisabeth asked with sympathy. She opened the gate. 'Come in for a minute or two, why don't you?' she said,

Cathy shook her head. 'I . . .I must get back.'

Elisabeth didn't press it but she could see she was concerned. Pity would be her undoing, she thought in desperation. *I can't bear anyone to feel sorry for me.*

To her relief Elisabeth said no more and she was able to walk the rest of the way to Lynch Cottage without meeting anyone.

CHAPTER FIFTEEN

Cathy arrived at school next morning deliberately early, hoping to get through the playground before any children were there. They would soon come pouring in, she knew, extra noisy because of the rising wind.

She had started lifting the chairs down from the tables when Karen came in looking pale with dark smudges beneath her eyes.

Cathy cleared her throat. She wanted to ask her how she was and if she could do anything to help but didn't dare because of the forbidding expression on Miss Bryer's face. 'Good morning . . .' she began.

'You're here early today.'

'Well, yes . . .' Cathy broke off again as Jenny came into the room with a bunch of scented lilies of the valley in her hand. With the other she pushed her wind-blown hair out of her eyes.

What do *you* want, Jenny?' Karen asked. 'You've no business getting to school as early as this.'

'I've brought some flowers.'

'Well don't follow me about. Take them into our own room.'

Jenny looked at Cathy and held the bunch out to her. 'For you, Miss.'

Cathy smiled tremulously as she took them, very nearly overcome by the sympathy in Jenny's eyes

'Outside until the whistle blows,' Karen ordered.

Jenny gave her a startled look and fled.

'I'd like tosee some exercise books, if you don't mind,' Karen said when she had gone. 'A cross section, please. Mickey Barnes, Pat Horlock and Maureen Barden will do.'

'Yes, of course.'

Cathy went to the set of low drawers at one side of the room and found the desired books. Today she didn't care if the standard of work wasn't good enough. She bit her lips to stop them trembling.

Karen opened one exercise book after the other. The silence was oppressive.

Cathy moved her weight from one foot to the other. She looked at the sweetly-scented lilies of the valley she had placed on her desk. She would get them in water in a minute and place them where she could see them all day long.

Karen snapped the last book shut and put it with the others on the nearest table. She looked at Cathy without saying anything for a moment. 'You seem rather miserable today,' she said at last. 'Is anything the matter?'

Cathy shuddered. 'Nothing I can't cope with.'

'Then see to the nature table. It looks a mess.'

'Yes yes, I will. I hadn't noticed . . .'

'And I want another look at your scheme of work for the term. You've kept it up to date, I hope?'

Cathy immediately felt guilty for no reason. She had spent time over this and knew that it gave a good, rounded syllabus such as the college had insisted should always be done well.

They heard the outside door open. Robert came in bringing with him a breath of air that seemed to lighten the atmosphere and bring instant warmth. He smiled at Cathy and she smiled back because she was aware of his concern for her. She thought of what he had said, *you are not alone*. Comforting words that had seemed true when he said them yesterday.

She wished they seemed true again now.

* * *

To Karen his smile seemed to linger on Cathy far too long as if they had a secret understanding. Seeing it she felt such a sinking of the heart that she couldn't remain in the room a moment longer. She had looked forward to Robert's coming in to school as she always did but now she felt cheated, only too aware that in less than an hour he would be gone again.

She went quickly into her own classroom and stopped short on seeing Jenny. 'What are you doing here, Jenny? Didn't I tell you to go outside?'

'Please Miss, I was only . . .'

Karen stared at her. 'Didn't you hear me?'

'But I only . . .'

'Do as you're told.'

'But . . .'

Karen leapt forward and grabbed her. Then she thrust her away from her and Jenny crashed into the partition with such force it rattled.

Robert appeared in the doorway, stern-faced. He helped Jenny up and passed her to Cathy for comforting.

Karen leaned on the nearest desk, pressing down hard with both hands. She took deep breaths to calm the roaring in her ears. She was finished now. This was unforgivable. She must get out, go home, go away somewhere where she wouldn't see the child again or Robert either.

She looked up and saw that he was deeply concerned.

'You're ill. You're not yourself,' he said with a quietness that seemed deadly to her. 'I insist you go home for the rest of the day.'

She began to shake. 'I . . . I . . .'

'It's Friday. You have the weekend. You were foolish not to take more time off when your mother died. Take my advice now, Karen, and don't argue. There will be time to talk about this in due course.'

'Yes, well . . .' She raised her eyes to Joe Barden's painting on the wall. She had struggled to get through to the boy for year or more and Elisabeth Turner had accomplished it in one day. Or so it seemed. And Robert admired her for that.

She heard Jenny crying in the next room and Cathy's comforting words. She went to her desk and picked up her whistle. 'I'll get the children in first.'

He took it from her. 'Leave everything to us and don't worry. Just go home and rest for the next few days, as long as it takes. Your doctor will advise you.'

She nodded, not meeting his gaze now. She couldn't think for herself any more. She felt empty, bereft.'

There was only one thing to be done when she felt stronger. She would put as much distance between herself and Mellstone as she possibly could.

Later she would think about it. Not now.

*   *   *

Cathy rang the bell on the front door of Marigold Cottage and stepped back, remembering the wet day she had brought Jenny home from school suffering with flu. Elisabeth had been happy and excited when she burst in, fresh from arranging the exhibition she was now busy working for.

She hated to do this to her at this time. Or at any other, come to that, but Mr Moore had thought it best and she had agreed because she knew he was right.

The door opened. Elisabeth looked surprised to see her here in the lunch hour.

'Jenny's all right,' Cathy hastened to assure her. 'It's just that . . .'

'Come in, Cathy. I was up in my studio.'

'I'm sorry to disturb you.'

Elisabeth wiped her hand down the front of her painting apron. She looked pale again today and there were streaks of blue paint on her face. 'It's a bit untidy indoors. Shall we go outside?'

There were shrieks and laughter from the playground next door but the atmosphere was nicer out here in spite of the wind.

'There's been a bit of a scene in school,' Cathy said quietly. 'We thought you should know because it involved Jenny.'

'Jenny? What has she done?'

'Nothing except being in the classroom when she should have been outside. Miss Bryer lost her temper with her. She knocked her against the partition. But Jenny's not hurt.'

'She's .. ?'

'Really she isn't,' Cathy said quickly. 'Not even a bruise.'

'But why ..?'

'No one knows. Mr Moore and I were in my room with the door open before school so we almost saw her do it. I took Jenny in with me and Miss Bryer went home.'

'But Jenny must have done something she shouldn't.'

'She gave me some flowers, some lilies of the valley, that's all.' Cathy looked across the grass to the overgrown flowerbed in the corner. She could almost smell the sweet perfume from here.

'And you're sure she's all right?'

'I wouldn't lie to you.'

'Of course you wouldn't, Cathy. I know that.'

'Mr Moore's helping out at school today and of course I'm there and Mrs Hill, the dinner lady, is there now. We're trying to keep things running as normal. But we thought you should know before the rumours start.'

Elisabeth rubbed her hand across her face. 'Yes, I see. Thank you, Cathy. There'll be plenty of that.'

'I'm afraid there will. And I've interrupted your work. I hope it's going well?'

'Nearly finished now. I'd show you but you won't have time.'

'I'll see the exhibition,' Cathy said. 'I'm looking forward to it.

Next door the whistle blew and there was instant silence.

'I must go,' Cathy said. 'Mr Moore will come and see you later. Jenny's all right, really and truly.'

Elisabeth nodded. 'Thank you, Cathy.'

'I'll see myself out.'

'Yes, yes, of course. And thank you for coming.'

Cathy slipped round the side of the cottage and into the front garden. No one was about in the lane. It seemed a dead and dismal world, she thought as she hastened through the windy playground.

* * *

Elisabeth stood at her studio window and looked out at the garden, thinking hard. What she had just learned was disturbing, especially as the vicar and Cathy thought it necessary to tell her about it personally and at once even though Jenny hadn't been physically hurt.

258

Suppose there was something deeper here they weren't telling her? But surely not. She couldn't believe that Cathy could tell a lie to save her life and presumably neither could the vicar. Karen Bryer, obviously under stress after the death of her mother, had been sent home after losing her temper. Jenny would not fall foul of her again in the meantime for whatever reason. It did no good dwelling on it.

Elisabeth turned her back on the window and surveyed the room in which she had spent so much of her working life these last months. Soon it would be empty of the paintings prepared for the exhibition and she would be free to lead a more normal life.

The practical details of getting her work to Hilbury had been taken care of by Martin Varley who was all set to transport them there on Saturday. She would go with him, of course, to hand them over personally so that the professional hangers could talk to her about each painting as it was placed in position. It was good that they were taking such a personal interest in their artists. No wonder the exhibitions they mounted attracted customers from all over the region.

And while this was going on Jenny would be with Jean Varley's sister-in-law who had invited her to go with her and her two children to Stourford Fair for the day, a treat she was looking forward to.

'All *day*?' Jenny had asked in wonder when

259

Jean Varley invited her on their behalf.

'All day,' Jean had replied solemnly. 'Make sure you are ready at nine o'clock when they come to pick you up.'

There had been no doubt from Jenny's rapt expression that she would be ready and waiting.

Elisabeth smiled as she thought about it. Soon she would have time to set everything to rights about the place, weed the borders and mow the grass and then be able to sit back and enjoy her handiwork. A different sort of handiwork from what had engrossed her for the last few months but to be valued none the less.

And of course she could spend more time with Jenny. Robert Moore would call at Marigold Cottage later and she would have the chance then to question him closely about the disturbing events at school this morning and discover how it might affect Jenny's future at the school. She needed to know far more than Cathy could tell her.

With the exhibition up and running she and Jenny could plan a short holiday . . . a visit to Bella in St Ives perhaps who would be delighted to see them.

Elisabeth looked round the studio to check that all was in order, resisting the temptation to do a recount of her canvasses. Once she had checked that Jenny really was all right there would be nothing else to worry about.

Robert arrived soon after tea was cleared away and Jenny settled on the window seat in the living-room with Children's Hour on the wireless in the corner. She was totally engrossed and hadn't heard the doorbell.

He stepped into the hall. 'I won't disturb you for long, Miss Turner. I hope Jenny is none the worse for what happened today?'

'She's listening to the goings-on at Cherry Tree Farm at the moment. D'you mind the kitchen?'

He followed her through.

'Jenny didn't say much about it except that Miss Bryer was angry with her when she was in the classroom instead of the playground. I didn't press it.' She looked at him enquiringly. 'I gather there was more behind it than that?'

'I think so.'

'Miss Bryer then went home?'

'She's agreed to take sick leave next week.'

'It seems that Jenny was in the wrong place at the wrong time?'

He hesitated.

Elisabeth picked up a cup from the window sill and then put it down again. She looked up at her studio on the back lawn and sighed.

'It won't happen again,' he said.

'How can you be sure of that?'

'I can't, of course. But I have reason to

261

believe that Miss Bryer deeply regrets what happened. I hope she will come to see you about it . . .'

'Oh no.' Elisabeth was horrified. 'That won't do at all. I'd rather see how things go with Jenny and decide what's best for her then.'

He looked at her in silence and she wondered what was going through his mind. He seemed tired and out of his depth. Karen Bryer's problems weren't hers but she felt a brief flash of sympathy for her and for him too having to deal with this.

'If you're sure about that?' he said.

'As sure as I am about anything.'

'Thank you.'

Smiling, she watched him go and then joined Jenny. Suddenly she was filled with deep weariness and was glad to lean back in her chair, eyes closed.

*　　　*　　　*

Much later Karen drove back to Mellstone, unable to rest until she had seen Robert once more to find out what had happened in school after she left this morning. She could have telephoned but it was important to see him face to face to say what she had to say.

It had taken her all day to reach this decision. She was only too aware that it was far too late to be calling at the vicarage but she no longer cared about her reputation. Who would

262

see her anyway unless they were skulking in the vicarage grounds?

Deeply she regretted her sudden outburst, to Jenny of all children. It would be all up with herself if the child had been seriously hurt, and probably even if she wasn't.

She couldn't apply for another headship anywhere else now. How could Robert give her a testimonial after what he had witnessed? She remembered the expression in his eyes as he saw what she had done and she could hardly bear it.

Full of shame, she had lain on her bed replaying the disgraceful scene in her head for hour after hour, filled with a strange lethargy until she had suddenly decided to take action and do something about it.

She drove in through the vicarage gates and stopped with a squealing of brakes. As soon as she pulled the bell rope the door opened immediately as if Robert had been expecting her.

'Come in, Karen.'

Inside the hall he looked at her gravely and she caught sight of her ashen face in his glass-fronted bookcase as he ushered her into the warmth of his study.

'Jenny?' she whispered.

'Sit down,' he said, doing so himself in the leather armchair opposite hers. He leaned forward. 'Miss Mellor, Cathy, calmed Jenny and afterwards the child seemed none the worse as far as we could tell.'

'As far as you could tell?'

'Indeed.'

Karen couldn't stop shaking and when she looked down at her hands she could see the tremor. She took a deep trembling breath. 'I . . . I'm so sorry, Robert . . . It was unforgivable.'

He stirred a little and then sat with his hands held together as if in prayer. 'You need a rest, Karen, as I've said before.'

'I can't come back.'

'That needs to be discussed. You need time to adjust to what's been happening lately. What you did was a terrible thing and must not be repeated. But unforgivable? Surely not in the eyes of God if you are genuinely sorry.'

She stared down at her clenched hands. His words seared her with pain.

'Can you account for what happened?'

'She was disobedient and I let rip. I couldn't seem to help myself and I'm bitterly ashamed. That painting on the classroom wall . . .'

'Painting?'

'The one Joe Barden did.'

His eyes brightened in comprehension. 'I know the one. A talented lad. Miss Turner seemed to inspire something in him when she kindly helped us out.'

She nodded, unable to explain her sudden fury but deeply afraid that he guessed the truth.

'The Education Office are sending someone to take over at school on Monday.'

'Who?' She bit her lip.

He ignored the question. 'Miss Mellor made a point of explaining to Miss Turner what happened this morning and I called in to see her afterwards. She understands the position exactly and why.'

Karen buried her face in her hands and the ticking of the pendulum clock on the wall stirred the silence.

'Since there's no harm apparently been done I believe she will accept your apology. I assume you intend to make one?'

She knew she should do this but it would be hard, too hard. She sprang up, her heart pounding. She must get out of the room quickly before she made a fool of herself. Tears sprang to her eyes. 'I'm sorry, Robert, you can see why I must leave Mellstone. I can't stay here after this.'

Reaching the door before her, he stood with his back against it, a gentle expression in his eyes. 'Wait!'

'No, I . . . '

'When I came to Mellstone I knew I was being given an easy parish because of the state of my health. This was a bitter thing but I had to accept it and live accordingly. I . . . '

'Please let me go!'

To her relief he stood aside. She stumbled out in to the hall and he made no attempt to follow. She would not give way to tears in front of him. He knew her now for what she was, a bully and a coward. But he would not see her anguish at the prospect of moving on and not seeing him again. That at least would remain her secret.

That night passed in a muddle of unhappy dreams that left Karen exhausted. She got up as the sun rose above the hornbeam hedge at the bottom of the garden. The sky was a symphony of pale lemon and orange with a crimson streak beneath a mauve flurry of cloud.

She stood at her bedroom window watching the colours merge into each other and then fade away, unable to feel the beauty but only to see it.

It was early yet, too early to drive to the post office in Mellstone to get her letters away requesting application forms for posts of assistant teacher in two or three schools in the Midlands, far from Mellstone. She had no hope of any of them but felt she must try.

She went downstairs dressed in her Saturday gardening clothes and made a pot of tea which she carried into the garden with a mug and jug of milk. The wooden chairs on the terrace were damp but she didn't care. A cobweb on the early dahlias twinkled in the sunshine and somewhere behind her a bird sang.

She poured her tea and then let it get cold. She didn't really want it. And trying to eat something would choke her.

At last she got up and went indoors. The papers on the kitchen table needed tidying, copies of *Teacher's World* most of them, left there last night after her diligent search for the right teaching post.

Gathering them together she piled them in the bin. It was a waste of time applying for posts she didn't want but she needed some activity away from Haymesgarth to keep her sanity. And the post office would soon be opening.

She was aware that her pain at moving away from Robert swamped her regret at hurting Jenny. In fact she hadn't thought of the child for hours until now.

CHAPTER SIXTEEN

Jenny liked the feeling that the silent world belonged only to her. Lifting her eyes high above her head she twirled round and round on the front lawn of Marigold Cottage. Early morning light shone through a cobweb on a rose bush and the leaves had heavy drops of water on them. A blackbird's clacking call split the air and the sky was a pale dusky red tinged with turquoise.

Red sky in the morning, shepherds' warning, Jenny thought. Red sky in the morning was unlucky but not today. She laughed as she thought of Stourford Fair. Suddenly the excitement seemed too much to bear.

She flung her hands above her head and began to leap wildly about. With half-closed eyes she saw spangles of light fly round her. She wanted to sing and shout as twirled.

And now the sun was really up and the garden flooded with sunshine that streaked across the grass and turned the cobwebs to sparkling tinsel. Jenny, breathless and dizzy, leaned back against the fence. She was glad she had jumped out of bed as soon as she woke and come out here to this lovely world where glistening snail trails decorated the brick path.

'Lucky, lucky, lucky,' she chanted.

She began to scuff across the grass, leaving her own trail through the unfolding daisies. She picked handfuls of them and sat down on the doorstep to make herself a crown and a necklace. Most of the flowers were only half-opened. Their fresh daisy scent hung on the air.

When she had finished, she hung one daisy chain round her neck, placed the other on her head and walked regally round the cottage into the back garden. Here the sunshine was flickering on flowers and grass and dewdrops hung glistening. Bees began to hum and a butterfly came lazily over the wall. She watched it fly high in the fragrant air and wished she could do the same. She would fly up to Larksbury Rings and pick the cowslips that Judith Wintle said grew there.

Up there the air would be clear and the sun higher in the sky. Down here parts of the garden were still in shade like the bit between the school wall and the studio.

And there was something else, too, something to do with Mr Ellis and his waiting until after the exhibition. Jenny didn't know how she knew this, only that it was true and the paintings in the studio had a lot to do with it.

She started to dance again but this time it was different. There was no exhilaration now and the grass was cold.

The studio is watching me, she thought.

She glanced up at it. The large window was looking down on her as if it knew that as soon as the paintings were sold everything would be different. But she didn't want them to be different. She wanted everything to be the same forever.

Miserably she walked through the damp grass and imagined how it would feel to break those paintings and scatter the pieces on the studio floor. She ripped the daisy crown from her head and trampled it underfoot and then did the same with the necklace. That's what she would do to the paintings, she thought with a wild excitement that tinged her cheeks with warmth.

She ran to the side of the studio near the

wall to find the key that was hidden there. From here she could see the door and paused in surprise to see it hanging open.

Uncertainly, she walked towards and went inside. It was just as she imagined, canvasses ripped and broken and thrust aside. Jenny cringed back in awe. What thing had known what she was thinking and done this for her? Aghast and tearful, she stared at the damage.

Then she began to cry in great gasping sobs. She hadn't known it would be like this. She hadn't known that the paintings would look so sad lying in ruins on the floor. Desperately she wanted them whole again.

Blindly, she stumbled out of the studio and ran in to the front garden. She grabbed her sandals that she had left by the gate and put them on. Then with a determined click she opened the gate.

Sobbing, she ran down the lane.

*   *   *

Elisabeth gave an exclamation of annoyance as a cup slipped from her fingers and smashed into pieces on the kitchen floor. She could feel the tension rising in her and knew that in a minute the rest of the crockery would follow suit unless she kept a tight grip on herself.

Going on like this was stupid but she couldn't help it. She bent down and picked up the pieces and felt a prick of pain in one finger. A tiny red globule formed and became larger by the second. She couldn't have blood dripping over her work. She pulled out several drawers before the cotton wool came to light. Quickly she dabbed at her finger and then wound her handkerchief round it as tightly as she could. Everything seemed against her this morning. She reached for another cup and poured herself some tea.

For a few precious moments she sat down on the stool, forcing herself to be calm. With the exhibition so close it was hard not to panic sometimes. Sometimes she wondered what drove her on and hardened her purpose so she could think of nothing else. Apart from Jenny, of course. Perhaps the desperate need to prove herself arose from the constant criticism she received.

Even John had criticised and that had hurt. Was respect for what she was trying to do as well as love too much to expect? She didn't think so.

She drank her tea in scalding gulps, resenting as always the things that kept her from her studio even when the work was virtually done. As she shut the back door behind her and hurried up the steps she was aware that she had barely an hour before preparing breakfast and calling Jenny.

The grass was wet on her toes in her open sandals and her feet slid about as she crossed the grass. The morning was beautiful and still after the winds of yesterday but she had no time to linger and enjoy its freshness.

She reached the shady side of the studio by the wall and saw the door hanging open. Inside sunshine poured through the picture window, illuminating upturned jars and brushes among the debris of mauled paintings that yesterday had been placed neatly against the walls.

For a moment she couldn't believe that it was her studio in this horrific mess. She stared in stunned horror the destruction before her. Then, stumbling forward, she snatched up a ravaged painting and held it protectively against her.

The exhibition, she thought. *I have nothing for the exhibition.* Pain seared through her in waves of anguish. *Nothing.*

Outside in the sunlit garden a bird sang a piercingly sweet song that stung her with its beauty. For long moments she stood there rocking the broken pieces backwards and forwards. It had come to this then. Nothing was left to her from her months of hard work but this shattered mess.

She must clear it up.

She sank to the floor and tried to gather up the jagged pieces to fit together like a jigsaw puzzle. But it was no good. It must all be swept up and thrown out with the rubbish. With shaking fingers she picked up a chain of daisies from the floor, fingering each separate flower. Then she let it slide from her fingers.

272

She leapt up and sudden anger blurred her vision. Who would do this malicious thing? Who could hate her so much that they destroyed something she held most dear? She clenched her hands, wanting to grab the culprits and grind them to dust. The police must be fetched. She would not rest until someone was brought to justice.

But revenge . . . what good was that when she was ruined? Nothing could alter it. Revenge wouldn't help her. The mist cleared from her eyes as she threw herself to the floor and wept for her loss.

Outside all natural things were coming to life. The sun rising high now above the trees in the corner shone glaringly into all parts of the garden.

At last Elisabeth struggled to her feet. She rubbed her face with the paint-smeared sleeve of her blouse and then ran her fingers through her dishevelled hair, attempting to smooth it.

The life she had tried to live in Mellstone was finished now. There was nothing left to do but to sell up and move away to somewhere far-distant. Coming here to live was the biggest mistake of her life.

She dragged herself across the lawn and down the steps. The kitchen looked just the same but different as she gazed round her with new eyes. Such a little time she had left it but it seemed strange to her now because of the wreckage in the studio. Someone else would live here. Someone else would wash up at the sink and look out at the cedarwood chalet at the top of the garden and wonder what the previous owner had used it for.

She must lay the table . . . open the drawer to find the blue and white table cloth, remove the vase of meadowsweet and willowherb that Jenny had place on the table in the living-room and spread the cloth. Back to the kitchen to find the tray and load it with cutlery, two plates, two cups and saucers, two cereal bowls. To the living-room to place all this on the table and return to the kitchen again.

She looked in surprise at some fragments of crockery littering the floor. What did a broken cup matter now?

The marmalade jar, milk jug, Cornflakes packet, sugar bowl, bread and the small square of butter left in the butter dish. She had everything. The kettle must go on.

It was too early yet to wake Jenny. Back in the hall she stared at her reflection in the looking glass, expecting to see some other person staring back at her. She must change her clothes, she thought as she saw the dirty blouse and skirt she had thrown on earlier. But it wasn't important so she did nothing about it and instead returned to the kitchen to remove the kettle from the stove before it spluttered boiling water everywhere.

It was a good time to put property on the market at the moment. Someone else would appreciate Marigold Cottage as she had done. It was May over a year ago when she had first discovered the cottage and fallen for its charm. How could anyone fail to fall in love with Mellstone when everything around was so beautiful?

But not the tree, of course.

She opened the front door to stare down the lane, remembering how she had sat beneath the branches of the Tidings Tree painting on more than one occasion. And now those paintings had been destroyed. She wondered if it would ever grow again and if she would ever see it in the future as it had once been, tall and proudly handsome.

How would Jenny react to all this? Would she be glad to move to somewhere different? She realised to her shame that she didn't know.

*　　　*　　　*

'Of course my dear,' Jean Varley said, her voice deep with sympathy. 'Martin's phoning P.C Hallen now. He'll be here soon. I just came along to check you're all right."

Elisabeth nodded, glad that someone was taking over. She had gone to Ivy cottage when she knew Mrs Cameron would be about and told her what had happened. Immediately her friend had gone to the nearest phone at Varley's farm and returned soon after to

Marigold Cottage with Jean Varley.

'Is Jenny up yet?' Jean said. 'Why don't both of you come back with me for a good hot breakfast. And afterwards Jenny will be there ready and waiting to be picked up at nine. Martin's guarding the bacon and egg on the stove for me. What d'you say?'

But Elisabeth shook her head. 'Jenny's still asleep. I have to wake her. I need to stay here.' She didn't want to discuss what had happened with anyone else at the moment. Time enough to do that when the police arrived.

'Fair enough then. I'll get back. We'll talk later.'

When she had gone and Mrs Cameron with her Elisabeth dragged herself up the narrow staircase to wake Jenny. To her surprise there was no red head on the pillow with the blankets pulled high.

She went out on to landing. 'Jenny,' she called but there was no answer.

Downstairs again, she checked the bathroom, kitchen and her own bedroom. Then she went upstairs to look in dismay at Jenny's discarded nightdress. Her best clothes were gone. Elisabeth took a deep breath, her mind whirling.

The garden! She raced downstairs and out through the back door into the honeysuckle-scented air. There was no one out here or in the wrecked studio.

Suppose whoever had trashed it had

snatched Jenny away too?

*   *   *

Karen drove into the village a little later and diverted to the school to park her car there so she could walk down to the post office. To her surprise she saw Pete Hallen, Mellstone's policeman, disappear round the side of Marigold Cottage. His bicycle was leaning on the front fence and near it was parked an unfamiliar car. She drew up behind it. What were the police doing here at Marigold Cottage? It was disconcerting to say the least.

As she snapped shut her car door Mrs Cameron came down the path, a flowered apron over her grey skirt and her hair awry. She clutched Karen's arm. Her face was flushed. 'Have you found her?' she cried.

At Karen's obvious perplexity the hope in her eyes faded. She ushered her up the path and through the front door of Marigold Cottage, obviously assuming that it was Karen's intention of calling here.

Elisabeth was standing by the window in the living-room holding her hands clenched together. She seemed unsurprised to see Karen who hesitated in the doorway, unsure of what her next move should be.

'A terrible thing about those paintings,' Mrs Cameron said. 'All smashed up and no exhibition now.'

277

'And Jenny's gone,' Elisabeth said.

'Gone?' Karen said. 'But where . . . when?' She looked at Mrs Cameron who was clutching at the hem of her cardigan and twisting it into knots.

'She got up early,' said Elisabeth in a small clear voice. 'They think she must have gone out somewhere on her own. But she wouldn't do that, not today.'

Karen had a swift vision of Jenny's ashen face yesterday as she threw her against the partition, and shuddered. This was her fault, her entire fault. She looked round wildly. 'Where are the police?'

'They're up in the studio with the smashed paintings,' said Elisabeth and now her voice trembled. 'They think she'll come back soon on her own. They want me to stay here.'

Karen nodded. 'Jenny likes exploring the village on her own.'

'But she wouldn't go off anywhere today,' said Elisabeth. 'Not today when she was excited about going to Stourford Fair. I know she wouldn't.'

'You think we should take this seriously?'

'She wouldn't have gone out on her own today,' said Elisabeth. 'No one will believe me.'

'I believe you,' said Karen.

Elisabeth was still for a moment. The she nodded. 'Thank you.'

'I'll help find her.'

'Martin Varley's already having a look for her down the lane,' said Mrs Cameron. 'And Jean too and others. And the vicar's coming. They'll have phoned John as well to see if she's gone down Nether End way.'

Karen turned towards the door as she heard Robert's step in the hall. Her breath caught in her throat and she had to force herself to stand still and not run away.

He came into the room like a comforting giant, his vibrant voice seeming to bring warmth with him. He went straight to Elisabeth and drew her down beside him on the window seat. 'Perhaps we could have some tea,' he said.

Karen escaped to the kitchen with Mrs Cameron and stood silently while the kettle was being filled at the sink and the gas lit on the stove.

'Tell me about it,' she said. 'I want to know all the details.'

Mrs Cameron's hands shook as she placed some cups and saucers on a tray. She was only too glad to pour out all that had happened in little bursting gasps of information that at times were almost incoherent. She sank down on the stool and rested her arms on the table. She looked as if she hadn't been to bed for a week with her untidy hair and shapeless cardigan.

'Elisabeth found her studio all wrecked,' she said over and over again. 'And then Jenny

279

gone.'

Steam began to pour from the kettle and she struggled up to attend to it. 'D'you think you could take it in?' She said. 'My hands are none too steady.'

'Of course.'

Karen picked up the tray and carried it into the hall. There was a tap on the front door and John came in. He looked as he always did in his working clothes but there was something else there too, a kind of suppressed energy that gave momentum to his movements. At the same time Robert emerged from the living-room and took the tray with a murmur of thanks.

'Where is she?' John said and moved towards the door. 'What do the police say?'

Robert cleared his throat. 'They're in the studio at the moment, I believe.'

'I'd like to see Elisabeth.'

'One moment, if you please. She doesn't want to see anyone. You've heard about the damage to her paintings? She thinks you will assume that Jenny did it. She doesn't want to see you.'

The lines on John's face deepened. 'I see,' he said quietly.

'Thank you. And Karen, I think you should be at home and not here. Officially you're on sick leave. Mrs Cameron will be staying here with Elisabeth and she'll do all she can.'

Karen knew she deserved little else. She

bowed her head.

Robert backed through the door with the tray and pushed it shut behind him.

'That's it then,' said John. 'There's a job to be done.'

'Someone has to convince the police that this is serious.'

He shrugged. 'Someone has to find Jenny and soon. I'll have a word with the police before I go.'

'Can I come with you?'

'You heard what Robert said, Karen. Go home. You don't look well.'

'No.' She brushed her hand across her face.

'If I can I'll keep you in touch with all that's happening.'

'Where are you going?'

'I'll tour the lanes. She might not have gone far.'

Karen marvelled that the police hadn't started a full-scale search already instead of pussy-footing about in Elisabeth Turner's studio.

She left Marigold Cottage feeing totally rejected.

*   *   *

Alice Pengold pushed open the church door and went inside. This was a fine old pickle and no mistake, the little maid gone and no one knew where. She had searched the churchyard and paused by Bert's grave thinking he'd have been down on his knees up there by the altar. But not she, not after her prayers went unanswered and Bert died. She had never darkened the church again for all the vicar's words. Except to clean every Friday.

But now as she stood just inside the church door, Alice hesitated. Suppose the little maid was hiding here, frightened and alone? Tight-lipped, she began to search but she was nowhere, not crouching in the pulpit or behind the lectern or in any of the choir pews. Alice stood at the altar rail and unaccustomed tears filled her eyes. Someone must know where she was. Someone must know what she was doing now. Inside her head she seemed to hear Bert's voice.

She moved back and sat down in the nearest pew and stared at the stained glass window above the altar. For the merest second the sun seemed to burst through the lowering clouds and brighten the glass to glorious Technicolor.

Find her. Find that poor little maid before it's too late.

Robert, entering the church a moment later, saw Alice sitting there, her lips moving. He knew he must not move or make the smallest sound. He hadn't long to wait before she struggled to her feet and came to the door.

'Oh it's you, Vicar.'

'Good morning, Mrs Pengold,' He was careful to sound unsurprised. To find Alice in the church building without her cleaning gear was truly remarkable.

'Not good for some. It's getting dark. It'll be raining afore noon.'

'You haven't seen young Jenny anywhere?'

'She'm be up the Hollow, like as not.'

'Why do you think that?'

'I've seen her up there once or twice.'

'The Hollow? Thank you, Alice.'

He held the door open for her and followed her out.

It was worth a try and he felt useless here.

He hurried ahead, up the lane to the trunk of the tree and then down to the main road past the vicarage. It wasn't worth getting his car out. By the time he'd done so he could be well past Meadow Cottages and starting up the track. For all he knew he might meet the child on her way back.

*   *   *

Karen came out of the main school door and locked it behind her regretting that she had set foot in a place that reminded her so vividly of her display of temper the day before that had had such catastrophic consequences. She didn't know quite why she had done it instead of going home.

For a while she had sat at her desk with her head in her hands replaying in her mind all that had happened. But what good had that done? Robert's reaction made her heart-sick but she was no nearer apologising to Elisabeth Turner as he said she must. Something held her back, some deep feeling that maybe now the score was equal and she had been justified.

But how shameful was that? How degrading?

She had remained there for a long time, thankful only that the cane had been safely locked away in the cupboard at the time. Suppose it had been to hand? She shuddered. What could she do to show remorse for her recent behaviour? Nothing it seemed.

Now as she left the school building and crossed the playground she saw that the bright look about the day was fading and clouds moving up from the west. It was not yet nine o'clock on Saturday morning but already it felt as if it were late afternoon.

Alice Pengold came stumbling along the lane towards her as she shut the gate. Karen looked at her in alarm. 'Are you all right, Mrs Pengold? You don't look well.'

'As right as I'll ever be,' Alice said shortly. 'Better when the young maid's safe and sound. Vicar's gone up the Hollow to bring her back.'

Karen was alarmed. 'He's gone up there? But it's steep.'

'As steep for him as anyone.'

'But . . .'

'Go after him, then, like I went after Bert when I wanted him.'

Silenced, Karen stared after her as she marched towards her garden gate. Then she got in to her car, reversed it and set off at speed.

CHAPTER SEVENTEEN

John saw Miss King attacking some rogue dandelions outside the fence of Lynch Cottage and drew up alongside her.

She straightened and called a greeting as he wound down his window. 'Are you looking for Cathy?' she said. 'She's just getting ready to catch the bus into Hilbury. I'll get her for you.'

'No, wait.' An extraordinary woman, John thought. Why should she think that he was looking for Cathy Mellor?

It took moments only to explain the reason he was here and then Miss King was all fluttering concern, rushing to open the door and call for Cathy and Miss Buckley to alert them about Jenny's disappearance. Miss Buckley caught hold of Benjy's collar to stop him escaping through the open gate.

'I met Jenny up in Hodman's Hollow the other day.' Cathy said breathlessly. 'She was telling me about somewhere special, somewhere she likes to go.'

John frowned. 'So where is this place?'

'I'll go and look there now,' said Cathy.

'But what about the bus?' said Miss King.

'That doesn't matter. Brooklands, Jenny called it. It's further down the lane through a gate on the right and down a sloping field to the brook.'

'Jump in then,' said John. He leaned across and opened the passenger door for her. 'I'll come with you.'

He pulled in on to the grass verge where Cathy indicated. They walked quickly down the field to an overgrown marshy patch in the corner thick with thistles and white fluffy flowers of meadowsweet among the rushes.

'It doesn't look as if anyone's been here,' said Cathy doubtfully.

'I wonder why she liked it?'

'The butterflies perhaps and the dragonflies,' said Cathy.

The sound of the brook was loud here but there seemed no way in through the impenetrable brambles bordering it.

'She said there was a secret path alongside the brook.'

'Then we'll find it.'

It took them far longer than John would have liked to force a way through and even then he had his doubts. If Jenny were here there would have been some signs and there were none.

He called and Cathy joined in but there was no answer.

'It looks as if we've drawn a blank,' he said.

Cathy didn't reply and he could see her disappointment turning to hopelessness from the way she scrambled out and stood looking down at the ground with her shoulders slumped.

'We had to try everything,' he said. 'There are other places.'

She nodded. 'Of course.'

He wouldn't let despair take over just yet and neither must she.

'I'd better carry on down the lane,' he said. Maybe you could see if there's anywhere else needing to be searched.'

She nodded and brightened. 'There's somewhere else she talked about, Larksbury Rings.'

'Then that's the place for me,' he said and thought of Elisabeth sick with dread and of his aunt hysterical with worry. Cathy might be better there than coming with him to search the hill which he could do adequately on his own.

'I'll drive as near to it as I can get and walk the rest of the way. I'll drop you off at Marigold Cottage on the way to check how things are there.'

To his surprise Karen's car was parked in the place he had in mind, just past Meadow Cottages where the lane stopped and the track up Hodman's Hollow began. So he was wasting his time here too because it was likely she had someone with her. He got out of the

287

car, undecided, fingering his pipe. Heading for Larksbury Rings seemed a strange thing for a girl to do, even one like Jenny. He wondered that Elisabeth condoned the child's wanderings. She must be regretting it now.

He made up his mind suddenly. Jenny could well be there and there was a wide area to cover. By why so early in the morning and without telling anyone?

He strode up the chalky track. A few drops of rain began to fall and he pulled up his jacket collar. If rain had come earlier there might have been a few footprints to alert him as to her whereabouts. Now the rain was merely a nuisance obscuring the view ahead in a frustrating sweep of mist and beginning to turn the ground beneath his feet into a chalky mess.

He reached the top of the track and climbed the stile into the field where the footpath led across to Larksbury Rings. There were sheep here. It was as well he had left Fly at home or they might have all been rounded up by now with Fly looking expectantly at him for approval.

Ahead of him some of them scattered with a few startled bleats and he saw a distant motionless figure with a smaller one alongside. His heart leapt. He ran up towards them. 'You've found her!'

Karen looked bleak. 'She won't come with me.'

'Jenny?' She looked back at him, her pale

288

face mutinous.

'Why is that, Jenny?' he asked, his voice tense. Relieved as he was that she had been found apparently unharmed he was aware the Elisabeth, sick with dread, needed to know as soon as possible.

She didn't answer. He struggled to find the right thing to say and do.

'I've got to find Robert,' Karen said through white lips.

John looked at her sharply. 'Robert's up here as well? Did you see him, Jenny?'

She shook her head and pressed her bunch of cowslips to her face. Her hair, darkened by rain, was stuck to her head and she had streaks of earth down one side of her skirt.

'Robert's up here somewhere,' Karen repeated. 'I need to find him. I'm worried about him.'

'Then do it,' John said. 'You don't need me to tell you. My car's down below. I'll get Jenny home straightaway.' *But how, short of using force?*

He watched Karen trudge back into the mist to look for someone he wasn't at all sure she would find in the wide expanse of hillside. But his attention must focus on Jenny now.

'I used to pick cowslips up here when I was a boy,' he said.

'Judith Wintle said they grew here.'

'And that's why you came?'

She shook her head. 'I can't go back to

Marigold Cottage. Ever.'

'But it's raining. We'll both get soaked. Why can't you go back, Jenny?'

She trembled violently. 'The studio.'

He had forgotten the studio. 'But surely you had nothing to do with that?'

'I wished for it and it came true,' Jenny cried. 'I didn't know it would be like that. I didn't know so I can't go back.'

He struggled to understand her reasoning. 'Jenny,' he said with emphasis. 'We don't know who wrecked the studio but whoever it was won't hurt *you*.'

'But he will, I know he will.'

'D'you know who did it?'

She shuddered. 'He let down your car tyres. He threw stones at the studio. He'll know that I know and he'll get me.'

'The police are there now. They won't let anyone get you, Jenny. Promise me that you believe me.'

He saw the disbelief in her eyes gradually give way to resolution.

'All right,' she whispered.

'And you'll come home now? Your mother is going to mind very much about her paintings. She needs you there with her.'

To his relief she nodded. They set off together to the stile and into Hodman's Hollow. The chalky track was lethal in the wet and they were soaked by the time they had slithered down to his car but he smiled as he put it into gear.

'Good girl, Jenny. I'm proud of you,' he said.

The front door of Marigold Cottage was wide open and the increasingly heavy rain was beating in. Elisabeth saw them at once and ran out to meet them. As she hugged Jenny John saw that her face was wet with tears.

'Oh Jenny,' she breathed, unable to say more.

John smiled briefly, hesitated for a moment and then left.

*   *   *

Karen suspected that once Robert had got to the top of Hodman's Hollow and hadn't found Jenny he would climb the stile and head across the field on the foot path that led to Larksbury Rings to search for her there. That he hadn't found her was worrying because he would have got here before the visibility worsened..

Head down against the swirling mist she plodded on. She had discovered Jenny sitting on the damp ground on the first embankment, arranging her cowslips with her head bent in concentration. When Karen called to her she had looked up, startled, but although she got to her feet she made no move to join her. She went to her, relieved that Jenny didn't run away.

'It's time to go home,' she said as gently as she could manage.

'I can't, Miss. Joe Barden will get me.'

'What nonsense is this?'

But Jenny would say no more and it was then that Karen had seen John like an apparition through the mist. Her relief was enormous.

But where was Robert? Hodman's Hollow was steep. Desperately worried about Jenny, he would have rushed up to the top faster than he should with his heart condition. It might well be too much for him. He could be lying somewhere now, out of sight and needing help and she didn't know how to find him.

She gave a stifled sob as she climbed up the first embankment, slithered down into the dip and then climbed the second, higher one. She had always found the place ominous and now it was even more so.

There was still no sign of him. She thought of the school meeting that had got out of hand because of her insulting remarks. He had suffered something very like a heart attack after that and it was her fault. She had done nothing but bring him harm.

And then she saw him close to her. She cried out as she ran to him. 'Oh Robert, Robert!'

He caught her to him and for a moment held her close.

She took a deep gasping breath. 'Jenny's safe,' she whispered.

'Thank God. Where was she?'

'I found her and John's taken her home. I

came to look for you.'

'You should have gone back with them too.'

'I knew you were here somewhere. I was afraid for you.' Her tears welled up suddenly and she struggled for control. She bit her lips to stop their trembling.

'Then let's go,' he said, releasing her. 'John Ellis will want to know we are back safely, Cathy Mellor will too.'

There were still things to be sorted out with Cathy, she thought. An apology for the curt way she had dealt with her when appreciation might have worked wonders. Apologising to Cathy would be easy. It was the one she had not yet made to Elisabeth Turner that was the stumbling block. It seemed that Robert thought she had already done that and was satisfied.

He took hold of her hand and pressed it warmly in his. It seemed as if all his energy and care flowed in to her.

*   *   *

'We've just heard the good news,' Miss King said, her face shining with enthusiasm. Behind her Miss Buckley loomed holding Benjy on a tight lead.

'Jenny's fine. A bit wet and tired. . .' Elisabeth paused in alarm at the whine of machinery that burst suddenly into a roar from the direction of the Tidings Tree. With a lurch

293

of her heart she thought of the gale that had brought down the branch all those months ago and of the noise then when the tree had been shorn of its remaining branches.

Benjy set up some frantic barking and pulled at his lead in an effort to investigate and nearly had Miss Buckley flat on her face on the brick path.

'How very freak!' Miss King cried.

Other people came running out of their homes. In full cry, Benjy led the ladies along with them as they streamed towards what was left of the tree. Mellstone, a quiet place a few moments ago, was now a hub of activity.

Elisabeth closed the front door to deaden the sound and returned to the living-room.

Jenny looked up from her jigsaw puzzle. 'What's that horrible noise?'

'I think they're cutting down what's left of the tree.' Elisabeth tried not to be dispirited but she couldn't help the hopeless tone in her voice. 'I suppose they thought it as good a time as any and they have the afternoon off as it's Saturday.'

She sat down on the footstool near Jenny's chair. 'Why did you do it, Jenny?' she said. 'Why did you run away?'

She was alarmed to see the child's face whiten and wished she had let the matter alone. Jenny was safe now and surely that as all that mattered?

'I didn't go to the fair,' Jenny murmured.

'There'll be other fairs.' Elisabeth had forgotten the fair because to her it no longer mattered. As soon as John brought Jenny in an hour ago and then quickly left it had been all action. A hot bath, a bowl of porridge and finding something to occupy Jenny while she dealt with the wet muddy clothes and tried to forget the devastation inside her studio.

Jenny picked up a piece of jigsaw and then put it down again. 'But I found the cowslips. I picked a big bunch and then it rained and there was mist everywhere. I didn't know what to do.'

'So you waited there all alone on Larksbury Rings?'

'I thought Joe Barden would get me.'

'But why?'

'Because of the paintings?'

'You saw the mess in the studio?'

Jenny nodded.

'But why didn't you come and tell me?'

Jenny stared down at the half-finished jigsaw and didn't answer.

Elisabeth looked across at the windowsill on which she had placed the jar of cowslips Jenny had brought back from Larksbury Rings and felt a deep sense of failure. The flowers' yellow heads were drooping and they looked a sorry sight. She hoped the water would revive them. Jenny had wanted to climb Larksbury Rings from the first and they had never got there because her work was paramount. And in the process Jenny felt lonely and abandoned.

'Mr Ellis said the police won't let him get me,' Jenny said at last.

'That's true,' said Elisabeth. 'They're coming back soon to get the proof they need and then all this will stop. I promise you that. Jenny.'

'I don't like it here anymore,' said Jenny.

'You don't?'

The roar outside stopped suddenly and then started again but this time it was a dull, monotonous sound that echoed round and round in Elisabeth's head. She sat still, thinking of what Jenny had said. She wasn't the same child now as the one who had leaned out of her bedroom window the day they moved in exclaiming in delight. Her own feeling of guilt lay heavily on her. Coming to Mellstone to earn a living for them both in such a precarious way had been a mistake. She had expected the lack of security to be difficult but not that it would make such heavy demands on Jenny as well as herself and in the end be impossible.

'We'll talk about it, Jenny,' she said quietly. 'But not today.'

The uncanny sounds outside stopped again and there was something ominous in the silence. Their first morning here she, too, had been enraptured by the scents and sounds of Mellstone and had gone out to sketch everything in sight. She had not been aware then of all that was involved, the unceasing

296

hard work from dawn to dusk and utter fatigue of mind and body not only day after day but month after month.

She wouldn't do that to Jenny again.

In any case she had failed. It made no difference that it was not, in the end, her fault. Suspecting that the wrecked studio was the work of young Joe Barden had hurt. She had failed there too.

She got up and moved to the window and saw the door of Ivy Cottage opposite open and Mrs Cameron come out and cross the lane. She flew to the door to meet her.

Mrs Cameron stepped inside, puffing slightly. She looked troubled. 'How is that poor little girl?'

'Go in and see for yourself, Mrs Cameron. I'll get the kettle on.'

Overcome suddenly by the kindness of all those who had helped and consoled her through the hours of Jenny's disappearance, she sat down on the kitchen stool, rested her face in her hands and let the tears flow. She wished she had thanked them properly, Karen Bryer who had never liked Jenny but had been the one who found her, Cathy and Robert. And John in particular. She hadn't known such kindness existed.

But she didn't deserve it. From now on Jenny must be her priority as she should have been all along. She had thought she was doing this for her in order that she should have a good life growing up in the country, picnics on the downs while she sketched, breathing in the good fresh air.

Bella had wanted her to join her as she set up her art centre because she needed a resident artist to tutor classes she planned. But there wouldn't have been the freedom to paint full time and she had wanted to strike out on her own. But what was freedom when it came down to it? Peace of mind wherever you were, the soaring of your spirit in the knowledge that you were in the place you were meant to be. She had thought that was Mellstone but perhaps she had been wrong.

The kettle shuddered on the gas ring, boiling now. She got up to make the tea, feeling a deep heaviness of heart.

The doorbell rang again and this time it was Cathy looking anxious as if she feared she wouldn't be welcome. Elisabeth hastened to put her at her ease and ushered her in to the living-room too.

'Everything looks just the same,' Cathy said, looking round the room in surprise.

'And why shouldn't it?' Mrs Cameron said, brusquely for her.

'Well yes . . . I mean . . .'

'A cup of tea, Cathy? There's plenty here. I'll get another cup.'

Yes, everything looked just the same, Elisabeth thought as she opened the cupboard door in the kitchen. Except that it wasn't the same beneath the surface. There were issues to be faced now that hadn't been there before.

By the time Elisabeth returned Cathy was seated at Jenny's side, helping with her jigsaw.

Mrs Cameron made a move towards the door. 'I'll get back home now then and get a letter in the post,' she said. 'Muriel's coming to stay for Whitsun.'

'That's good news,' said Elisabeth..

'But first there's the studio to clear up. I'm going to help you with that so mind you don't start it on your own.'

'Not yet. I can't face it yet.'

'When those policemen have gone and let you alone, dear.'

Elisabeth shuddered. She must find her insurance certificate and check what could be claimed.

'It has to be done and the sooner the better,' said Mrs Cameron.

Her friend was right, of course, but to do so seemed like the end of everything. 'It won't be long, I promise,' Elisabeth said as she gave her a hug.

*   *   *

On Tuesday morning Karen had been at her desk for some while before Cathy came in and paused in the Junior Room on her way through to her own.

She smiled. 'Good morning, Miss Bryer. It's

good to have you back.'

'Is it? I'm not sure everyone will think so.'

Cathy moved her bag of exercise books from one hand to the other. 'I saw Mr Ellis just now. He didn't look well. He did so much searching on Saturday morning.'

'And you were with him.'

'I knew Jenny wanted to go to Larksbury Rings but I thought she was more likely to be in another place as we wasted time looking there.'

'You knew about her liking Larksbury Rings? Then why didn't you say so right away and save a lot of trouble?'

Karen broke off on seeing Cathy's stricken face, immediately ashamed of her harsh words. 'Oh my dear, I'm sorry. I've no right to interrogate you. If it wasn't for you she might not have been found as soon as she was.'

'And it was you who found her.'

Karen shrugged. 'Ironic, don't you think?'

'Jenny told me about both places when I met her in Hodman's Hollow one evening. You see I had just heard that the man I'd hoped cared for me had gone away for good and . . .' Cathy broke off, her voice tight.

'I'm sorry.' Karen felt suddenly humbled, knowing how hard she had been on Cathy these last few weeks.

'I tried not to let it make any difference in school.'

'You had more control over yourself than

300

I had.'

'You don't think . . . you can't . . ? You know that Jenny blamed herself for the paintings being destroyed and that's why she ran away?'

Karen stared at her, unable to speak for a moment for the surge of thankfulness in her heart that it wasn't because of her. For the first time she noticed Cathy's pallor and the pain in her eyes and felt deeply ashamed that she hadn't noticed before.

'I didn't actually see what happened that morning,' Cathy said hesitantly. 'I know you didn't mean to hurt Jenny.'

'I don't deserve your kindness. I'm afraid I did intend to hurt her, at the time.' Karen laughed bitterly. 'That's a confession I thought I'd never make. But it's only too true. Never let pride rule your life, Cathy. Pride does terrible things to people. I know that now. And that's why the school will need a new headmistress in September.'

'You're leaving?'

'I'm leaving. I couldn't stay after this. It's time I moved on.'

'I'm sorry.'

'Thank you, Cathy. You're kind and loyal too. You'll do well in your teaching career. I hope you'll stay on here for many years. The children love you.'

Cathy flushed.

The first of the children to arrive burst into the classroom.

'Outside until the whistle blows,' Karen ordered. But although she sounded as stern as she usually did when they tried things on she felt lighter of heart than she had for a long time.

CHAPTER EIGHTEEN

Towards the end of the week Elisabeth knew she couldn't put off clearing her studio any longer and when Mrs Cameron called soon after breakfast was glad to accept her offer of help.

Outside in the garden she gulped down breaths of sweet-scented air before opening the door and confronting the damage inside. She expected that the same sense of shock experienced on Saturday would overwhelm her now but to her surprise she felt nothing.

Mrs Cameron sighed. 'Such destruction, such waste.'

'But it's only canvas and paint,' Elisabeth said. 'That's all.'

'But all your hard work . . .'

'Yes, there's that.'

But nothing mattered compared with Jenny's safety, Elisabeth thought. During these last busy months she had become hard and unfeeling and for what?

She propped open the studio door and flung

the window wide open to let in the pure air. Then together they started to gather together the broken canvases to pile outside against the back wall where they would be hidden from view.

'All I want now is for the place to be as I first saw it, empty and sterile.' Elisabeth said.

Mrs Cameron looked at her in concern. 'But you'll do more of your lovely paintings, dear?'

'It's too late for the exhibition now. Martin Varley notified the organisers straight away . . . Breaking my contract has put them in a difficult position and they won't rely on me again.'

'That's not fair. It wasn't your fault.'

'They're running a business. They have to be professional.'

'But what will you do if . . .'

'I don't know. I really don't know. At the moment I feel I never want to paint again.'

Mrs Cameron looked horrified. 'Oh my, oh dear, that's terrible. I hope you're not thinking of going away?'

Elisabeth shivered. 'I don't know. I must think of Jenny. I don't know. How can I know?'

Mrs Cameron took a shuddering breath and then for a long moment looked at the bags of smashed painting they had put by the door. 'You'll know when the time comes,' she said as she picked up the last piece of broken jar and held it carefully.

Looking at her, Elisabeth saw her courage and dignity in facing something that would be hard for her but not allowing her true feelings to show because she cared for Jenny and herself. She felt humble in the realisation of what it must cost her.

Mrs Cameron sighed. 'And now we hear that Miss Bryer won't be headmistress at the school any more . . .'

'She's leaving?'

'That's what they're saying. Come the autumn there'll be somebody new in her place.'

Elisabeth left what she was doing and put her arms round Mrs Cameron and gave her a hug. She looked round and saw one of her paintings that hadn't been knocked about as badly as the others. She picked it up and looked at it critically.

'What's that you've got there, dear?'

'It's for you, if you'd like it.'

Mrs Cameron took it from her and exclaimed in delight when she saw what it was. 'It's the track going up the hill behind John's house. It's beautiful. You're kind dear, so very kind.'

'Kind?' Elisabeth laughed, surprising herself at the sound.

'I'll be able to show Muriel when she comes. She'll love it as much as me. It's a scene she knows so well from when she was a girl.'

She sounded happy now and Elisabeth

was glad.

Their work was finished here for the time being. All she wanted now was to go back indoors and forget about it. She locked the door and pocketed the key and Mrs. Cameron, pleased with her gift, carried it back to Ivy Cottage.

But instead of going indoors Elisabeth sat down on the top step at the edge of the lawn and thought of John who would feel justified now in the advice he had given her. He had been appalled at her financial position and had never understood the power of creation that was so much a part of her life. He had said she should be hard and ruthless but she failed to see how either quality could have prevented this fiasco but maybe he wouldn't see it like that. In any case his criticism of what she was trying to do meant that he disapproved of her as a person and that had hurt.

The sun broke free from a bank of cloud and looking up, she saw him coming round the side of the cottage.

'John?'

She got to her feet and moved down the rest of the steps, confused at seeing him so suddenly.

'Elisabeth. Aunt Ruth said you were here.'

'She's been helping me.'

'In the studio? So she said.'

There was silence for a moment and she wondered why he had come.

'I haven't thanked you for what you did on Saturday,' she said. 'I'm so grateful to you, John.'

He nodded. 'I should have done more.'

'No one could have done more.'

'Perhaps not. But it occurred to me you might need help now dealing with the insurance people.'

She shook her head. 'I've filled in the form. Martin Varley checked it for me. I can claim only for the price of the canvasses, that's all. I think I knew that. That's all my work's worth. John. You were right in saying that in doing it I wasn't being fair to Jenny.'

He looked surprised. 'You say that now?'

'I don't think I can go on with it anymore. I'm beginning to see things differently. I failed in what I set out to do.'

'There's no question of failure, Elisabeth. You don't have to prove to anyone that you're capable of producing a large number of paintings by a given date. You've already done that.'

'But that not they could be valued by others and make my fortune.'

She turned away and looked up at the studio.

'There are more ways of obtaining what you want than living in penury,' he said.

'There are?'

'With no money worries and with me to take care of you and Jenny you'll be able to do it

306

all again, perhaps at a slower pace in between other things. My dearest Elisabeth I'm asking you to become my wife.'

She looked at him in a silence that seemed to last forever. He was offering security, the chance to paint with peace of mind, the knowledge that whatever happened she and Jenny would be looked after without any need for striving to prove something important to her. It had been hard living as they had for the last few months but it was harder still to face this blinding temptation to do as he wished.

'You might like some time to think about it,' he said, his voice gentle.

'I don't . . .' She stopped, unable to go on for the tears in her throat.

He smiled. 'Nothing would make me happier than to have you at my side. But please, say no more now. We'll talk of this again. I think you're still in shock from the past few days and need time to adjust.'

He left her then and she went indoors. For the rest of the day she thought deeply about what John had said. Perhaps she had needed her time here in Marigold Cottage to discover what life really meant. She knew now. It was no longer a dream. She knew that there were things that still held great importance for her and one of them was Jenny. She must have her full consideration now.

* * *

The church was full on Sunday morning. Although it was the Whitsun weekend Cathy had decided to spend the holiday in Mellstone so she could take part in the bellringers' outing on Whit Monday and also ring on Sunday morning for the special Whit Sunday service. There had been some opposition from home but for once she had been adamant. She was surprised and relieved that they had accepted it because she couldn't have faced her sisters' derision about Arnold leaving her. Not yet, anyway. She would need to feel stronger for that.

Before the service began they had rung a touch of Grandsire Triples with Cathy on the treble. Now all eight ringers were seated in the back pew. That they were all staying for the service must be some sort of record, Cathy thought. Maisie, the young girl Arnold had liked, sat next to her.

The service began.

Cathy knelt, her head bent, conscious of Maisie beside her and wishing she hadn't stayed for the service after all. Arnold hadn't been interested in Maisie any more than he had in her but it was obvious that Maisie didn't care. Cathy wished with all her heart she didn't either. She had to accept that Arnold's words when he said he loved her meant nothing.

Her bitterness was like a heavy weight pressing down on her in everything she did.

Oh please, please give me peace from it, she thought. *I don't want to feel bitter any more.*

She felt in her pocket for Arnold's letter but didn't pull it out because she knew the words by heart.

There's no time to see you as I'm off tonight . . . keep your fingers crossed.

How dare he assume that she would condone his uncaring action enough to cross her fingers for him and wish him luck! The arrogance of it! He had no conception of her pain on his leaving her without even saying good bye. How could he do it to her? She had believed him when he said he loved her, of course she had believed him. And yet he was planning something like this. But why hadn't she suspected this, picked up on some clue or other? She had been stupidly naive. No, she hadn't. He was the one whose actions were contemptible. He was the one, older than herself, who should have respected her trust. He should have told her face-to-face that his feelings had changed. He was the coward. She clutched the edge of the pew. A crimson mist blinded her and she was finding it hard to breathe.

Beside her Maisie moved a little and then looked towards her. 'You all right,' she whispered.

Cathy raised her head. The mist vanished. The church seemed filled with radiance. A huge weight seemed to have lifted from her shoulders. How could this be? Her thought had become a prayer that was immediately answered.

'I think so,' she said in wonder at the sudden feeling of release.

'Good for you,' Maisie whispered and then put her finger to her lips as the man in the pew in front turned round and frowned. No so long ago Cathy would have cringed back in her seat at his implied criticism but today she didn't care. Her sense of freedom was empowering.

She stood up with the others to join in the singing of the hymn before Robert climbed the steps to the pulpit. For a long moment he stood looking down at his flock before giving them the text from St Paul's letter to the Galatians. *Since we live by the Spirit let us keep in touch with the Spirit.*

Feeling calmer than she had for days, Cathy leaned back to listen as he spoke of travelling through life fulfilling individual daily purposes and feeling guided all the way so that you knew the right place for you. She liked that, and the idea that each person would use their special abilities to help others. The trick was to know what your special abilities were and she wasn't at all sure she knew hers.

She glanced around at others in the congregation. Perhaps they, too, were having the same trouble. Not Elisabeth, of course, because her talents were obvious. But surely it didn't matter what your abilities were as long as you were aware of them and used them?

Now the vicar was talking about new beginnings and the importance of an open mind. Yes, that was true, she thought. An open mind. An open road.

'And we shall soon have a new Tidings Tree as a new sapling takes over from the old,' Robert concluded.

There was a sudden stir among the congregation as the significance of his words sank in.

He smiled. 'Indeed, the new tree, a young oak, is to be planted very soon, a significant moment in the history of Mellstone.' He waited until the shuffling of feet and the murmuring of voices ceased and then he said, 'Now we shall sing the offertory hymn, number 356, *New every morning is the love our wakening and uprising prove.*'

The singing swelled until the roof seemed, to Elisabeth, to be lifting with it. Or maybe it was her heart doing the soaring and her imagination was taking over? In any case she had felt a lightness of spirit as she listened to Robert's words about feeling fulfilled in your role in life by knowing yourself and what your strengths were. That was the hard bit, of course, truly understanding yourself.

Her lips moved automatically as the hymn progressed but her thoughts dwelt on ideas that hadn't occurred to her before. She was aware, since the fear of losing Jenny, that her happiness lay in Jenny's well-being. In taking part in the exhibition in which her reputation could have been made lacked, for her, something important to her that she must have known subconsciously but hadn't known what to do about it.

Now she felt she was on the verge of making a discovery that would bring ultimate content to them both.

*   *   *

'That was a bit of a bombshell about the tree,' Ralph Varley said as he followed Cathy out into the sunshine.

She turned to him and smiled, liking the way his cheerfulness seemed to brighten his surroundings.

'The centre of Mellstone looks bare without the Tidings Tree ,' she said.

'Nature abhors a vacuum,' he agreed. 'So true. And the village is doing its bit to help nature along. I wonder that Dad didn't say anything. He's on the Parish Council. He must have known.'

'But it would have spoilt the vicar's surprise.'

'I don't suppose that would have entered Dad's mind for a minute. More like he didn't think it important enough to mention. That's Dad all over.'

'You can't say that,' Cathy objected. 'How do you, a mere mortal, know what's in anyone's mind?'

Ralph grinned. 'Fair enough. It jolted everyone awake anyway. And now just look at them.'

People stood about in talkative groups and only two people were walking away down the path. Cathy gazed after Elisabeth as she hustled Jenny out through the lych gate, obviously wanting to escape before anyone set upon them. At least that's what it seemed like. Although, come to think of it, Elisabeth looked more relaxed than she had for the past few weeks.

'Looking forward to the Ringing Outing tomorrow, Cathy?' Ralph asked, his eyes gleaming. 'Some of those Somerset churches are worth seeing. I've rung in most of the ones on the itinerary but not all of them. And the food laid on is always amazing. Worth going for that alone.'

Cathy laughed.

'I haven't seen you do that for ages. Laugh, I mean.'

She was surprised he had noticed. He looked so eagerly boyish and good-humoured that she felt better for talking to him. 'I hope the weather's like this tomorrow,' she said.

'It will be. An early start, don't forget. We've got a long way to go.'

*　　　*　　　*

313

Elisabeth was in the garden when John walked round the side of Marigold Cottage. He paused for a moment and looked up at her as she cut some pink roses from the climbing rose growing against the wall. The sunlight shone on her hair in auburn highlights. She wasn't wearing her painting clothes today but a pink blouse the same shade of pink as the flowers and their sweet scent seemed to surround her.

She didn't see him at first but when she did she smiled and came forward to meet him at the top of the steps holding the roses close to her.

'They're beautiful,' he said, looking at them. 'Are you going to paint them?'

Her face clouded and he knew he had said the wrong thing. He had said many wrong things, too critical and condemning. His wish to protect her had gone too far.

He cleared his throat. 'I'd like to be your friend, Elisabeth,' he said, his voice husky. 'But a great deal more than a friend too. As I said the last time we spoke I can offer you security and time to paint without worry. There will be no need to strive as you have done up to now. You won't have to work so hard.'

She said nothing but gazed at him in such a way that he knew he had failed.

'Jenny will be able to run free in safety at Nether End,' he said quietly.

'She can run free in other places if she chooses.'

'But not here. Not in Marigold Cottage.' This was no place for her now with the continuous threat from hooligans whom the law had not yet caught up with.

'Not here,' she agreed.

'I love, you, Elisabeth, with all my heart, deeply and truly.'

'But what of respect, John? I have to be true to myself and not pretend to be other than I am. There's no happiness without that. How can I be true to you if I'm not true to myself?'

She buried her face in the roses and he could see she was close to tears. He longed to take her in his arms.

'What can I say other than I want you to be my wife?'

'But how can that be when you have never understood what painting means to me?' she said.

'I could try.'

'You have to be true to yourself too, John.'

'And that's all you have to say?'

'I'm sorry, truly sorry.'

She seemed to droop and he stepped forward and put his arms round her. 'I love you, Elisabeth, always remember that.'

For a moment she leaned against him but he didn't try to hold her when she pulled away.

'So what will you do now? Where will you go? You surely don't plan to stay here after what has happened?'

'This is my home, and Jenny's. I promised

her once that I wouldn't make any decisions to move away from here without discussing it with her first.'

'But she's just a child. You spoil her . . .'

She flinched. 'I shall keep my promise,' she said quietly.

'I wish you well, Elisabeth.'

'Thank you, John.'

He left then and walked away from her with a heavy heart. He had been so sure of what was best for her and it seemed he was wrong. He unlocked his car with a shaking hand. This wouldn't do. He needed time, that was all, to regain his composure and get on with the life to which he had become accustomed. Fly was waiting for him at home expecting a long walk before lunch.

He drove down to the main road before he remembered the message for his aunt. This time when he returned he parked directly outside Ivy Cottage and hastened to her door without glancing across the road.

Mrs Cameron took one look at him and, concerned with what she saw, ushered him inside at once.

He made no demur as she fussed round him without any of her usual questions as to his welfare, perhaps suspecting what had occurred over in Marigold Cottage.

She was obviously preparing to go out because her highly polished shoes were waiting by the door and her coat hung over the back of a chair instead of on its usual hook.

'I met Martin Varley,' he said. 'Jean's not well. Only a cold but she's infectious and not seeing anybody. He had some idea you might call in this afternoon.'

'That's so,' Mrs Cameron agreed. 'What a shame. It's likely she'll have to miss the planting of the new Tidings Tree tomorrow,' she said. 'I'll be going along, of course. Half the village will be there.'

'But not Elisabeth,' he said, a flat tone to his voice.

'No, lad, not Elisabeth. She's taking young Jenny for a picnic up on Larksbury Rings to be out of the way,'

He nodded. 'I went to see her. She didn't . . .' He broke off, unable to go on.

She got up, puffing, and picked up her coat. 'Things change,' she said. 'Sometimes we think they're not for the best and don't see it till years later. But Muriel knows it's right for her to come back here to live as soon as she can find somewhere.'

He took the coat from her to replace on its hook.

'Thank you, John,' she said. 'You're a good lad.'

'And you're a good aunt,' he said. 'I'm glad for you that Muriel will be near.'

317

CHAPTER NINETEEN

'There is something I wish to discuss with you, Karen.' Robert said.

He stood in the drive at Haymesgarth in the late afternoon sunshine and Karen, in her gardening clothes, had found him there when she came to the front garden to weed the rockery.

'I felt I was in no position to do so before, Karen, especially at this time when you are still grieving for your mother.'

Speechless, she stood and stared, her trug in one hand. Grieving still? And yet it was such a short time. She felt a stir of anguish for the mother whose life at the end was so difficult for them both.

Robert looked at her steadily, a small muscle moving at the side of his mouth. 'Indeed, I've surprised you. I didn't know how to say this. I'm expressing myself badly. I've received an offer of work that would mean moving away from Mellstone.'

She took a deep breath. 'What sort of work?'

'It would involve a fair amount of consultancy work that it seems I'm considered fit for. I've been given time to consider.'

'And would you like that?'

He hesitated for a moment. 'Indeed I want to hear your reaction to this, Karen. It's important to me.'

She was silent.

'The Living I've been offered is in Somerset, a smaller village than Mellstone. It was felt to be more suitable for my health's sake.'

He sounded so humble and accepting that her heart was touched. He was a good man. He deserved to be happy and she wanted that more than anything.

'I've had time to consider another matter too, and now believe I was wrong in suppressing my feelings for you,' he said. 'You seemed so vulnerable on the hillside in the rain after you found the child. I knew then that I wanted to look after you, to make things easier for you.'

'It's not raining now,' she said.

'No indeed. I've long known I wanted to share my life with you, such as it is. I was afraid to tell you because I thought it unfair to you.'

'You felt like that?' she said in wonder.

'I should like you to come with me, my dear Karen, as my wife.'

She raised her face and for a moment allowed the joy his words gave her to flood her. But she knew it wouldn't do. 'I can't, Robert,' she whispered. 'You deserve so much better.'

He smiled. 'If I believed that I would not be having this conversation. I love you, Karen, and I hope that you can find it in your heart to love me?'

'Oh Robert.'

'Will you do me the honour of becoming my wife?'

'Yes, oh yes.'

So engrossed were they that they didn't hear at first the sound of tyres on gravel until a vehicle pulled up not far away and a car door slammed.

'It seems I'm interrupting . . .' John Ellis made a move to go.'

Robert stepped forward and held out his hand, turning at once to Karen. 'I have asked Karen to be my wife,' he said.

'And I hope she's accepted?'

'I think so,' Karen said with a quiver in her voice.

'Then I must congratulate you both.'

Karen was glad to see that he looked pleased for her. She smiled. 'Shall we go indoors?'

'Not me,' said John. 'I mustn't linger here. I have something important to do in the estate office before I see my solicitor tomorrow. It involves someone I care about very much. I think you'll understand.'

Karen looked at him gravely. She understood only too well that it was Elisabeth Turner he meant and wished she didn't. As she watched him get into his car and drive away she was filled, for a painful moment, with envious hurt and was dismayed that she should feel like this when her happiness was not with John but with Robert.

'I've been a fool,' she said.

320

'We've both been fools. But not now.'

'I'll make you happy, Robert. I'll do my very best.'

'I know you will.'

She dropped her trug with a clatter and moved to him. The next moment she was in his arms.

*   *   *

The pink of wild roses in the hedgerows, the scent of new-mown hay through the open car window . . . Cathy remembered them with pleasure as she trudged up on Larksbury Rings on Tuesday morning. She had liked the sudden cold gloom of country churches and the anticipation of catching hold of the sally as she pulled on the unfamiliar bell rope in each place, not knowing quite how the bell would handle. When they had rung a touch or two she had liked emerging into brightness outside again and on to the next place.

The meal Ralph had promised was good, laid out on long trestle tables in the village hall of the last place they visited. Ralph, at her side, made sure she ate her fill. His own plate was piled high too. It had been a good day and she was surprised she had enjoyed it so much.

Today, the last day of the Half Term break, was one of challenge. Larksbury Rings was the place where Arnold had promised to take her and where she had gone with John Ellis to search for Jenny in the rain. Now she would go alone. She needed time to think undisturbed, to try to work out in her own mind just what was wrong with her relationship with Arnold.

She had tried so hard to please him, to be the kind of girl he wanted.

Miss King, knowing her destination, had pressed a packet of sandwiches on her. Miss Buckley had presented her with a map of the area, drawn by herself in such detail that Cathy had exclaimed in pleasure and promised to take the greatest care of it. Their kindness was amazing.

Arnold hadn't always been kind. He had made hurtful remarks about her progress in learning to ring the bells in front of the others sometimes so that her cheeks became hot with embarrassment.

As she climbed up and down the embankments the air up here felt balmier on her face than it had down below. There were no sheep grazing the soft turf today. Although it was misty in the distance Mr Wintle's place, Downend Farm, showed up clearly. But her gaze moved on to Nether End instead and the lane leading to the village.

Up she climbed and then stopped, heart fluttering, as a black animal came streaming towards her. Bruno, the Varley's dog!

'What are you doing here?' she cried. 'You're a long way from home.'

His tail wagged so rapidly she felt the air

stir. She caught hold of his collar with one hand while removing the belt she wore round her waist with the other. This made a fine make-shift lead.

'You won't escape again,' she told him.

He didn't seem to mind. He was being himself, a dog who liked a spurt of freedom every now and again. He licked her hand.

Maybe she should have been herself more often when she was with Arnold. Maybe she had tried too hard to be someone she wasn't.

She set off back the way she had come, Bruno pulling her up the banks at record speed. As they topped the last one she saw Ralph plodding up towards them. He let out a piercing whistle. She stood still and waited as he came up, not yet having see them. Bruno barked.

Cathy laughed at the expression on Ralph's face.

'You found him?' he said, puffing slightly.

'He found me.'

'Wise dog.'

'I remembered that Larksbury Rings is his hunting ground every now and again. I didn't dare let him go.'

'Wise girl.'

Ralph took the make-shift lead from her. 'I knew where to look. Mum was concerned in case there were sheep up here. The truck's down below. Fancy a lift home?'

'Not yet, thanks. I didn't get quite to the top.

I came for a long walk.'

'Not a bad idea. 'Can I come too?'

'If you want.' She looked down at Bruno who gazed up at her, tongue lolling. She patted his head. 'You rogue,' she said, smiling. 'You don't deserve this when you've led your family a fine dance.'

'We don't all get what we deserve,' said Ralph. 'But when we do we make the most of it.'

Cathy smiled. 'I've got sandwiches here,' she said. 'Miss King made them for me. Enough for six at least.'

'That'll do nicely,' said Ralph, his cheerful face shining with enthusiasm. 'And we don't need six. Two of us are plenty to be going on with. And Bruno, of course.'

She didn't quite know what he meant but he seemed satisfied.

'Let's go,' he said.

* * *

Elisabeth and Jenny left Marigold Cottage at eleven o'clock, anxious to be right away before people started gathering for the ceremony of the planting of the oak sapling that would one day grow into a new Tidings Tree.

The June morning was beautiful. Mellstone at its best, Elisabeth thought. Jenny skipped along at her side, happy to be going to the place she had long wanted to visit because something about the Iron Age hillfort of Larksbury Rings had caught at her imagination and wouldn't let go.

'How many people d'you think lived there?' Jenny asked.

'A lot, I should think. Something no one knows for sure,' said Elisabeth.

'A secret?'

'Hidden knowledge.'

'Is it buried in the hillside? I didn't see anything when I came. It started to rain so hard. I couldn't see anything.'

'You were lucky Miss Bryer found you.'

'She was crying.'

'You didn't tell me that.'

'I think that's a secret too.'

'A deep secret.'

'I'd cry if you died.'

Elisabeth laughed but her heart was touched. 'Let's think of happy things,' she said.

'Butterflies,' said Jenny. 'And flowers like all these the pretty mauve scabious and these yellow ones.'

'Toadflax,' said Elisabeth. 'Remember the antirrhinums in our garden? These are wild antirrhinum. I used to like picking them as a little girl and snapping them open and shut when I visited my aunt and uncle in Wiltshire.'

'Aunty Bella?' asked Jenny.

'Not Aunty Bella, Jenny. A different side of the family.'

'Can we go right up to the top when we get

325

there? I couldn't see the highest ridge when I came the other day.'

They started to walk across the field at the bottom of the hill. Elisabeth moved her laden picnic bag from one shoulder to the other and raised her face to the sky, listening for the trilling sound of lark song.

'I can hear it singing,' said Jenny. 'But I can't see anything up there. What do larks look like?'

'They're small brown birds,' Elisabeth said. 'You wouldn't think it, would you from the lovely sound they make?'

'You'd think they'd be blue and gold and silver and sweet dusky red. And proud like the swans on Poole Park lake, or pretty like bluetits. It's more fair though. Little brown birds with a beautiful sound instead of being beautiful to look at. It makes me think of big spaces going on and on forever. Like the sea.'

Elisabeth smiled, unable to follow the reasoning of Jenny's flights of fancy. But it didn't matter because that was how Jenny was.

They climbed on until they reached the plateau that was the summit and Jenny was satisfied. But they weren't the only ones here it seemed, for in the distance Elisabeth saw two figures and a black dog. Could it be Bruno, the Varley's dog who liked to wander off every now and again? It seemed like it because now she could see Ralph Varley and Cathy with him. So Cathy had got to Larksbury Rings at last, just as she had, and by the way she was laughing with Ralph it seemed as if she was having as good a time.

They were both too engrossed to notice anyone else and soon they were out of sight and she and Jenny had the hill to themselves.

They chose a spot for their picnic overlooking the way they had come and settled down to enjoy the solitude that felt healing to Elisabeth after the trauma of John's visit to Marigold Cottage yesterday.

She unpacked her bag, laying out the container of sandwiches. She had brought biscuits too and a ginger cake Mrs Cameron had made. There was some of her lemonade to drink, lemony and sweet because Jenny liked sweet things.

Afterwards Jenny wandered off a little way, not too far so that Elisabeth could watch her concentrating on picking flowers. When she had enough she came back and Elisabeth saw that the delicate blue harebells in the centre were fringed with yellow toadflax.

Jenny flopped down at Elisabeth's side. Her face was a little flushed and her eyes bright. 'We can see a long way from here, can't we?'

'Miles and miles, Jenny.'

Although it was beautiful it tore at Elisabeth's heart as she thought of yesterday morning. She had sent John away because of her conviction that it was the right thing to do but the decision had left her shattered.

She said no more but let it wash over her as she gazed across the vale that had come to mean so much to her. Bees hummed nearby and the heady scent of bruised grass was satisfying. She knew she had done the right thing, that she and John couldn't be happy together because of the differences between them that were core-deep. She hoped that he would accept that too.

'It'll always be here, won't it?' Jenny said. 'Larksbury Rings?'

Elisabeth smiled. 'I don't suppose any one will take Larksbury Rings away. Can you imagine how many wheelbarrows would be needed to cart it all off? They'd be going backwards and forwards for months.'

Jenny giggled. 'And cowslips and all the other flowers will grow here every spring forever and ever?'

'I can't quite promise that.'

'I'll come back and see.'

'We'll come again,' Elisabeth promised, though her heart wasn't in it. And neither, it seemed, was Jenny's.

'It's a long way,' she said.

'No longer than it was today.'

Jenny picked a piece of grass and nibbled the end. A small blue butterfly fluttered close. 'It's the same colour as the sea,' she said, watching it.

'The sea changes. All different shades and tones of blue. Green too sometimes and

328

turquoise.'

'I wish we could see it.'

'We could. We could stay with Bella.'

'For always?'

Elisabeth gazed at her thoughtfully. 'You would like that would you, Jenny?' she said at last. 'Are you really sure?'

'We could go and see the kittens, couldn't we, the ones the lady wanted you to paint? They live in Cornwall.'

'They won't be kittens now,' said Elisabeth.

'We could have our own kitten.'

Elisabeth smiled. 'We could choose to do a lot of things, Jenny.'

'Good things?'

'If we make good decisions.'

Jenny leapt up. 'Let's go back now.'

They said no more as they walked down over the soft turf to join the chalky track and eventually the lane that took them back to Mellstone but Elisabeth was thinking deeply about what Jenny had said. There was much to consider. They would talk more about it, perhaps go down to Cornwall for a holiday and decide finally what to do then.

As they passed it the new Tidings Tree moved gently in the breeze.

'It's waving goodbye to us,' said Jenny.